IN HER SERVICE

'I'm bad, Franklin. Worse than you could ever imagine. And I should be punished for hurting you. You have every right to hurt me. You could never touch my heart, but you could put your pain into my body.'

She looks up at me. Her face is happy and sad at the same time. 'You know what I'm saying.' It's like she's asking a favour. It's like she's pleading with me. 'Take your belt off, Franklin. The thick, black, leather belt, Franklin. And hurt me.'

She stands up and walks across to the dresser. Bends over. Places both hands on top and looks into the mirror.

IN HER SERVICE

Lindsay Gordon

This book is a work of fiction.
In real life, make sure you practise safe, sane and
consensual sex.

First published in 2005 by
Nexus
Thames Wharf Studios
Rainville Road
London W6 9HA

www.nexus-books.co.uk

Typeset by TW Typesetting, Plymouth, Devon

Printed and bound by
Clays Ltd, St Ives PLC

ISBN 0 352 33968 3

You'll notice that we have introduced a set of symbols onto our book jackets, so that you can tell at a glance what fetishes each of our brand new novels contains. Here's the key – enjoy!

cp (traditional)

cp (modern)

spanking

restraint/bondage

rope bondage/hojojutsu

latex/rubber/leather/enclosure

fem dom

willing captivity

medical

period setting

uniforms

sex rituals

Part 1

Chapter One

We're not supposed to be doing this. Which makes it twice as good.

I can't believe it's happening. I mean, I'm looking down my body and watching Mrs Berry's beautiful face between my thighs. Mrs Berry! Who I've had a crush on for, like, years. Like forever, man. And now, right now, she's ... It's hard to even say it. She's sucking me. Kneeling down on the floor with me in her mouth. Her eyes are half closed and her white fingers with the red nail polish are stroking my tummy.

I'm like embarrassed and scared of getting in trouble, and don't ever want to die because it feels so good and I want this to last forever.

I try and slow my head down. Just watch. Enjoy it. Stop thinking. Nothing else matters but her and me in this hotel room. Me standing up with the trousers of my dinner suit around my ankles, my shorts strung between my knees, bow-tie really useless and just hanging around my neck like the fake thing it is, my hands hovering, scared to touch her – I mean, is that allowed? – but not wanting to drop them at my sides either, because then I'd feel hopeless; just standing here, getting my cock sucked like I'm waiting for the bus or something.

Now she's purring. Her cheeks are all sucked in. I'm really hard. Longer and thicker than I've ever been before and she's moaning because she's pleased by how I've grown inside her mouth. I go all hot and tingly with pride and excitement. Her eyes are wide with surprise and her long lashes flutter a bit. She puts a hand on my cock. The sight of those ghost fingers makes me dizzy. She looks up at me with green cat eyes and sucks until her pretty nose goes thin.

'You should be very pleased with yourself, Franklin. You have a beautiful cock.'

Oh, man. To hear a dirty word like 'cock' come out of her red lips makes me sway. It's a word that's banned in high school. Me and the guys only whisper it when no women are around. Women just don't say stuff like this because everything is proper and clean in the new order. You dream they do and then feel really ashamed and guilty for it. But Mrs Berry came right out with it. And here she is on all fours in a hotel room.

'I can tell you, Franklin, when we women get to a certain age, we have limited patience with things that don't work properly. With little things that don't do their job. We know what we want.' And then her mouth widens and I see her perfect teeth before she swallows the big, purple end of me.

Closes her eyes again, purrs. Tickles my balls. Rises on to her knees. Moves her whole head up and down my shaft. Opening her jaw to take even more of me inside her pretty head. Moving me right to the top of her slender throat.

I can smell her lipstick and perfume, the cigarettes she smokes, the wine she's been drinking.

It's too much. Can't help myself, but I start talking to myself, to her, to anyone. I don't care. 'Oh, ma'am. Oh, ma'am. It's so good. Oh, ma'am.' I look down at her chest. Milky breasts pushing out that black bra, all silky and tight looking. Pearl necklace, sinews working in her neck.

I'm terrified of her. Am crazy about her; have been since I was a kid watching her going in and out of her

2

house across the road, wearing those black suits with the tight skirts and white blouses. Sunglasses in her hair. Shiny legs in the sunlight. Better looking than every girl at school and most every teacher too.

Oh, man. How many times have I dreamed of this? The two of us together. She must have known what I was thinking all these years. Read my thoughts behind my blushing face. Women are so clever. We don't stand a chance. They know everything we're thinking; sometimes even before we do. And she must have been thinking about the same things too. That's the sexiest thing. Especially since I started to 'fill out', and since they've been calling me a 'young man' and shit like that at high school.

Most times when she comes over to see my mom, her best friend, it's like I don't even exist. She just says, 'Hi,' to me and then talks with my mom. But they always whisper stuff with their heads close, while snaking their feet around and dangling their high heels off their toes; drinking cocktails and smoking cigarettes with their legs crossed on the leather sofa, while I pop in and out to steal looks at Mrs Berry – her thighs, her feet in the black heels, her chest, her mouth. Then my mom will say something like, 'In or out, Franklin. Make up your mind. We're trying to talk, darling.' And I'm like, 'Sorry, mom. Sorry,' and shit like that. But if I think about it, Mrs Berry always has a sly smile on her pretty mouth. Sometimes she watches me go out of the room. I can feel her staring.

And now she's my Mentor. Every guy in this town gets one when they turn eighteen. For your last year of high school before you go to Finishing College, a Mentor is supposed to show you stuff. But not this, man! They're supposed to tell you about a husband's duties to his wife. Get you ready for the commitments, and fine tune all that annoying guy stuff left over from hanging with your friends through school. But beside all

3

the jokes that start at around thirteen about losing your virginity with the Mentors, which is such a big cliché and totally not true, being Mentored is something you have to take real seriously with a lady your parents choose. So this is why my head is on the spin cycle. This is not supposed to be happening.

What about her husband? Karl would be pissed. My mom? Don't even want to think about that. My dad would be jealous; I've seen his eyes when Mrs Berry pops over. Peeking at her from the kitchen while he cooks dinner, or looking in through the French windows as he does the garden. And if word got out about tonight in the hotel room, my whole family would be ruined by the shame.

But then I think, has she done this before? Sucked cocks, young cocks, in hotel rooms? Or in that black Mercedes with the tinted windows? It makes me jealous and excited at the same time. Slut. The word comes into my head. A hot, bad word that makes me shiver. Mrs Berry you are a slut, I say inside my head and hope she hears. I look at her face and then her legs stretched out behind her, all shiny in stockings and spiky in black shoes.

'Oh,' she says and pulls her mouth back a little bit. Her eyes go wide. Holding my pulsing cock, she aims the sperm on to her tongue. So much of it. Shooting then plopping on to her chin, teeth and tongue. My whole body is shivering. She licks around her lips. Then cleans the end of my cock with her wide mouth. 'Mmm,' she says. 'You taste nice, Franklin. Fresh. Young. I like that,' with a whisper. And her eyes look at a faraway place for a bit with her head tilted back.

She stands up and lights a cigarette over by the table near the window. Shakes her hair out. Smoothes her stockings up her legs with both hands, because they're creased from all that kneeling. One leg first, then the other.

4

'Take your clothes off,' she says with her back turned to me. 'We don't have much time left. I have to get you home before eleven.'

I'll never forget the day my Mentor was announced. Dad was real nervous, but tried to hide it from me. The door to the lounge was closed, television was switched off. Outside a lawnmower grunted into life. Some kids raced past the house on bikes, yelling. In the conservatory, mom started to sing. Off in the cool summery spaces of our house, I heard her voice drift, faint and sweet like a lullaby, only broken by the sound of her martini shaker. Closer to me, across soft carpet the colour of brown rice, was dad's breathing. Wheezy.

'Franklin, it's your birthday tomorrow,' he said, but avoided my eyes. Looking down at the floor, with his white shirt sleeves rolled up and tie removed, he seemed anxious, like he does whenever mom goes away on business.

Almost feel sorry for dad, but like mom I have this impatience with his reluctance to say what he wants. Like now. I just want to dissolve the big hot lump of fear and excitement inside my chest and express everything clearly like the Saviour Councillor at school. If only I could find the words and speak to dad. But not in the 'son' voice you use on the back seat of the car when you've helped carry the holiday luggage, or in the garden when you've been trusted to light the barbecue. I hate the 'son' voice. It's so fake. With women you always get right to the nitty-gritty.

Takes after his mother. Got her good looks and sense. Everybody says this about me.

Dad looked all hunched up and small in his chair. I stayed quiet. He had to do the talking; it was a special job that mom gave him to do.

'Your mother and I have put a lot of thought into next year.' He made a big sigh and looked up to the wall above my head. Above the family photos, and the little pot with bus change and rubber bands inside, is the painting of Our Saviour. Maybe her eager smile with the painted lips and the clever eyes with the big lashes remind him to stop pussy-footing about and to say what he must.

'Everything has been arranged for you,' he said, keeping his eyes on Our Saviour. 'After lunch, you'll take Confirmation with Chaplain Mitchell. And I want you to listen to everything she has to say, it's very important' – his eyes drifted back to me and looked harder – 'she'll bless you and get you ready. Now there's to be no nonsense. I guess you boys think you know it all, but you don't.' His voice went quiet. 'This is a serious matter. After tomorrow you'll be a man. It's an important year for you.'

Dad took a deep breath. This was the crucial moment: who do I get for Mentor after Confirmation? I hoped like hell it would be Mrs Berry. It was my turn to look at my feet. I was trying not to do a silly laugh. Anticipation made me go all stupid inside. The side of my mouth was twitching and my shoulders were about to do the little shrugs. I could feel these big whooping hysterics coming up through me. Can't lose it, I told myself, which only makes it more likely to happen.

Talking with dad is only the first stage. Communion's coming up and then Initiation with the Mentor they choose for me, which is just a meal, but it's made into a big deal in this town. A religious occasion.

I managed to get my lips straight. Dad looked right into my eyes. Please say it, dad. Mrs Berry. That's all I want to hear. Me and the guys have been talking about my eighteenth birthday for a year, analysing every woman in the congregation, careful not to criticise each other's mothers, but it's rare in our community if you get your friend's mom.

'Your Mentor has been selected.'

Oh dad, let it be Mrs Berry. Our Saviour knows I've dropped enough hints and I know she and mom have been having coffee like twice a week for ages. I can see Mrs Berry now, out on her lawn in that flimsy summer dress tight to her breasts, with that cold look on her smooth face while her husband washes her car. Or climbing out of the Mercedes after work; long shiny legs ending in high heels that always come out the car door first. So slowly they hypnotise me. Then the long body follows in a dark suit and she always has sunglasses tossed into her hair. Oh come on, pops. Please, please, please let it be . . .

'After careful consideration –' he dabbed his forehead '– taking into account her maturity, experience and . . .' Oh dad I feel sorry for you, man, but please don't keep me hanging on. My face was hot, I couldn't see straight, and it sounded like someone was hitting a snare drum inside my head. 'We feel it's best your Initiation is supervised by Mrs Berry.'

One thousand guitars tuned up inside my head.

For the sake of Our Saviour I tried to keep my face straight. Don't look keen. Don't grin. Stop it!

'Mrs Berry is honoured to accept our proposition and has already made plans for evening supper and . . .' Dad never finished, he just cleared his throat.

Floating out of my seat, I found my feet. It was like electricity was humming beneath my skin. Helium in my feet but lead in my head. Heavy head, helium feet. This feeling must be like drugs, not like we'd ever know in our town. Like Christmas morning when you're a kid but more intense, and better than the time we got the song *God Gave Rock'n'roll To You* just right in the double garage where my band practises. Oh this was too much. I wanted to hug my dad. He'd done his best, like all the other dads do at this time, and like I'll have to do when it's my turn to select the Mentor for my son.

7

There was no hug. We cleared our throats at the same time and tried to look at each other. He offered a solemn hand. After extending my sticky fingers, cool air rushed into the palm of my hand to dry the sweat. There were nail marks on my skin. We shook hands. Dad's big rough hand, with the black hair on the back, had a little tremor to it. I glanced at his white knuckles and then took my hand away. He stood there looking at me. No one said a thing for ages. There was no way he wanted me to have Mrs Berry. He's been weird about her ever since she moved in across the street. I wonder if he knows something the rest of us don't. And my mom is like her little sister now; she really looks up to Mrs Berry. So Mrs Berry must have decided she would take me on and be my Mentor. Which is so scary but so irresistible.

'Thanks,' I whispered, and did a false cough. After a quick swallow I felt a bit better, but not much. I was blushing and couldn't stop. My shirt was stuck to my back. Something itched inside my nose and I gave it a little rub. I made a stupid grin and mentioned my band practice later. Dad took a peek at his watch. 'Better get the dinner on,' he said.

Maybe he thought the father-to-son, man-to-man bit had fallen flat. I wanted to say how happy I was, but it would have been inappropriate. Dads don't have much say in anything and I know these talks are really important to them. Since the card games stopped and the bars closed down, they don't get much male company either. Coffee mornings are not quite the same. But what could I say? I know he suspected me of having the hots for Mrs Berry and probably thought I should have had mumsy Mrs Mullins as Mentor, but mom must have fought my corner. She secretly asked me who I would like about two months ago and I said Mrs Berry.

Just recently, my parents had been muttering in these hushed voices downstairs when the house is quiet and

I'm supposed to be sleeping. Through the floorboards, I'd hear my dad raise his voice, but I'd be unable to make out the words, and then mom would speak, calmly. Common sense and a clever argument would come out in her husky voice; you can tell by the tone of voice. Makes dad feel like a fool. Mrs Berry is mom's best friend and mom's choice of Mentor. Maybe dad suspects I know this and feels bad, because it's another defeat.

'Son?' he said, as I turned to leave. Then he sighed.

'Dad?'

'There are things . . .' And he couldn't finish what he wanted to say, but I knew it was about Mrs Berry. 'Never mind.'

I took off for band practice.

After turning off the main lights in the hotel room, she switches the bedside lamps on. They are set at an angle to illuminate the bed. The rest of the room is murky around the edges, but the bed is bright and she is lying on it, smoking and watching me. I'll be naked if I take my shorts off. But even after she sucked me, I feel self-conscious. Being naked in the same place as her feels inappropriate.

Sitting forwards, she unhooks her bra and lets it fall away from her white shoulders and down her slim arms. She tosses it on to the floor. Then she opens her compact and runs lipstick around her lips while I just stare at her breasts. She looks calm. Doesn't even seem aware of me. It's as if being in a hotel room with your best friend's son, who you are supposed to be Mentoring into a fine, upstanding man, is no big deal to her. Like she doesn't care. She's dangerous. I always knew it. I always liked it.

'Shall I come over then?' I say like a dork.

'Do what you like,' she says, arching her eyebrows and staring into the little mirror, checking her make-up.

'I meant . . .'

'Franklin, we have an hour left and at least fifteen minutes of that will be consumed by me washing my perfume off your body and my lipstick off your cock. Now, I know you want to fuck me. In fact, you need to fuck me. And probably really hard too. Which would be nice. But if you keep hovering over there with your shorts on, you might as well head for the showers.'

'Sorry.'

'Don't say sorry. Be a man, Franklin.'

That comment makes me feel lousy. Kind of angry too.

She raises an eyebrow. 'Franklin, right now I want you to forget everything your teachers ever told you. Can you do that? I want you to do exactly what you want to do. And nothing else. OK? It's in there somewhere. You just have to dig down and find it.'

I nod. 'Sure.'

She puts the compact down on the night-stand and stretches out on the bed. Closes her eyes. Parts her legs. I swallow and stare. She is wearing a shiny black panty girdle with four suspenders attached. Underneath I can see her panties. They are black but you can see right through them. I can see her pussy. Pinkish and rumpled. My breath catches in the back of my throat. I feel light in the head. I want to eat her pussy through those thin panties and stuff her white breasts in my mouth. Suck, lap, nip. Grip her flesh and leave red fingerprints. Maul her like a tiger with a slender, freckled deer between its claws. Be a man, she said. She wants me to just take her. To be a man on top of her. Just going for it. She would get pleasure from it. It is too much to comprehend. It is an unacceptable idea. I can't move.

She raises one knee and moves it to the side. Opens herself up to me. Suddenly, it's hard to get my underwear free from my erection.

She keeps her eyes closed and I'm glad of it. She does it for both our sakes. To have her green eyes penetrating

10

me while I crouch undignified with my mouth on her sex will make me clumsy and shy all over again. I think she knows that. Or she just wants the pleasure without seeing the clumsy geek between her thighs. Maybe the sight of me will remind her of all the reasons she's ended up here, in a hotel room with a teenager.

I lower my head, get closer. The smell of her sex surprises me. I pause, in shock at the hot animal scent of her pussy. This strong meaty smell has nothing to do with this perfect, soft, shaven, elegant lady.

Warily, I extend my tongue and just touch the front of her flimsy panties. I hear her draw her breath in hard. Her legs tense. Then I put my mouth against the slippery material and my lips touch the folds of her sex. She says, 'Oh, God,' quickly. Then 'Oh, God,' again, and she sounds so young.

I get used to the harsh smell and push my tongue gently up and down the front of her panties. So salty. She moves her hips off the bed and pushes her sex against my face. The bed dips behind me as she presses her high heels into the mattress. This is good. I feel so happy because I am pleasing her. It's the most import-ant thing in a man's life: to make them feel special and to make them happy. To give them pleasure. That is what my whole upbringing and education has been for. This is the purpose to our lives. Everything is training for these opportunities to make their lives easier, to create happiness, make them content. Even though she wants me to be some grunting, mythical man figure who takes what he wants, it's in our nature to please them.

Her gauzy panties are wet and stuck to my nose and lips after all of my lapping and nuzzling of these incredibly soft ripples of skin. And then I want to put my tongue inside her. To press into the fullest flavour and pinkie tissue, maybe even drink from her. If I touch my cock, I'm sure I will come, disappointingly, over the bed.

As I peel her panties off her pussy and peek through the space I make, she must know what my intention is. Especially as the air rushes in to tickle and make her pussy feel vulnerable. Rolling her head into the pillow, she hurriedly whispers, 'Yes. Yes.' And I push my aching, tired tongue through her wet flesh and find this slippery passage into her body.

I can barely breathe when she presses her groin on to my face and rubs her sex against the hard bones. She folds her legs across my back and I feel her spiky heels touching my buttocks like spurs. The weight of her legs pushes me down into the bed. I suck and smear my face like a savage eating a big joint of greasy meat, until my neck aches and I want to sit back and breathe, but I stay put and keep on lapping until her whole body locks and she makes these hard sounds from deep inside her chest.

With her spiky shoes she pushes me away from her. She folds her body into a foetal position with both hands clasped between her thighs. Making the coughing sounds and jolting like she is being electrocuted, she stays like this until the tremors die down and her face goes all dreamy.

Then one of her eyes notices me. I'm lying beside her, too polite and cautious and respectful to touch without permission. 'Do what you want with me,' she says in a hard voice.

Earlier, in her car, on the way to the hotel where we had dinner, I knew something had changed between us. It was real subtle. I told myself not to be stupid, that it was down to my nerves, that I was kidding myself because I wanted to believe something was going on. But I was right.

It wasn't like I was that stupid kid from across the road any more, and Mrs Berry wasn't just my mom's friend either. We were suddenly two adults all dressed up for an evening out alone. And it was so intense in that car, even though no one was speaking much. Even more powerful somehow than the sex that came later. There was this kind of anticipation of something about to happen. This gravity was keeping me pressed into my seat. I mean, most of the time I couldn't even feel my legs.

It started as soon as we left our street – driving past all those perfect green lawns and tidy gardens and white houses with my mom and dad waving from the drive, all proud their son was eighteen and beginning Confirmation with his Mentor.

Maybe it was the new suit and haircut and aftershave that made me feel weird. Maybe it was all the familiar things disappearing in the rear-view mirror. And maybe it had something to do with Mrs Berry. She looked so hot, but in an elegant way. No expression on her face, no music in the car, just staring ahead and driving me away from home. At first, I had this lump in my throat. Wanted to stay young for a bit longer. Got a bit scared. But that was just the kid in me. I know that now. The other part of me that had been kept down by a tight chain for years and years, like some big growly animal on a cement floor behind bars, who just wants to break out of his corner and sink his teeth and claws into soft girl flesh, was checking out Mrs Berry. And doing it more and more the further we drove away from the neighbourhood.

Glances at those perfect hands on the steering wheel. Red nails on black leather. Her profile with the smooth white cheeks and charcoal eyelashes. You could see the pretty girl she once was; a girl that would have made your tummy turn over if you saw her in a corridor at high school. But you could see how getting older had made her sexy in a way no girl could ever be.

Stern but beautiful. Lips so red and shiny they looked wet. The chest looking hard and tight in her black dress.

13

No sleeves on her slender arms. Little golden hairs on her forearms that I could see in the late sunlight that came through the side window. Her shiny hair, immaculate. Smelling so good, like the air in a room that a beautiful lady has just walked through without even noticing you. Out of my league. It made me ache. That smell of her perfume made me hurt in a nice way. It made me dreamy and hot and drowsy too. I would have been happy just looking at her and inhaling her for the rest of my life.

Soon, my eyes started to drop down and stare at her lap. Her dress was black and shimmery. Satin, I think. And tight against her legs. If I stared hard enough I reckoned I could see the little bumps her suspender clips made on the front of her thighs. But then maybe they were just creases from sitting down. You just don't know for sure with those indentations. And down in the footwell, her legs tapered into her high heels and looked so streamlined. They had the hard, female curves of sports cars and jet planes. Her stockings made them look like they were made from polished glass. Dark stockings. Not black, but a kind of chocolate colour. And I couldn't stop looking at them. Until I realised she was watching me. I looked up and saw her eyes for a moment, staring right at me.

I went so red, couldn't swallow and quickly looked out of my window but saw nothing. Could just hear the rushing of hot blood in my ears. She never looked offended, or happy to be admired either. Just totally indifferent to me. Next time I looked across, she had moved her eyes back to watching the road, like it had never happened.

'What do you want from me, Franklin?' she said, after we had gone a few more miles.

'Ma'am?'

'Tell me, Franklin. What do you want from me?'

'From the Mentoring?'

14

She smiled to herself. Laughed, at me. 'Mentoring,' she whispered in a mocking voice and shook her head.

Then there was more of the silence as we rode the smooth tarmac, the sleek tyres whispering, taking me away from everything I knew and into a place that made me feel stupid and clumsy. I mean, what should I be saying or doing? I couldn't be natural and spontaneous or anything like I am in the band with the guys. What does she want from me? That's what I wanted to know.

Do what you want with me.

Her saying that makes me excited again and it makes me feel aggressive at the same time. Of course I don't want to hurt her, but I want to eat her. Devour her white body. Be rough with her. Pull her feet into the air and thrust myself against her. She looks so vulnerable and inviting in her black underwear. She has shown me the most secret part of herself. But this thing between us is only half finished. Until I am inside her it won't be complete. Even though my rational mind is saying 'Stop!' because this is everything I have been told never to think about.

I lose control of myself for a while. Find myself licking her face and holding her shoulders down in the pillows. I feel like a big cat, tenderising its prey before the ripping and tearing. Biting her spongy pink nipples and rubbing her wet panties against her sex with one hand, I make her do the girlish sounds, like she is crying. It surprises me, but not enough to stop trying to get all of her into my mouth and stuck on my cock at the same time.

I'm so clumsy. I leave some bruises. Make her wince once or twice. Squash her. Make her squeal. And I just can't get inside her. This deep and wet place I have just gorged myself on has vanished beneath the surface of so many tricky folds of skin.

15

She raises her legs. Grips my cock. Puts it in the right place. 'Push.' And I do. 'Ow. Not so hard. Not to start with. Slow. You're big,' she says. Closes her eyes.

Slips her long fingers behind her knees and places her spiky feet on my shoulders. I slide out twice and curse myself. This makes her giggle. I get so mad at myself for being a klutz, I start to go soft and think about giving up on the whole thing. But she shushes me and moves her tongue around her lips while keeping her eyes half closed. Smiles in a wicked way. This makes me grow through her, deep inside.

And soon I am staring down at Mrs Berry while my cock is stiff inside her. She's moaning every time I push myself deep. Her breasts shudder a little each time. She has this frowny face but is enjoying it. Her eyes stare right through me. She doesn't look like Mrs Berry any more. Has a different face. A red, kind of mad, beautiful face that makes me even more eager and I start to bump and thrust against her while she sucks her own fingers. Doesn't take long before I feel dizzy and know I can't hold it back much longer.

She seizes my hand and holds it across her face. Sucks at my fingers.

I feel the tingling, the head swoops, the first hot surge.

She puts my hand over her eyes. Holds it there tight. Then she is pulling at my hand, struggling to take it away, but holding it there too, like it's me pushing down. I think this is really strange and I don't know why, but it drives me crazy. Makes me thrust faster and harder. Mrs Berry is moaning and saying, 'No. No,' with my hand held over her eyes and mouth like she is smothered and blindfolded. Just struggling but holding it there, biting the palm of my hand.

'I'm coming, ma'am. Inside you. Too late. It's all inside you.'

She sighs and seems to relax. Her whole body goes loose. Her fingernails dig into my buttocks. 'Stay

16

inside,' she says. She lets go of my hand but keeps her eyes shut.

She hardly touched her food during the meal. Just drank wine and watched me. I smiled at her, but she never smiled back.

Waiters in white smocks came and went. Filled her glass and offered her different foods. But she never looked one of them in the eye. Dismissed them with a shake of her sleek head.

A man played sad music from a piano in the corner. Around us there were mostly female couples eating, or groups of women talking and drinking.

I wondered when she would start telling me about what I'd have to be as a grown man, what I would have to do and say. My role, and shit like that. What women feel and want and need. What men must do. You know, outlining some plan about her intention to teach me how to be a good companion, when to speak and offer support, when to keep quiet, to anticipate my future wife's needs. That kind of thing. At Finishing College I would get taught how to manage a home, how to cook, how to clean, iron, garden, fix things around the house, shit like that. But a Mentor teaches you the more sophisticated stuff. The psychology, from courtship to the emotional support of marriage. So you won't be a total jerk like men always were before the Graceful Revolution. But Mrs Berry said nothing about what we would be doing. She just looked a little sad. Wasn't too keen on me talking either.

'So what will we be doing first?' I said, trying to look keen and interested but secretly fancying her like hell and trying to conceal it.

She didn't like me asking that question. Seemed bored with the whole thing. Drank some more wine. I looked at my plate and ate tiny mouthfuls. I could feel her staring at me with no smile on her face.

17

'What did you feel when your parents told you I was going to be your Mentor?' she asked, totally out of the blue..

I'd drunk a lot of wine and my tongue felt thick in my mouth. My thoughts wouldn't form properly and there was a big gap between them and my mouth, like my voice was a boat that had floated away from a dock. I giggled like a chump.

'Stop laughing like that. You're not a boy any more.' Her voice was sharp. I wanted to die.

The two women at the next table must have heard. There was a pause in the sound of their cutlery on the china. 'I asked you a simple question. I believe I am entitled to an answer. After all, I now have to deal with you for a year.' She said it in such a way as to make me feel like shit. I couldn't stop her from seeing the mean look in my eyes. It seemed to please her. She smiled like I was an amusing fool.

I shrugged.

'Don't sulk. Don't pout either. That's not what a woman wants to see over dinner. God knows I've had enough of that.' She lit a cigarette. Was she talking about her husband, Karl? 'You haven't answered my question, Franklin. I don't have much patience. You must answer me truthfully at all times. Think about your answers to my questions, sure, but never, ever say anything but the absolute truth. Never say what you think you should say to me. Do you understand?'

'Yes, ma'am.' I felt out of my depth. I'd never seen this side to her before. Used to find the sulky face sexy, but now I wasn't so sure. I lost my appetite and hoped no one was listening in, or watching from one of the tables nearby.

'So what did you feel?'

I was smarting. I said nothing.

'Would you have preferred Mrs Pritchard?'

'No.'

'Maybe Annalise Brown? Good tits, Annalise?'

Totally shocked, I said, 'No. Nothing like that.'

'Mrs Hythe-Parker? Stuffy, stuck-up cow, but nice legs. You like legs, Franklin?'

'No. I mean, yes. I mean, no. I didn't want Mrs Hythe-Parker.'

'You were glad you got me?'

I nodded.

She smiled and drew on her cigarette. 'I know you were, Franklin. You've wanted me for years. And I've been waiting to see what you turned out like.' I couldn't look her in the eye, just stared at the table feeling my face fill with blood.

She called the waiter over for the bill. 'Finish your food. We haven't got much time left,' she said as the waiter walked away with her credit card in a little silver dish. But it was only eight and I hadn't had dessert yet. There was like three hours before she had to drop me back home. What was going on?

'Don't follow me right out. Wait here for a few minutes after I've gone. Then come to room 27.'

I'm sure the dining room was moving around my head when she said that. Then I decided there was a rational explanation, and that we were just going up to a room to talk about the Mentoring.

She slipped a mint into her mouth and excused herself from the table. I stared at her retreating body – long and slim, her dark legs and tight bottom, her white hands holding the clutch bag. Then I looked around to see if anyone was watching. No one was even looking in my direction. I waited for like ten minutes and then left the table. One of the waiters, an old guy with a tired face, smiled at me, nodded. I grinned back and nearly tripped over my own feet. My stomach was alive with nerves and I wanted the toilet. I felt sick. It was too much to take in at once and I was sure I couldn't go through with whatever she wanted me to do.

19

But then I thought some more about Mrs Berry's legs in the car, and her pretty feet in black heels pressing the accelerator pedal down. And I thought about her red, sulky mouth across the dinner table. I looked around the restaurant at the elegant ladies in nice dresses and high heels, the little hats, the occasional veil with smoky eyes behind. I wondered what they had done as Mentors, in plush hotels like this. My throat got all choked up with emotion and I dropped my hand over my groin to hide the swelling. Then I made my way to the stairs. I would walk up.

And in the half-light of that hotel room, as I lie in the bed too tired to get up, Mrs Berry curls around me. She kisses my neck and shoulders. Whispers to me. I close my eyes. Feel her heartbeat. Soon, it's like my heart thumps at the same time. A slow rhythm. Soothing me. I fall in and out of sleep. Feel pleased with myself for what I've just done.

Sleep, sleepy, sleep. I dream of her. Wearing a black satin suit at a wedding; her eyes over the top of a wine glass, turning my guts to a shiver, my cock to stone; crossing her legs on a couch, one hand stroking her shin, the hand loving the leg, up and down, hypnotising me; from my bedroom, watching her legs uncoil from the car across the road, a hundred times and now all at once; skirt riding up shiny thighs, maybe a glimpse of pale flesh above the stocking, then it's gone and she's tall and straight like a statue; goes into her dark house, no lights come on.

Tongue tip moves down my spine. Licks around my waist. Kisses on my tummy. Hot breath around my nipples seeps into my heartbeat.

I gasp. Eyes flash open. A sharp pain. Goes deep. Try to pull away. Gripped by slender legs and arms too strong for such a delicate body. Holds me tight. The pain dims. A love bite?

Dizzy and drunk now. Pins and needles prickle my body. Red rivers crash through me, froth hot to the pain, sweep it away. All my strength drains through the little hole she has made in me. Pours into her sucking mouth.

I smile. Weigh nothing at all. My body wants to float to the ceiling. She holds me down. Strokes my cock hard again with a gentle hand. Rolls me on to my back and rises over me. Moves down my body to the hardness I poke into the warm air. Grips me with her lips, works me with determined fingers. Feel her nose breathe in my floss. So good just to drift and spin inside while she pleasures me. Every nerve in my cock head tingles until it hurts with a sweet pain. A sweet pain that empties me into her body again. Then it goes numb like the bite. I sink through the bed into never-ending softness and warmth. The world is red under my eyelids.

Settling her soft weight and feline limbs across me, like a tigress with a fresh kill in some steaming forest, she relaxes into my slow breaths and quiet heartbeat. Presses me down like she's collapsed drunk on my young body. She talks to herself. I can't hear the words. A happy murmur. I drop again, down, down, down into the velvet.

Chapter Two

'Franky musta got laid.' Brad says, smiling. 'He's not been the same since his Initiation.'

'Yeah, right,' I say, not meeting his eye.

Thick grey walls and the spider-webs up in the dusty rafters, beneath the low ceiling of the garage, shrink our voices. When I'm singing, I have to really scream into the mic in here to be heard over the drums and guitar amps. But his voice isn't quiet enough for my nerves. Once, a Chaplain called Brad 'indiscreet and vulgar'. She was right.

I throw a hand towel at him. He ducks, twisting to the side and nearly falling over his bass amplifier. Davey does a drum roll on his kit, ending with a crash against his high-hat cymbal and points a drum stick at me. 'So who'd you get, stud?'

'If you got Berry, I'm gonna kick your ass,' Gretchen pipes up, without looking at me. He stays in the same position, hunched over his guitar. Gretchen is sitting on his hundred-watt Marshall amp, tuning up. He's been eighteen for two months and is having a real dull Mentoring with a lady called Mrs Willows who always wears white gloves.

'Keep it down!' I say. 'My mom's in the conservatory and the door's open. You know the rules. If she knows half the shit we've been saying about women, we'll get our asses kicked out of here.'

'Don't be soft, man,' Brad says. 'We wanna know all about it. Who'd you get?'

I grin. 'Well, it ain't Mullins.'

All three of them call me a dork.

'I knew it,' Gretchen says, still watching the tiny silver strings running up his maple fretboard. 'He got the cherry, boys. So you guys miss out. The women never initiate more than once a year.' He raises his face, which I can't read, and stares me right in the eye. 'You did, didn't you?'

My smile answers the question.

'Bastard,' everyone in the band says in turn.

'This prick gets everything he wants,' Brad says, shaking his head. 'He's not content with being the track and field star, or a straight-A student. He's just gotta get Mentored by hot-legs Berry too. It's not fair.'

I laugh. 'Not my fault you're such a loser. And it's not like I had anything to do with it. My parents chose her.'

'Loaded dice, brother,' Davey says. 'His mom pulled strings,' he says to the others.

'Ain't that the truth,' Brad says. 'Whereas, I'll get Mullins. I just know it.'

We all laugh. Then I shake my head like I'm tired of all this talk about Mentors. But it feels good to have success acknowledged. I've had a good couple of years at school and in athletics. Maybe that's why Berry chose me; the better you are at stuff, the more women seem to like you around here. And I like pleasing women.

'So?' Gretchen says. 'Spill.'

I shrug. 'What do you wanna know?'

He exchanges glances with Brad, like I've just asked the most stupid question in the world.

'What you friggin' think, dumb-ass?' Brad says. 'Did she? You know?'

'What do you think, shit for brains? Huh? How sexy does dinner and a polite chat get? Who do you think she

23

is? Like she's going to throw away her reputation on some scratcher like me.'

They all laugh, maybe with relief.

'Yeah, but did she dress up? Did she look hot?' Davey asks.

'She always looks hot,' I say, which comes out the wrong way and I know I've lost some control and given something away.

'Woah! See, he's got it so bad for her. But I don't envy you, buddy. It's not like you can touch or anything. She just gets to tease you for a year. Just eye candy, that's all,' Brad says. Davey laughs along with him, but Gretchen looks at me with narrow eyes. I stare down at my guitar and tune it when it doesn't need tuning.

'Anyway, are we gonna rehearse or what?' I say, desperate to change the subject. 'I got this new song. Just came to me this morning.'

'OK, butt-munch, let's hear it,' Brad says.

I jab at the effects board with my toe and turn my guitar acoustic. Play the opening arpeggio. This whole song just came out this morning. I woke up late after my Initiation, totally drained. Felt like I could have slept for days. Had a really thick head too, but my dad kept shouting up the stairs for me to get out of bed. He sounded pissed off. While I was in the shower, just standing there under the hot water in disbelief that I'm no longer a virgin, and seriously doubting it ever really happened until I saw the purple bite above my left nipple, this melody just crept into my head. Words came soon after. I had to get right out the shower and write it all down before it disappeared. The best songs come to me when I'm not thinking about music, or not thinking at all, and I'm totally unprepared.

I skipped breakfast, but went down to lunch and struggled to keep my face blank. My mom was at work but my dad kept asking me how it went with Mrs Berry. Man, he was like really staring at me. Freaked me out.

I just shrugged and grumbled a few things like the whole deal was a pain in the ass for me. But I could hardly eat. I was terrified we'd get found out, but desperate to do it again, and unable to get her out of my mind. It was like my stomach twisted and shrank whenever a thought of her popped into my head. Like the song I came up with, she just kept taking me over like a daydream.

From the opening chord progression, I turn the distortion on and play out the first verse. Man, it's the best riff I've ever come up with. All the hairs stand up on my arms and neck. I close my eyes and sing the rough lyrics that are still forming and fitting into the spaces. Brad starts a bass line. Davey kicks in with the drums. And I just know Gretchen is watching my hands on the frets so he can work out the scale and chords I'm using. He starts to strum a rhythm real quiet, then a bit louder. They're all getting good. We just come together now on most songs.

I take them into the chorus. It has a great hook and I hit the top notes without even thinking about it. So far, this is all I have, but then I work out the bridge as we play. I can hardly breathe; this is like our best song. I'm sure of it. Mostly we play covers, but we have about six rough songs we're working through. None of them are this cool.

When I stop playing nobody speaks. The amps hum. A cymbal tinkles.

'Dude, whatever happened last night must have been inspirational,' Brad says.

'That's a killer melody on the chorus, dude,' Davey says.

'Nice riff,' Gretchen says in a quiet voice. 'What you calling it?'

'*In Her Service*,' I say.

After practice, I have a quick word with Gretchen. 'Buddy, what was your dad like, when he gave you the Initiation spiel?'

'Pissed.'

'Yelling and shit?'

'No. He got the shakes and kept licking his moustache like he needed a drink.'

'Mine too, kind of, in his own way. They don't like it, do they?'

'Nope. Not a one. But my old man's different. He just misses the booze and the sound of his leather belt off my back. Fucker can't do shit now. And I'm glad.'

'Never thought I'd hear you say a good thing about the Saviour system.'

'Keeps daddio in check, but I never liked what happened to Isaac. Where we gonna get another guitarist like him from? You guys think I'm good but I don't know shit compared to Isaac. He taught me everything I know, which was like five per cent of his repertoire. What good is his talent stuck in the reformatory? And the Chaplain shouldn't be able to tell us what we can listen to. Chicks don't see rock'n'roll the way we do.'

I nod. Isaac was such a cool guitarist, but his wildness scared us. He used to fail tests at school, stay out after curfew, steal his mom's booze and even wink at girls in church.

'So tell me, lover boy, anything happen with you and Berry?'

I can't stop smiling. 'Dude, you guys have got one-track minds.'

He doesn't smile. 'You'd tell me, right? We tell each other everything, right?'

'Sure.' I nod.

He looks away. 'She's something else, buddy. Anyone can see that, but she's weird too. You know it. She's just different.'

I swallow. Can't speak, but I'm desperate to tell him everything. I hold myself back.

Outside the garage, in the back garden, where the bright colours of so many flowers hurt your eyes, I punch fists with Gretchen and say 'Adios'. Through her sunglasses, mom watches us from where she's stretched out on the lounger in her silver bikini. She smiles at Gretchen. He blushes and nods to her before walking down the side of our house and back into the street. Gretchen wanted my mom for his Mentor. I can tell by his silences. He had Mrs Willows instead. Gretchen would have had my mom if he wasn't my best friend. I think that has come between us in a small unspoken way.

Chapter Three

Another afternoon, another motel room.

Her black Mercedes is parked on the forecourt outside of number six. Beside the red door, there is a machine that dispenses Our Saviour Soda.

The door is unlocked.

It's dark inside.

On the night-stand beside the bed, a cigarette smokes in the ashtray. There is a whiskey bottle beside the ashtray, uncapped. Her suit is draped over the back of the chair beside the little dressing table. Curtains are drawn against the orange sun. Mrs Berry stands in the doorway of the en-suite bathroom. Her long fingers curl around the edges of the door frame, the nails dark against the white paint.

'Hello, Franklin.'

I swallow. 'Hello, ma'am.'

Her eyes have a wild look about them. I don't stare at them for long. Instead, I am distracted by the sight of her long body coming out of shadow. One leg first. The leather of her shoe catches what little light there is. Like her stockings, her shift is black and very sheer. So see-through, the pale skin underneath is almost luminous. The parts of her that are showing, like her shoulders and throat, look white as milk.

The room smells of liquor, cigarettes, perfume and

sex. A thick salty smell, same as in the other three rooms I left last week. The smell of sin.

'You're late.'

'Sorry. Had relay practice. State finals next month.'

She raises an eyebrow. 'How nice for you.'

I don't like her tone one bit. 'I – I got you these.' I hold out the red roses I bought from Saviour Mall.

'Sweet,' she says, without looking at them. 'Are you going to close that door, or do you want people to watch us fucking? It would be nice, but I don't think you're quite ready for that yet.'

'Sorry.' I push the door shut. I can't swallow and my heart is banging against the front of my chest. Every time I meet her, I drown. It never gets easier.

'Don't say sorry unless you've done something wrong.'

'OK. Sorry.'

She sighs. 'But you're incapable of doing anything wrong. Isn't that right, Franklin?'

'Depends.'

'Too busy getting top grades and winning races. Or playing guitar in your little band,' she says in a pissy voice, then slowly walks into the room. She sits on the bed. 'You wouldn't know how to put a foot wrong. What a marvellous product of the system you are, darling.'

My breath goes short. I feel weak and hot all over. She's wearing stockings with a seam up the back, like from old black and white movies. No bra either, under the swishing shift. Pink nipples and white curves of breast tremble when she moves. My mouth fills with saliva.

I want her to like me. To smile. Even though she's dressed like this I never know if she'll let me make love to her; she seems so bored and dismissive all the time. 'Maybe I'm not such a goody-goody,' I say. 'Wouldn't be here otherwise.'

She shakes her head. 'You are here because your Mentor told you to come to a motel room and fuck her. You were following orders. Obeying the will of a respectable member of our perfect little society. If she had told you to eat horse shit, you'd start setting the fucking table.' Throws her head back and laughs and looks sexier than ever.

I go hot all over. Feel giddy with anger. Feel small and stupid, like some tiny little thing that runs around the floor and lets itself get crushed by a shoe. Want to slam a door or smash something against a wall. I have no voice. She's right. If she tells me to go now, I'll go; obedient and sulky. All I can do is drop the roses on the floor. They make a pathetic rustle against the carpet. Then I say, 'Sorry.' Grit my teeth. 'Fuck!'

Her laughter goes on and on. Her eyes don't focus. She drinks some more from the glass. 'Franklin, my treasure, be careful or you'll get into real trouble. Maybe Our Saviour heard you. She hears everything, you know. Even your thoughts. You better go and make a confession to the Chaplain, you little blasphemer, before you get damned. And while you're there, say a prayer for me. Ask the Saviour to save a slut.' She kicks her legs out and wets her lips. Then straightens the seam of one stocking. 'Oh, I'm a sinner, Franklin darling. A real sinner. I've been bad today. It's not even three and I'm drunk. And it's lucky you were late. You missed the others leaving.'

The room moves backwards and forwards. I hear her voice like an echo. Hear her say it three times even though she only said it once. The back of my neck goes cold and prickly. I feel nauseous.

'Oh, precious, your face is a picture. Just adorable, darling. Don't tell me ... No, you thought ... Oh, sweetheart, how simply divine. You thought I was your girl. That you are my only lover. But I thought it was obvious. I mean, you know I love to fuck. To be fucked.

30

Did you think a college kid in a motel room is all I can get? All I need?'

'Slut.' I just said it. It was barely a whisper but it feels like I just shouted it out.

Mrs Berry stops talking. Her mouth is open in surprise. 'Darling. I never knew you had it in you.'

I'm breathing hard like I've run the two hundred metres on a hot day. The room seems so small now. I can't breathe. I have a pain in my chest. My guts are full of frost. If I leave now, I'll be crying before I get to the bus stop. My body starts to shake.

She watches my face. She is cold and beautiful. I love her.

'I'm bad, Franklin. If you could watch my memories, your hair would turn white.' She smiles again. 'And your cock would never go soft.' She crawls across the bed to the night-stand and pours a drink for me. 'I think you're just beginning to realise what I am, Franklin. That hurts, doesn't it?'

I swallow. 'No.'

She smiles, looks into her glass. 'You have feelings for me. I know. And I knew if I seduced you they would get stronger. I couldn't resist it. Couldn't resist you. But I'm bad, Franklin. Worse than you could ever imagine. And I should be punished for hurting you. You have every right to hurt me. You could never touch my heart, but you could put your pain into my body.' She looks up at me. Her face is happy and sad at the same time. The spiteful, hard angles of her laughing, sneering face have gone soft. 'You know what I'm saying.' It's like she's asking a favour. It's like she's pleading with me. 'Take your belt off, Franklin. The thick, black, leather belt, Franklin. And hurt me.'

The horror and confusion that wells up inside me shows on my face. I can't hide it. I shake my head.

Her eyes look moist. 'Do it, darling. You're a good boy. Your Mentor is a bad girl. Punish her.'

31

She stands up and walks across to the dresser. Bends over. Places both hands on top and looks into the mirror. In the reflection, she watches me over her shoulder.

Seems like the sun has gone behind the clouds. Feels like winter, but it's the hottest part of the day.

She watches my hands. They are shaking, but manage to unbuckle the belt. I slide it through the loops on my Levi's. It hangs from my fingers. There is no strength in that arm. There is no way I can do it. When I realise this, I feel relief.

Her voice comes from a distant place. There is no emotion in her words. 'I picked the first one up at the supermarket. Can you believe that? By the female toiletries. I was buying lipstick. For you. Looking for something dark and red to please you. And he was pretending to look at the shelves near me. He was taking quick little peeks at my chest. My blouse was tight. He could see my black bra through it. And he was staring at my legs. At the seams on the backs of my stockings. But he shouldn't have even been in that section. He'd followed me there. Saw me outside in the parking lot and followed me inside. I could feel his desire. His need. It was dangerous. It burned.

'I saw inside his head and saw what he was imagining. He was holding my wrists down and pushing his cock into my mouth. Holding my waist with hard, squeezing fingers and thrusting his body against me. Making my whole body shake. He never cared for my pussy. No, he wanted to go deep inside another place. So I decided to let him. I just said, "Follow me," in the store. I left and he walked after me. I never even looked him in the eye. Wasn't interested in his face, who he was. Just what he wanted to do to me. How he wanted to use me.'

I take a step towards her.

'I drove out here earlier than I'd planned. Cancelled a meeting for him. For a stranger who wanted to use me.

32

He followed me in his car. I went and got the keys from reception and then let myself in. Before I'd even dropped my handbag on the bed, he came up behind me. Put his hands on me. He was hard with me. Rough. If you look at my back you'll see the marks his fingers made. He had big hands.'

I take another step. I wrap the belt around my knuckles. Hold the leather so tight it hurts my hand.

'He fucked me on that bed, Franklin. On the bed I rented for us. I couldn't wait for you. I needed something quick and aggressive and dirty from a man. A stranger. It had to be a stranger.'

My doubled-over belt strap smashes across her buttock cheeks. Sounds like a wet foot slapping on a tiled floor. Her whole body flinches. Through the black nylon panties I can see a red mark already. I go to say sorry, but hear her sigh with pleasure. I look at her face in the mirror: teeth biting the bottom lip, eyeliner smudged, cheeks red, like she is when I'm inside her.

My voice trembles. 'Did you like it?'

'Yes.'

The questions just come out of me. I don't even have to think about them. 'Did he fuck you hard?'

'Yes. Once. Very hard. Like the world was going to end and he had to do it fast and quick before it was too late.'

I don't know why, but my cock is holding up my loose jeans. I can't remember feeling this turned on, ever. I bring the belt down twice, harder than the first time against her bottom. She squeals and steps from one foot to the other like a prancing horse. 'You bastard. You pretty bastard,' she says.

I look down at the long seams on the backs of her legs. I know I'll do anything in the world to be inside a motel room with Mrs Berry. I hate myself for it. I strike her again.

'I betrayed you. Betrayed you in our room. In our bed.'

33

I bring the belt whipping in. Over and over again. Make her shout and slap her hands against the dresser.

'Slut,' I say. 'Slut. Slut.' I like the word. Like to say it. To let it surge up and out of me, trampling over all of the restraint and thou-shalt-nots of the Saviour. I know I am damned. Feel guilty. Enjoy the guilt. Wonder if I'm crazy. Know that I am weak.

'There was another,' I say, between the panting breaths that make my whole body heave.

'Yes. I went back into town for another. I needed more. I drove around looking for a man. I couldn't see anyone. They all looked away when I stared. Like they were frightened of me. It's like they knew what I wanted. It's like I had a disease. But I eventually found a man who couldn't avoid me, who couldn't look away. A parking attendant in a little booth. A young man who has been made to stay in a hut and give out tickets. In the hot sun, he sits in there and gives rich, beautiful bitches tickets. Drops change into their soft, manicured hands. Looks down from his counter into the cars. Sees their legs. He told me they often show him things. Pull their skirts up or widen the splits when they drive through. They never smile at him or talk to him but they show themselves to him. One lady shows him her naked pussy every Friday at noon. It's the only reason he can stand the job. She parks next to his booth and complains about the litter in his carpark. Asks him what he is going to do about it and all the time she is showing him her sex. Sitting with her legs open on the leather seat of a Mercedes Benz and playing with herself. Under the counter he gets out his big cock – oh, Franklin, it was huge – and strokes it. Isn't that beautiful? They've never touched but they go through this every Friday.'

'And you had to have him?'

'Yes. Back here. I told him to close the carpark and I brought him back here. He cried like a baby while I sucked him. I put him in my mouth and sucked away

34

all of the pain and frustration of his life in that little booth. I drank his suffering. All of it. Every last drop. Every desperate dream he has ever had of fucking the cold, rich bitches who buy tickets from his booth slid down my throat.'

The sound of my belt against the buttocks of my mother's best friend spanked off the walls of this hot room. That was the last time I struck her with the belt. She could never be punished enough. It is futile.

I unzipped my jeans and used her like the other two men who had been in here today. And no matter how hard I thrust into her – so fast she even tries to climb on to the dresser in her excitement and loses one shoe – I know I'll never be enough for her. I'll never stop thinking about what she's doing when I'm not around. It will be torment. Already I am being punished for being a sinner.

Chapter Four

She looks out the window of the diner. Stares at the highway. Across the table I eat cheeseburger and fries, with a malted shake and a basket of onion rings. She hasn't touched her Caesar salad.

'Go on, ask me,' she says, without taking her eyes from the highway.

'What?'

'The question you are dying to ask me.'

'I don't understand.'

She kicks me under the table with her pointy shoe. 'Remember what I told you about telling the truth. I won't have anything less. It's important. Then there can be no games beside the game of dealing with the absolute truth.'

I swallow a mouthful of burger and take a slurp from my shake. 'What you said about the men. Is it true?'

'Every word. Do you want me to take photographs in future? I will if you need proof.'

I look down at my plate. 'Have there been many?' My voice is barely a whisper.

She laughs. Looks at me. Taps ash from the end of her cigarette. 'I'll tell you about them all. Each and every one, if you like. Though sometimes I was drunk. Took too much. Things are hazy.'

Took too much? The bite on my buttocks she gave me in the shower of the motel room feels like it's glowing.

She smiles. 'Overindulged. Was greedy,' she says, like she can read my mind. 'And no,' she answers my next question that is only half formed and hurts as it takes shape. 'You don't mean nothing to me. You're not just a statistic in my black book, darling. I like you. I like you a lot, Franklin.'

I feel my face go hot with a blush. It's the best I've felt in ages.

'Does . . .'

'Say it.'

'Does my mom know?'

'About the other men?' She smiles to herself. 'Your mother is an angel, Franklin. Don't worry, she's nothing like the lady from across the street. And don't underestimate your father. He's a good man. He looks after her. Adores her. She'd never need anyone else. She'd be lost without him. She's good with accounts in the city, Franklin, but needs a lot of love at home. Your father gives her that. This is the truth. But we shouldn't talk about them any more.'

I nod. Secretly pleased and relieved with what she said. I guess I knew it anyway.

'And you know it anyway. They'll always be all right. It's how you're going to deal with the world now that counts, Franklin.'

'Yeah. But don't figure I'll have much say in it.'

'That's what they all say. What do you want to do?'

'Be in my band.'

She laughs. 'And you're not joking either. It's not the last of your youthful affectations. You actually want to be a rock star.'

'Wouldn't mind,' I mumble into my burger.

'Then be one,' she says in a straight voice with a straight face.

I nearly choke. She's said some pretty crazy things since my Initiation, but this is just the most outrageous. My turn to laugh. 'Sure. Yeah. I might just do that.'

'What's stopping you?'

'Like you need to ask?' She frowns. I adjust my tone. 'Best I'm going to do is to go to Finishing School, get an arranged marriage and play for the church orchestra. Maybe they'll let me do a guitar solo in a hymn sometime.'

She laughs. 'Sounds wonderful, darling.'

'Don't it just.'

'But I'm not joking. You can be a musician if you like. I mean that.'

I shake my head and giggle away: she is just outrageous, but so cool.

She lights another cigarette. 'I'll help you.' She's not fooling around either. I begin to think she really is crazy. She looks right into me. 'I'm not crazy, Franklin. And I would have thought after all you've seen, and heard, in the last two weeks it would have been sufficient to remove your annoying habit of underestimating me.'

I nod. 'Sorry. Sure. Sorry.'

'But be sure being a musician is not only something you want, but something you need. What you absolutely have to do.'

I don't know what to say to that. I mean, she's talking about me leaving town. Defying my parents, the church, the system, everything. That's what it would take to play in a band.

'Everything would be at stake, Franklin. But you know that.'

Chapter Five

'Where are we going?'

Mrs Berry smiles, says nothing.

I want her, desperately. It's been four days since she drove me out to Saviour Mount and parked her car under the beech trees. Four days and nights since she gave herself to me inside the small, leathery spaces of her car: seat reclined, high-heeled feet on the dashboard, her pale face tense with pleasure at my enthusiastic fumbling, trying so hard to get at her flesh beneath the expensive silk. There is despair in my passion to stroke her legs, lick her breasts, suck her tongue and tickle her pussy all at the same time. I always feel like she is about to be taken away from me.

And it's been four days since she taunted me with more of the small details from her betrayals. As I thrust between her thighs, she confessed she'd taken two suburban husbands to quiet places outside of town and emptied them of their needs. Since then I have been haunted by the painful ghosts of faceless strangers using her long body. It makes me afraid; makes me angry; makes me hard. Now I want to bend her over the bonnet of this car and use my belt again.

No calls or messages either. Just glimpses of her across the street. Eight steps in spiky shoes from her front door to her car; and eight steps back from car to house when she gets home late. Whenever I'm in my room and I hear a sound from over there, my heart jumps and my skin gooses, even when I know it isn't her. I can tell now. Can sense where she is and what she's doing. When my gut twists and my spirit drops like a heavy stone through a dark lake, I know she's betraying me.

Sometimes it makes me cry. Other times I break stuff – the stupid kid's stuff in my room I used to think was precious. And sometimes I snatch up my guitar and make songs and lyrics that surprise and shock me. Surprise me because they're good; like I've found a secret place deep inside full of melody and poetry. Songs that shock me because of the strong words and evil images I write down. Most of this material I couldn't even show the band. I'd be ashamed and they might think I'm going crazy. We all used to be alike, but now they remind me of kids. All that horsing around and dumb-ass banter. They're just totally unaware of what goes down in this town and how intense life can be, out there in the world we're protected from. I'm sick of kid's stuff. All the shit and old toys in my room. I took the baseball and football posters down and pissed my dad off by throwing all of my sports trophies in a cupboard. I want nothing in my room but my guitar and my dreams; there's no room for anything else. No one would understand but Mrs Berry. But I doubt she cares much. She gets me so mad.

After school, I'm breaking track records. Coach doesn't know what's come over me. Never knew I could hit that track so hard myself, or just smash through the pain and keep on going, for ever. Nothing can stop me. And I have to keep going, keep burning myself out, so I don't go crazy. It's like, in just a few weeks, she's taken away all the stuff I used to know and replaced it with something hot and reckless I don't really understand and can't see the end of either. It scares the shit out of me. Sometimes I want things to be back the way they were before the Initiation. Just to goof around like a big kid again. But the regret and the looking back doesn't last long. Before long I'm thinking of her again – my head is so thick with pictures of her I'm ready to overload. And my whole body hums and vibrates with power and I fill up with so much white energy I think I'm going to combust. Then I know I could never leave this alone. Never go back to the way things were. Now I know why the Chaplains and the women in this town want to keep us men safe from sin; they know what's inside us and how good it feels. But it's too late for me; Mrs Berry has unlocked the door of my comfortable cell and now I'm long gone.

'Do you ever think of the future, Franklin?' she asks.

'Sure. All the time.'

'Of us?'

I look out the side window and mumble, 'Sometimes.' I feel sick to my stomach for being sulky. She hates it too. But I just can't help it. She is cruel.

'I won't be around for ever, Franklin. You know that. This is nice. But soon you're going to have to look after yourself and find the things you need.'

I stamp my foot; it's all I can do to stop myself from punching out the glove compartment.

She smiles. 'I'm such a bitch.' Shakes her head like she's amused with herself. 'Sometimes I forget myself. But it's important we move things along with your Mentoring.'

'So what's next on the syllabus: how to deal with a bitch? Seems like the most important thing a guy can learn in this town. Or is it a lesson on how to cope with being dumped on?'

Mrs Berry tilts her head back and laughs some more. 'Oh, darling, you're doing just fine. Believe me.'

'Maybe I'd have been better off with Mrs Mullins.'

She raises an eyebrow. 'That all depends on whether you want a private education or the public service like

41

every other poor fool in this town. Do you want to fuck like a rock star, Franklin, or learn to bake a cake?'

I shrug.

She slides her dress up her legs. I look down; can't stop myself. Stockings the colour of sand that sparkle when we go past a street lamp, and no panties. My crotch goes so tight I have to fidget my backside around on the seat.

'I have a surprise for you tonight, Franklin. I want you to see it as a kind of mid-term. You need to do well before you can progress to the finals.' She looks so excited. She looks a little crazy. I want her even more.

With a pointed, shiny foot she floors the gas pedal.

'Who is she?' I whisper. I can't move any further into the motel room.

Mrs Berry places one finger against her lips to shush me. Then smiles, but not in a way to make me feel comfortable.

I take a deep breath and look at the bed again. The tied-up woman turns her head in my direction. Blindfold, she uses her ears and angles the side of her head towards me and the open door behind me. She's older than Mrs Berry but real nice looking: short silver hair, lots of make-up and pearl earrings; stripped down to stockings and black underwear, her ankles and wrists are tied fast to the bedposts with what looks like thin ribbons. Her legs and arms are pulled apart. It's warm in here, but she's trembling.

Mrs Berry closes the door behind me. 'She's yours. Go to her. Take her.' Her lipsticky breath is hot against my cheek. A scent that makes me think of my mother's handbag at the same time as sex with Mrs Berry.

'But who is she?' I whisper across the short electric space between our faces. I still can't move my feet.

'Someone who needs you, darling. And someone you need. It's been four days. Give in to what you feel.'

That's easier said than done. Sure, it's been a while since that night on Saviour Mount and my need to thrust and maul is starting to turn painful, but this lady looks like someone's mother or wife, and she's tied down in a cheap motel room. I feel light in the head.

'She came here willingly,' Mrs Berry whispers over my shoulder. She slides both hands around my waist and massages my cock hard. 'She likes this arrangement. But don't take off the sleeping mask. She's a very important lady in this town.'

This makes my breath go all quick and my swollen cock seems to take me away from Mrs Berry's arms and drag me towards the bed. What have I become? A degenerate? That's what the Chaplain would say. But I like it.

I kneel on the end of the bed. It creaks. The mattress dips. The woman's whole body goes stiff. She whimpers. Can't endure the waiting any longer and pulls at the bindings. Moves her wrists in hopeless circles. Tries to close her knees and pull her feet up to her bottom, but can't do it.

I look over my shoulder. Mrs Berry smokes a cigarette. She watches me through the smoke. Nods her head.

I reach out. Stop. Then touch the woman's ankle, below the binding.

Her body jolts like my fingers are live wires. Her chest goes up and down real quick. Through the lace pattern on her bra I can see she has large nipples. They look so pink. I lick my lips.

Trace a finger up her leg. Follow the thin seam up her calf and behind her knee where her sweat has made her stocking damp, then along her thigh to the cold of the metal garter clasp. Brush the inside of a thigh with the back of my knuckles.

She sucks in air. Moans.

I move further up the bed, kneel beside her ribs.

43

Looking down at her big breasts, I unzip my jeans to release the pressure.

'Oh.' Then, 'Oh, God,' she says at the sound of the zipper.

I flop my cock out of my shorts. Feels good to have the air on the tingling skin. Reaching out, I touch her sex. Her panties feel warm, are moist. I slide one finger inside the black panties and then slip it inside her. The bindings go so tight on her wrists and ankles and cut into her skin. She's wearing so much perfume, I can hardly breathe.

'Slut,' I say. Can't stop myself before the sight of this strange, important woman in the black lingerie, tied up on a hotel bed, who needs a strange man's hands on her body.

Pressing the back of her head into the pillow, she writhes her body on the sheets. It's like the one finger inside her has made her whole body come alive. She liked what I called her too. I can tell. But shakes her head from side to side in denial.

'Yes,' I say.

I slip two more fingers inside her. She presses both hands down into the bedcovers, opens her mouth, grimaces.

I swallow saliva to take the dryness from my throat. 'You dress like a slut because you want a hard cock.'

She pants through clenched teeth. Moving the fingers of one hand in and out of her slippery sex, I use my other hand to play with her breasts. I pinch a nipple. Then the other. She slides her feet around. I pluck, tweak, squeeze, caress. Can't help myself, so I lick both nipples through the black lace. She does an 'Oh, oh, oh, oh' sound. Under her buttocks the bed is wet. Can feel it with the back of the hand inside her.

Push my jeans down to my knees. Straddle her face. Arc my body over her. Gently lower my cock to her lips. Her tongue darts out. Licks the end. Bad thoughts and bad words fill my head. 'Suck me like a slut. Don't spill a drop.'

Somewhere in the room, I hear Mrs Berry exhale.

Moving her whole head and her shoulders upwards, she swallows most of me. Tilts her head back to take me into her throat. Her breath rasps through her nose. Her moan vibrates up my length and travels into my stomach where it sinks and tingles my anus.

It's like she's starving; devouring me like this. Slowly, I move my hips up and down. Support myself with my arms and knees and sink into her wide open mouth.

When I notice the thick, gold wedding band on her finger, I hear myself say, 'Oh, sweet Saviour,' and I can't hold back. I go blind from the pleasure rush that makes my skin shiver and my ass shrink tight.

Under the blindfold, I know her eyes are wide open. As I chug and froth everything down her gulping throat, her forehead furrows. I pull up a bit from her slurpy mouth, but her head follows my cock, her tongue slapping and her cheeks hollow like she's terrified she might not get it all like I told her to.

Won't be long before I'm hard again with this woman. I wish Mrs Berry would be jealous. This woman is as bad as Mrs Berry. And there was me thinking my Mentor was one in a million.

From the jug on the night-stand, Mrs Berry pours me a glass of water. Mops my face with a white towel while I recover. The woman on the bed licks her lips. She's older than my own mother. But that just makes it better because it's more unacceptable. If she was tied face down, I'm sure I'd use my belt again. I begin to imagine she's a school teacher, or even a Chaplain. I stop myself. That's going too far. Mrs Berry smiles.

I take off the rest of my clothes and kneel between the woman's legs. Stroke her slippery thighs. Snap her panties from her waist and toss them on to the floor. Extend my tongue. Taste her. Look up at Mrs Berry's intense face with the narrow eyes. Hold my cock in my fist and trail the thick end through the folds of the sex before me. If I slip inside, I think, I will have slept with two women. This is forbidden. One man, one woman. A decree of the Saviour Church. Reform school awaits. I look down. Have to see myself go in. Slowly. All the way. Deep.

The woman groans. I hold her legs under the knee and begin to push in and pull out. Over and over again. She pulls her wrists against the bindings. Opens her mouth. Makes a deep moaning sound that comes from the floor of her stomach.

'Like it?'

She whips her head from side to side. Moans.

'You like it? Mmm, this young cock?'

'Ohh,' she says and presses her groin into me. Wanting more. Something harder.

I speed up my thrusts. Close my eyes. Lose myself in the red thoughts of madness. Never lose breath. Never get tired. I just thrust and thrust and thrust so the whole bed sounds like it's ready to collapse. She can't talk. The sounds she is making seem stoppered, stuck. Her face is screwed up and her body locks. She makes the sounds of a crying baby. I can't stop. Just keep pummelling into her. Want to put my mouth on her. Eat her white flesh as she comes. Suck her sinning soul inside me and keep it prisoner. She's not an elegant, mature lady. She's a lusty girl all over again. Only now, feeling shame is half of what makes her come so hard, so coughing, choking hard.

Inside my head I start to see pictures. Quick snap shots changing at speed. This lady is tied up on a bed and three men use her body. Hands all over her breasts and between her legs. One man stuffed into her mouth. Another turning her over to go in from behind. Bed after bed after bed – her glamorous body writhing and clawing and bucking up and down with so many men all over her. Blindfold, whipped. Bent over her car beside a highway at night, skirt over her hips. Someone being quick and hard from behind. I shake my head clear. Don't know where it comes from. It's like I've seen these things in the past and am remembering them all at once. They fade and she goes loose under me. I squeeze her thighs and let my cock burn and scorch and empty itself inside the tied-up lady.

I feel dizzy from the ecstasy of seeing so many bad things at once while doing something I would never believe happens in this town. But I'm doing it. It was so good, but I want something else. It's like a craving for sugar, but it's not sweet stuff I want. Like I'm hungry but not hungry either. Thirsty without needing to drink.

I hear Mrs Berry whisper into my ear. Her thin arms slide around me. Her chin rests against my neck. I inhale her perfume. 'Bite her. Bite the bitch. Taste her. Go on. Finish her.'

I don't know what this means but Mrs Berry pushes my head down to the woman's sex. No, to her thighs. 'Bite her,' she says. 'Bite her, darling. She wants you to.'

What she says seems to make sense when hot skin is close to my mouth. I lap and lap at her leg above her stocking top. Then lick at her sex and suck at the salt. That's nearly it. The hot taste of her secret place in my mouth. Unable to stop my mouth I slide my tongue between her buttocks and then clamp a cheek with my teeth. Want to bite hard. Stop myself. Drool with my watery mouth over the skin. Roll my eyes and then nip. Nip. Nip.

I taste something salty. So rich it makes me shiver like I've bitten into a lemon. My eyes water. I want more. More. So much more. I suck at the salty, rusty taste. Think of meat from a barbecue. Could eat the world I'm so hungry. I suck until my mouth is silvery with her and my throat burns from her sauce. Can hear a thump, thump, thump in my head, between my ears.

47

Fingers go into my hair. Clench. Pull my head back. I shout, 'No.'

'Enough!' Mrs Berry hisses. 'Enough.'

I struggle against her arms but she holds me tight. My head drops. A wonderful warm, sleepy feeling takes all the strength from my limbs. I see so many bright, blinding lights under my lids. I shiver. I start to cry. Never felt so good. So much pleasure is pain. I understand everything. This is God.

I wake up next to the tied-up woman. She is sleeping. My head rests against her bosom. She smells good. I lick her skin.

Someone is shaking my shoulders. 'Come on, up. Get up. Get up. Franklin, wake up.' It's Mrs Berry. I moan, feel cold, want to sleep some more. Forever. I was so comfortable. She slaps me. Helps me off the bed. Pushes me into the bathroom. Holds me up on my bare feet. This place is full of steam. I can feel every droplet on my skin. I want the water. I start to laugh. I'm so happy, I tell her. I love you, I tell her.

Water blasts off my face and body. All the smoke goes from my thick head. I can see thoughts becoming hard objects inside my head. All my bones and muscles reform and rebuild themselves all over my body. I can feel it happening. My skin goes tight over the rocks underneath. Now I'm stronger than ever. I feel like a superhero.

Chapter Six

Skateboard, basketball, stack of computer games, cycling helmet and the Saviour adventure annuals look like junk piles in the corners of my room. I'm going to stuff them all in the loft and garage. With the ghost of Mrs Berry stalking through my mind in black heels they are nothing more than silly coloured bricks – kid's stuff.

Lying in bed gives me time to think. The size of what I'm doing dwarfs everything I own, where I live, how I've lived, what I've done with my whole life. Everything here in this town is a version. But you can't hide behind biblical action figures, chemistry sets and heaven-seeker telescopes for ever. Not if you've seen another version.

A dark suit my mom had dry-cleaned hangs on my wardrobe door. Delicious hot and cold flushes start the countdown in my head. Pins and needles prick my stomach and I need a crap for the nerves. She's starved me of herself again; six days this time. But we're going out tonight. She said she's going to teach me how to hunt.

Being a man used to seem so far away – a different life – I never thought I'd run out of summer holidays, hanging with my buddies in the garage, eyeing women from afar. But now it's here and with it has arrived a huge cinema screen in my mind, flickering with fast edits of the pleasures and bright promises of excitement Mrs

Berry says can always be within my reach. My imagination is expanding so fast, my parents seem like tiny people in a doll's house. And this town is made from Lego.

Outside my room, in the street white with sunlight and green with trees comes the jangly, hurdy-gurdy sound of an ice-cream van. I go to the window and watch the kids gather and wait impatiently amongst discarded skipping ropes and fallen bikes. Those with money in their moist hands skip up and down or do little excited jumps. Others, caught short, race white-faced as if the devil were behind them, to beg from fathers hard at work with the preparation of evening meals. Ice-cream on their minds, with raspberry squirts on top and chewy bubblegum balls in the bottom of plastic cones that taste like blueberry for three seconds, the kids go at frightening speeds up swept paths to houses with bright faces – all smiles of tinted glass, solar panels and Scandinavian wood, three storeys high.

Out front of the gleaming houses, on broad lawns, smelling of cut grass and drowsy flowers, the fathers work – trimming, pruning, planting, washing, making everything real nice for the wives who work so hard out in Saviour City. Warm tarmac divides the big houses and white sidewalks like a black river. Two mothers return from work at the Corporation. As they drive slowly past with their sunroofs open, I can hear the tyres making pleasant rippling sounds on the road. I think about their pretty legs pushing the pedals like Mrs Berry. Thoughts of them clicking around that big black skyscraper in high heels and tight skirts make me shiver.

Two fathers appear at open doorways and smile, eager to talk about their day indoors. At number 217, Mr Karl Berry sets his sprinklers to pitter-patter against the blood-red roses Mrs Berry likes. Wins prizes for those roses and lavishes so much love on them to make my mom and Mrs Berry laugh when they drink coffee together, while their eyes do something different above the gold rims of black china cups.

Through the shiny silver ropes of clear water, Mr Berry stands tall. With the roses thick about his feet and the lawn mowed into stripes, he sees my beaming face at the window. Turns to face me. I retreat back into the dark of my room, not liking his stare.

Her Mercedes is gleaming on the drive, like a big purring black panther. Came home early today. She's a boss of something at the Corporation so she's allowed to bunk off. Somewhere across the road inside the massive dark house, she's there. It's like I can hear her breathing and can smell her perfume from over here. I wonder what she's doing right now. Maybe selecting a dark outfit for tonight, like the one that showed off her pale shoulders at my dad's birthday party, all low cut at the front with that tiny wisp of lace peeking out the gap. Or maybe she's taking a shower after work. Undressing her paleness and walking to the en-suite bathroom to make herself smell so good. For me.

My dad comes into the room. Drying his hands on a tea towel, he looks down at the boxes. 'Someone's growing up real quick,' he says.

I shrug. Don't want him in here.

He checks his watch. Then looks at the window. 'A watched kettle does not boil.'

I sigh. 'I'm not watching.'

He smiles. 'You look forward to your meetings with Mrs Berry.'

I nod. 'She's pretty cool.'

'She is. But she's only your Mentor.'

'I know,' I say far too quick.

He picks up my pitcher's glove. 'We should throw a few sometime.'

I nod.

'You hoping to play in the softball leagues after

college? It's important when you're married to keep up with your friends.'

I clench my fists. 'All we've got.'

'What?'

'Not like there's anything else to do.'

'There's plenty. You wouldn't believe how much effort goes into running a home and bringing up kids.'

'I don't doubt it,' I say, and let a little sarcasm slip into my tone.

My dad chuckles. Shakes his head. 'I knew this would happen.'

'What?'

'Suppose you think you're going to play in that band for ever.'

My face goes dark with angry blood; I can feel it. I have to look down. My jaw starts to shake.

'Your mother wouldn't listen. Some women should never be Mentors. They're too wild. Too fast. They should save that for the boardroom and the sales meetings. Young men need stability. Common sense.' His voice goes quiet. It's getting harder for him to speak. 'Your whole future's at stake. You got to keep your head together.' I've never heard him challenge one of my mom's decisions before. Least not in front of me.

'Mom thinks she's OK.' I feel like a shit for saying that.

'Mrs Berry is great. I'm not denying that. All I'm saying is you spend all your time mooning around this room, strumming your guitar, or hanging with the band. Which, let's face it, is going to have to call it a day when Finishing College starts. And you seem so restless. Bored. Not something you've ever been before.'

'What do you mean? I still go to training.'

'I know. And I expect you'll clean up at the state finals. But it's your attitude. I can see you're distracted.' He looks at his feet. 'Can't think about anything but Mrs Berry. And when she's not around, you watch her house.'

'That's crap!' I suddenly hate myself for being so obvious.

'Hey, keep it down. You might be eighteen, but that's no excuse for raising your voice to your father.'

'Sorry.'

'I'm worried about you, Franky. It's the only reason I'm bringing this up.' He goes to stand by the window and breathes out slowly. 'It's happened before, you know.'

I stay quiet. Just don't want to hear what he's going to say, because I know what he's going to say.

'Young men forming attachments to their Mentors.'

My whole head is burning. I'm red down to my tailbone. May as well grow a lobster tail. 'Man, it's nothing like that.'

He looks at me for a long time. 'Just take it easy. All I'm saying. Some things seem irresistible. But nothing really is. Things can't be the way they used to be for us guys, Franklin. They just can't. We had to give women a chance to do better than we did. We got a duty to stand by that.'

'Yeah, I know that. I know.'

'Good. Sometimes it's easy to forget.' He goes out.

I put my hands over my stupid, red face. I've been indiscreet. She warned me about this. But what do I know? I suddenly realise; I'm just a big, dumb-ass kid with a hard-on. I laugh at myself. Then sit up. But if this is all I am, why is Mrs Berry trying to undo everything? I know she hates the town. That's pretty obvious. But people notice stuff. She's taking a massive risk with me, and with everything else she gets up to. Everything goes along nicely here because no one is different. So when someone goes a little strange, everyone knows about it. 'Act like a kid. An older kid,' she told me. 'But not around me.'

Chapter Seven

This one has seen me checking her out, but hasn't run away from the look in my eyes like the last two did. I like her too. Sleek with the short black hair and sunglasses. Tight skirt to her knees, white blouse, hardly any jewellery, short legs with a nice shape in those sexy boots that stop at the knee. Mrs Jackson at school wears them in the winter and I find it hard to concentrate on her history lessons.

Maybe she's 'available to misbehave' like Mrs Berry said. But she's more than ten years older than me; it seems impossible that I can go speak to her and try to seduce her. The thought makes me feel sick. I'm not cut out for this. Like I told Mrs Berry: it's too early. But she won't listen; she's pretending to look at clothes on the other side of this store, but is watching me the whole time. I can see her between the racks of underwear. She catches my eye. Nods.

I walk behind the woman who is touching a black, see-through garter belt with her fingertips. I go to speak. My throat closes. Sweat runs in my palms and down the channel of my spine. I feel dizzy, sick. Clear my throat. The woman moves away and looks at a cream and white garter belt.

I wait a moment, then walk past her. 'You'd look . . .' I run out of words. Cough. 'You'd look real nice in that.' She turns on a spiky heel and stares at me with hard blue eyes.

Man, what have I done! She could call the store manager, the cops! I'm too young to be in here! Why would I be here anyway? I'm too young to be married and buying something for a young wife. That makes me a degenerate. And once they call you a degenerate in this town, you're finished. Some of them have to wear electronic tags. I read about the shoe-shop guy in a paper last year. The police took him away. He was incarcerated and rehabilitated. I got to get away. What was I thinking?

'Thank you,' she says. 'That's something only a fool or a very brave man would say.'

I do that stupid giggle, then pull my face straight when I see her look of disappointment at my dumb-ass sound. But she's not angry. 'Sorry. I mean, I didn't want you to feel uncomfortable, but sometimes you just can't help admiring someone pretty.' I blush hot and crimson and bow my head.

'How sweet. Thank you. But I don't think your mother or your Mentor would be pleased to know you were chatting to women in the lingerie department.'

Look them in the eye. Never break your stare. Look past their expression and right into the middle of their deeper feelings. Try to find who they can really become. Pick up on every nuance and change in the eyes. Put them at ease when they're insecure. Say something nice, and mean it, if they feel bad about themselves. I remember the advice Mrs Berry gave me. Too much to process, but I realise I haven't been looking this woman in the eye like I'm supposed to. I'm scared of her. Have no control of myself, or the situation.

I take a deep breath, look up, smile. Read her eyes. She finds me amusing, but silly. Is bored and is only entertaining me because this is highly irregular; men aren't allowed to bother women; especially us younger guys. Women know about our urges, but are not to encourage us.

'I – I just liked your style. And your hair. Most women wear it longer.'

She blushes. The hard frost in her eyes melts. She smiles and laughs to herself. Shakes her head. 'So what are you doing here?'

'I'm buying a present for my Mentor.'

She raises an eyebrow. 'In the lingerie department? That sounds highly irregular.'

I can think of nothing to say. Panic floods my guts and head. I break off the stare. Nearly cuss. Find her eyes again. She still finds me silly, but is curious why someone of my age is approaching her. From my humiliation and breaking voice, she can see I'm pretty harmless. Not like that Trapdoor Spider guy who used to operate in hotels and tie business women up. They never caught him.

I shrug. Look at her pretty face with the fine lines just appearing around her eyes. Admire her discreet make-up and long black eyelashes. Can't help myself or the swelling below. Dare myself to think of how this face would change underneath me. Think of how much I want to kiss her.

Like she's read my mind, her expression suddenly changes. Her eyes go bashful and her face softens. Then she composes herself in an instant. 'My, my, you are a fast one, aren't you? And I thought all the men in this town were so well behaved.'

I think of the lyrics to one of our songs. The one we play in the garage when my mom is out. I stare deeply, part my lips, find the part of me that always tells the truth. Think of her skirt up around her waist and me between her thighs. 'Rules are made to be broken.'

Her eyes go wide. Her chest looks a little pink. Her voice is almost a whisper. 'So where do you take them?'

What does she mean? I frown.

'No. This is silly. I'm sorry. I'm presuming too much.'

She's getting away. The real world of stores and courtesy and *how do you do* is creeping back and sealing over the narrow opening I have made between our eyes. 'I like to go somewhere quiet,' I say real soft, and don't dare break my eyes away.

'Have you been caught?' She sounds breathless.

I shake my head. I think of what Mrs Berry told me. 'I'm discreet. But passionate too.'

This seems to shock her. Her fingers twist a suspender strap around the knuckle; she doesn't know she's doing it. I think of how white her bottom would look and how the thin lines of her garters would cut across her curves. I think of her sex. I know it is pink without much floss. And very sensitive. I want to taste her down there.

She swallows and quickly looks around us. No one nearby. Neither of us can hear the store music any more. I can even feel how hot her face is by just concentrating. I know that even if she walks away, she'll do something wicked with her hands between her thighs tonight in bed while thinking of me.

In the distance I half see a tall black silhouette, pale face raised, standing absolutely still: my Mentor.

'How much time do you have?' the woman says in a hurry.

'Plenty.'

'OK,' she says. Then bites her bottom lip while she thinks. 'Wait until I've gone, then find my car. It's the red Saab near the big ticket machines.' And she's gone, walking quickly. I don't move or look at anything in particular. Just listen to the fading clickety-clackety sound of her heels.

'You did good,' Mrs Berry says from close by. She sounds relieved. But I can hear something else in her voice too. Sounds like anxiety. 'Go now. But don't take too much. Just taste her. You know what I mean. This is very important.'

57

I nod my head and follow the perfume-ghost the woman with the clever blue eyes left behind her.

'Do it here. Quick. Here. Don't take my clothes off.' Soon as we were through the door of her condo, she walked quickly into the little white living room and stood in the middle, by the black coffee table.

I follow her. My whole body is shaking. I'm desperate to take her, to taste all of her flesh; warm and perspiring under that hot black suit and boots. But I'm real nervous too. The lights are on but the blinds are open. I go to draw them.

'No,' she says, without looking at me. 'Leave them.'

I walk up behind her. My heartbeat deafens me. Close my eyes and inhale the perfume, soaps, moisturisers – I can smell them all. And her milky, salty woman smell from where it rises out from her collar. I breathe her in and out. Fill my body with her scent.

When I touch her, she jumps. Her whole body is trembling. 'I'm sorry. This isn't something I do every day.' Now it's her turn to do the silly laugh.

Trace the tip of my tongue across the nape of her neck. I breathe out; the ecstasy of this situation pushes all the air from my body. Slip my hands under her arms. Find her breasts heavy and trussed inside a bra. She lets her head fall back on my shoulder. Her eyes are closed. I undo the buttons of her thin blouse. It feels expensive. Kiss the outside of one ear. She moans. Starts to relax. 'This is bad. I shouldn't be doing this,' she says.

I go to reassure her, then remember the woman on the motel bed and realise this reticence could be part of her game, her role. Maybe a night-time fantasy has suddenly become real for her. Yes, I know it. And even though there is a husband in the suburbs, she often thinks of the young men in town. Has had little experience with us, but the very thought of us makes her feel desire and shame in equal amounts. I find her nipples and gently

58

press my hardness against her tight bottom, so she can feel its width between the valley of her tingling buttocks.

She starts to roll her head around on my shoulder. Says, 'Oh, God. Oh, God,' a few times. My teeth find her neck. So white, so soft, so full of mineral goodness. Lick it numb with my wolf tongue and shuffle her skirt up to her hips. My hands go into her panties real quick. Squeeze her bottom. Slip some fingers under and touch her sex. I smile when I find her panties wet. She shivers. Slide one, two, three fingers inside her. She bends forward and bows her legs. Puts her hands on her shiny knees. When I look down and see her stockings rising out of tight, shiny boots, I suddenly have to be inside her.

I rip at my belt and zip.

'No,' she says, head down, eyes closed. 'You're not going to. You can't. You can't do this to me.'

Holding her hips, I pull her buttocks up and slip my cock between her thighs. Rub it against her lips. She puts fingers in her mouth to stifle the sobs. My whole cock is so wet and, without hardly noticing, I slip right into her warmth. She makes hard croaky sounds as I slide further in.

I look to the window and see all the bright lights of the condos across the street, staring into her living room. She walks around this place naked and gets undressed in front of open windows. I know it. Can see her doing it in my head.

'They can see us,' I whisper.

She jolts like I've bitten her.

I slip my hands over her shoulders and pull her small body back hard against my groin so my cock really impacts into her. 'Someone is looking. I can see them. They can see a girl being fucked with her panties around her knees.'

She makes crying sounds, then hard, deep noises like she's trying to speak with her stomach. Holding her still, so she cannot squirm, I thrust into her as hard and fast as I can. She goes silent but pulls and twists her nipples through her bra. I can see her reflection in the television screen. 'I'm going to come in you. Fill you. There's so much of it. I saved it for you.'

She puts her hands on the back of her head and pulls at her hair. I hold her breasts and move my hips even harder so we nearly lose balance. When she makes the coughing lamb sounds and her legs lock, I let go. Long stream after long stream jets inside her.

As I'm catching my breath and wanting to kiss the back of her neck in gratitude and with affection, she wipes her eyes and says, 'Go now. You better go now.'

'OK,' I say. 'Just let me kiss you first.'

Staying hard inside her, I gently pull her up against the front of my body. Put my face on her neck. The pleasure of seducing and then releasing myself inside a woman is blinding. But there is more to be had and Mrs Berry showed me how to get it. Using the teeth after sex brings the second climax. 'I'll show you a secret,' Mrs Berry whispered to me our first time in a hotel room. 'How to extract greater pleasures from your lover. To take part of them with you for ever.'

I wet the nape of the woman whose name I still don't know. Lick down to the soft place where her neck joins her shoulder. She shivers. I know her eyes are closed. She's surprised at the cold numbing sensation of my saliva. But finds it pleasing. Caressing her breasts with my hands I want more of her inside me. Want to take her captive through the mouth. Absorb her secret erotic life into me like a special nutrient.

After a little gasp, her body goes loose in my hands. Supping through the little nick, I move my cock through her again. Hold her upright with my hard meat. It feels more intense for being slow. When I start to feel dizzy, I break my mouth away from her neck. It's hard to do, but I mustn't take too much. Little fireworks flicker under my eyelids. Sleepy warmth grows out of my stomach and fills my arms and legs to fingertip and little toe. I sigh and roll my head. I want to slump to the floor as her stolen warmth makes me float inside my own skin.

I know from the lump in my gut that this is bad, but it seems like the most natural thing in the world to do. There is no way a person should be doing this, but it doubles the pleasure of the sin.

I release the woman gently to the floor. She murmurs in her sleep. Don't have the strength to cover her legs with her skirt. Stagger away and scrabble at the door lock to get out. Mrs Berry is downstairs waiting. Through the dark, I can feel her. She's thinking of me. I know there will be no need to tell her about what has happened. Somehow, she has seen it all.

Chapter Eight

On the hard wooden chair outside the Chaplain's office, I sit and wait with only my fear for company.

I couldn't help myself and now I've been caught.

It's scary to lose control in a town like this. You just can't behave that way. I thought I was being discreet, but maybe someone was watching me the whole time.

Times like this, the Saviour System doesn't seem so bad. At least when you're bringing up kids and looking after the home like my dad, you don't have the terror in the guts that feels like ice melting when you mess up.

Got to learn to pace myself. 'Take it easy. Don't wear yourself out all at once, Franklin.' Maybe coach had a point. When I have no lover, I rip around the track and take the hurdles too, and I feel like I could scream to let the angry bees out of my head and could dig into my body with gouging fingers to release the electricity. Unless I love, I start to run a temperature and my skin burns too. This is the payoff; unless I can seduce and make love and take a good taste of a woman every few days, I'm like one of those junkies back in the days before the Graceful Revolution.

But the worst and the best part is the erection. I stay hard for days. At night it can be impossible to sleep. Even the brush of the bed sheet against my groin sets me off and I'm ready to come. And out through the window go my searching thoughts to find her across the street. Dark eyes, pale skin and her long body fill my dreams. Sometimes when I wake from the half-sleep, I am sure she's standing at the foot of my bed.

'Do you want to see the world differently, Franklin? Do you want to be better at everything? Faster, stronger, smarter? I chose you for this gift,' she whispered to me, the first time we were together. I know she wasn't only talking about sex. I even thought she was crazy, but I was too horny to care at the time. But she has changed me, and I welcome the changes in me. Living by your instincts when they are always right is so much better than having to work stuff out by thinking the way I used to do. I don't have to exist like other people anymore. I can feel the difference between the way their heads work and the way mine does. I can see their memories and hear their thoughts.

Sometimes Mrs Berry's Initiation scares me white, but in the end the excitement is always stronger than the fear. Maybe I'm her revenge on this town. She can't resist corrupting it. I fear Mrs Berry belongs to nowhere and nobody. She's a beautiful devil who seduces the innocent and I love her.

I guess she always knew I had darkness in me. Buried deep, well hidden, but there all the same and only allowed to live inside my head. Now I don't know where this journey is going, and this might only be the first of my troubles, because there is no way I can go back.

Some days, when the 'gift' she put inside me is strong, every woman I see I desire. Any tiny detail can catch my eye and get my heart thumping. It was real bad on the Day of Grace, which became the day of my disgrace. First thing in the morning I noticed the fresh orange lipstick on a woman at the mall while I was looking for a CD. She had good lips. All I could think of doing was tasting her mouth and unwrapping her plumpish body. Outside in the carpark, I spotted a beautiful hand hanging from a car door. It was all I saw of the woman – rings and red nails catching the sunlight and my eyes. I needed to suck those fingers then wrap them around my cock. I'm a beast: a panting, sniffing beast looking for the scent of prey. An animal that needs to mount the soft and fragrant creatures of my territory. Hand, foot, mouth – sometimes I would take anything as long as it belongs to a woman.

I think this is why Mrs Berry starves me for days on end – even for the whole week before the Day of Grace – so I am forced to go out and hunt for myself. Which becomes little more than aimless wandering around the streets and malls, and occasionally a crafty circling of a woman whose legs or neck or breasts in a tight summery dress have caught my eye. I'm shy most of the time without Mrs Berry around. This annoys her. 'Opportunities arise or can be created in the most unlikely situations with people you least expect to be interested.'

But it's easier for her: she's older and knows so much. And she is so beautiful it hurts to look at her. I'm just a dumb-ass kid with a hard-on. And I proved it last night at the Day of Grace celebrations. It was thick with dressed-up, sweet-smelling ladies. In a nice suit with a smile on my face I went amongst the herd like a hungry wolf.

The Day of Grace is the biggest occasion of the year in this town. Ladies love an opportunity to look even sexier than they usually do, and to be seen by everyone. Besides all the time wasted in church in the morning, when your ass burns and guts writhe and all you can think about is getting outside and ripping your tie off, there are dinners and stuff later: a marquee, a parade, and finally the big outdoor dance under fireworks.

For once I didn't want to hang out at the back with the guys from the band – none of us dancing, trying to steal alcohol. They couldn't believe it when I went off looking for girls to dance with. First, I went with Rebecca Howarth, who looked real hot in pink high heels and a long dress to match with slits up one side. But what I liked the most was the way she pinned her hair up and left her throat bare: milky white with a few freckles and smelling so good.

We made small-talk on the dance floor and she went through the boring routine of being indifferent to me while really liking the attention and flattery. When you've done things with an older woman like Mrs Berry, that Rebecca Howarth would be totally clueless about, you can get impatient. But she blushed and stopped being haughty when she felt my hardness pressing against her stomach. She wouldn't look into my eyes for long either, scared of what she might see there. I was trying too hard to turn her around to my way of thinking. I know that now. But I was so horny; sweating in a flood and going dizzy among so much well-presented woman-flesh that is totally out of bounds to young men. Rebecca didn't stick around for a second dance.

Same with Annabel and Ingrid. They got wise to my real intentions straight from the first steps of the dance and made their excuses. Just as I was considering going for one of the mothers, I spied Melody Watson talking to our music teacher by the big drinks table. She was wearing lots of make-up and had black seams running up the backs of her shiny legs. I felt faint. Had to take a few breaths and slow myself down.

Melody is the smartest girl in school but not too popular with boys. From a big wealthy family too. Still, I can't remember another woman moving me more that night. And why was she wearing a garter belt and stockings under a tight black gown? When she agreed to dance with me – looking surprised when I asked her, and then real suspicious, but too polite to say no – I could feel the secret lines and straps of her underwear against my body. And she just stared at me with disbelief when I told her she looked 'real chic'. Probably thought I was only a jock in a rock band who fluked a few good grades, or cheated. But she softened – I made her – when I relaxed and looked deep like Mrs Berry told me to, and then whispered through her glossy hair and into her ear. She stayed pressed against me for two more slow dances.

She looked a little afraid, as I manoeuvred her to the far edge of the dance area. But when I kissed her neck so swiftly that it was nothing but a brush of my lips on her throat, I could almost taste her weakness for a man.

'I want you, Melody. Have done for a long time.'

She swallowed and blushed, but didn't pull away from the shadows as I stroked her curves. 'Let's get away from all these people. Go someplace quiet.'

'I don't think that would be right,' she whispered. 'One of the clergy might see.'

'You ashamed of being seen with me?' She shook her head. I looked deep into the place she guards from men. 'I want to kiss you, Melody.'

She sucked in her breath. 'We shouldn't. We're not even engaged.'

'I'd marry you in a heartbeat just to make love to you.' Now this was going too far, but I was so out to sea on stolen booze and my need for a girl, I meant it. I was smitten with her: inhaling her fragrance, exploring her trussed softness through her dress and feeling her little bird heart struggling in the snare I'd laid. 'I want you so much. Been waiting ages to tell you.'

Her pupils were big and her whole face looked vulnerable and girlish under the make-up. I kissed her twice on the neck. She never pulled away from the hard part of me that must have felt like carved wood against her tummy. 'I need to be inside you.'

She was breathing hard and her cheeks were hot. Leaned against me until I realised I was nearly holding

66

her upright. Made me realise just how much power is in the stare Mrs Berry taught me.

I took her hand and led her away from the dancing, past the refreshments and outside the perimeter rope and into the field where the kids were fooling around on the funfair. Then out to the park and into the wooded part where it would be dark and silent.

'We can't. We should go back. Someone will see us.' I cut her off by looking deep and shushing. Then took her mouth with my own. A pretty mouth but a little clumsy and too wet. This was her first kiss. For a moment I felt a pang of shame, but then got to thinking about getting her dress up around her waist, and my better instincts just died right then and there. I just had to see under this long black dress. Had to feed on her.

Kneeling in the pine needles before Melody, I inched her gown up from her calves. Moved the palms of my hands over her legs. Smoothed her stockings up to the warm thighs that looked luminous in the moonlight. I could smell her sex and knew it was damp in readiness for whatever I wanted to put there.

'I never knew clever girls wore these,' I said to her, and stroked the thin stockings on her thighs.

She giggled, which was a welcome sound. 'You don't know much about clever girls.'

'You're right. But I want to know more. This is the nicest thing I have ever touched.' Through her panties, I tickled her sex with my fingers. Then applied my tongue to satin.

She leaned back against a tree, biting her bottom lip, her body tense. 'Don't be rough with me.'

Pulling her panties down to her stocking tops and seeing that little triangle of black fur, I said, 'I can't make any promises.'

She laughed, but then stopped at the same time I enjoyed the sharp, bitter taste of her sex. It drove me crazy. She started to grind her teeth when I pushed my tongue inside her and tickled her hot ring from behind with my middle finger.

Some people came close by. We heard their voices and she tried to pull away, but I held her thighs hard so she couldn't move and carried on licking her between the legs so she had to stifle her whimpers in the palm of one hand.

The voices died down, moving off into the trees and darkness. I eased Melody down to the soft ground and let her taste herself on my lips with her nervous nips and licks at my mouth. She clung to my shoulders when I moved her underneath me and got between her legs. Wouldn't let go. Clutched the back of my head and dug fingertips into my back. 'We can't. We can't. We can't,' she kept saying like a mantra, but didn't push me away, even when she felt the head of my cock against her naked sex.

Then suddenly in a breathless voice, 'Yes, yes. Put it inside me. Do it.' She imagined this moment all the time: I sensed it. Alone in her room, just like me, she had an appetite for beastly, sinner's things. It shocked me a little. I was in danger of making a strong connection with Melody that could prove tricky, but it just made the situation more exciting, like the sight of the wedding band on the woman's fingers in the motel.

When I broke inside Melody, her whole body went stiff and she wrapped herself around me like an animal clinging to driftwood in a swollen river. She made choking sounds and said, 'Oh, God,' a few times. I'd hardly done anything; it was like she made herself come with her own mind. The unexpected thrill of it all – to be in a forest with a boy – had brought her to a peak of pleasure straight away.

I had to break free of her clutching arms to move in and out of her, and to ease her into a comfortable position. Then I could go to the mad red place I had been salivating over for days. And once I was there I wanted it to last forever.

'Fuck me,' she said.

I was so surprised, I remember crying out, 'Oh yeah,' and she put a hand across my mouth. How had Melody heard such a word? It made me think that despite all our vulgar talk and desperate imaginings of what we want to do to the women in our town, we guys are the real innocents. Women have depths you never expect. It can be scary to go right to the bottom of them.

But I wanted to drown in Melody's depths: the smartest and most sensible girl at school was underneath me, writhing against my body and pushing her buttocks up at me as I thrust down, trying to swallow my whole cock with her hips. I squeezed her breasts out of her dress and lathered them with my hungry mouth. Rubbing those hard cherry nipples all over my face, I thrust hard enough to make her shake like a rag dolly in a careless child's hand.

On to my shoulders, I arranged her feet in the spiky black sandals. Just the sight of them, all shiny and poking into the air next to my face, made my hips speed up. I licked her silky toes.

We were noisy and clumsy and unco-ordinated down there on the ground in the woods for what seemed like ages, but we managed to give each other so much pleasure. Couldn't stop kissing and licking each other's mouths. I'll never forget Melody on Grace Day. When I think about her, my chest goes tight every time.

I got carried away. So did she. When I said, 'Drink me,' she knew what I meant. 'Now,' I called out, and pulled out of her. She wriggled about underneath me, while I was in the press-up position, and stuffed my shiny cock into her smudged mouth. I loved the little sounds of girlish surprise she made as I launched stream after stream of dammed-up liquid down her throat. Her very first time and she drank everything from my cock.

Her hair was all frizzed out from its arrangement and one stocking was shredded by a broken thumbnail of mine. But we couldn't stop laughing under the tree, with our chests going up and down like we just crossed the finishing line at a track meet. 'I can't believe I just did that,' she said.

'There's more.'

'I bet there is, you naughty boy, but I have to get back. My mom will be worried.' She took her shoes off. Rolled her stockings down her legs and pinched them off her toes. Then put her shoes back on.

'This won't take long,' I said, and started to lap at her wet, exposed thigh. Traces of her virginity tasted good. I got it ready for the bite.

Where it smelled of BBQ smoke and empty wine bottles behind the marquee tent, I said goodbye to Melody. Gave her a final kiss. Hoped I hadn't taken too much; she looked sleepy. Eyes vague like the others I'd been with. But I didn't get much time to enjoy the moment of triumph and the fresh taste of a girl in my mouth. No sooner had Melody slipped away to the Ladies' toilet – 'to put myself back together' – when someone put their hand on my arm.

As the first fireworks screamed to explode purple, gold and blue in the chilly sky, I turned and stared into the enraged face of Chaplain Skinner. 'I was curious as to why a young man, newly Mentored, would need to take the brightest girl in the county away from the celebrations and into the park.' She moved right up close to me. I could taste the liquor and lipstick on her breath. 'I heard you in there. If it wasn't for her sake, I'd have you arrested. You are disgusting.'

I stepped away from the pointy, meddling face. Her gloating was spoiling the euphoria of having slaked my thirst on a virgin. I couldn't have been thinking straight with so much of Melody's sweet soul pumping through my heart. I looked her up and down and wondered again why priests wear long silk dresses and high heels

70

on Grace Day. It is said to be in honour of the beauty of Our Saviour. But I think they just like to look hot and make men sweat.

'You stink of drink, and worse. Perhaps your Mentoring has been morally defective. I wonder if someone has been teaching you dirty tricks.' There was panic in my eyes – I couldn't help it – with this mention of Mrs Berry. 'Eighteen is an awful age to come unstuck these days, my lad. Your whole future can suddenly seem a lot closer and a lot less appealing.'

I tried to look defiant. 'Don't know what you mean.'

Her eyes went narrow and her voice made me feel cold. This lady was just as strong as Mrs Berry. She could hurt me. I knew it. So did she. 'You interfered with her, didn't you?' That hurt. What we did was good. Had nothing to do with a Chaplain. I would be damned before letting this vinegar scarecrow with the frosty face take me down so easy. 'Tell me what you did to her,' she demanded.

I unhooked the belt of my trousers and unzipped. It was her turn to cringe. I was drunk on excitement and rage. 'I put this inside her. She asked me to. And it was nice. Real nice.'

Not even in the fight I had in third grade did I get hit so hard. Chaplain Skinner slapped me from east to west so I ended up looking in two places at once. The sound of her hand against my face deafened me. I could feel the whole shape of her hand and all the bones in her fingers too, burning in a sticky way.

'Animal. Put yourself away.'

'Sorry,' I said. This slap had snapped me out of the sullen, delinquent dreaminess. Now I felt ashamed.

She turned away, her shoulders shaking. 'Go home. You're not welcome on our holy day.'

And with my shoulders all hunched over and rounded like a turtle, I tripped and stumbled away, through the park. When I looked back, the Chaplain had gone. I

71

started to curse myself. Then took a long piss on the statue of a Graceful Revolution Martyr.

Chaplain Skinner only told my parents about sending me home for being drunk and disorderly. Didn't mention Melody. My mom thought it was funny. My dad said nothing and kept ironing. I was so relieved, I almost wept in front of them. I'd had all night to lie awake and think about the repercussions. By daybreak I had exhausted my mind and convinced myself I'd have to run away from home. Otherwise I'd be castrated and sealed off in a hospital for degenerates. Most of all, it was the thought of the shame I had brought on my parents that made me sick with nerves.

Between the curtains, I watched Mrs Berry's house for most of the night. I'd not seen her at the celebrations. There is supposed to be a final dance between New Men and their Mentors, but I don't think she was even there. I got bored looking. At two in the morning, her husband came home alone. I know how he felt: abandoned.

She wasn't there the next day either. She was supposed to come with me to see the Chaplain for a meeting about my behaviour. I had to miss band practice and go alone. Mrs Berry couldn't be reached so my mom dropped me off. I told her I'd walk home alone.

And now, with jiggly feet and wet palms, I'm waiting outside Chaplain Skinner's study at the big Saviour Centre downtown. My mouth is so dry I can't swallow. Three times I've had to take a pee.

The door to her office opens. She doesn't even look at me; just stands there holding the door handle. I get up. Swallow. Can't feel my legs. Head is thick with panic and shame. I walk in, real slow, trying not to stumble. Look down at my feet. But as I pass close to her, the smell of her perfume hits me. It's strong and feminine. I used to love this smell. Always found it

comforting. It's the fragrance of authority and responsibility: with these women in charge you know everything is going to be fine. That's what I always thought.
It's a smell I liked to be around and I always wanted to
make the women who wore it happy. I wanted them to
like me for being so polite and successful and reliable.
For being obedient. But were my motivations to please
so different from my current ambitions to seduce? I
wonder if, ultimately, it was the same thing.

I glance at her legs. Can't help myself: I'm a
degenerate.

Not bad. Slim but with a good shape in flesh
stockings and black court shoes. All the Chaplains wear
black Chanel suits with a white blouse. In the past, it's
been a struggle not to fantasise about the clergy. So
smart, so elegant, so perfect, so untouchable, so holy. I
clench my teeth and concentrate my thoughts to hold
back the thoughts of sex. I'm here for punishment, but
already I can feel the tingling of my skin, the widening
of my eyes, the excitement fizzing in my blood and the
desire to stare deep.

Snap out of it!

'Take a seat,' she says, and walks around her desk.
Her skirt and slip whisper against her shiny legs. The
fact that she's here to discipline me, disapproves of me
and probably finds me disgusting, but looks good in
that clergy suit, has a thrill all of its own.

She's not what I would have called pretty. But the
mumsy hairstyle and the discreet make-up on that cold,
unsmiling face make me think of transgressions too
obscene to put into words. 'At the very least, what you
did at the Day of Grace celebrations would warrant
your being held back for one year to attend counselling.
I'm referring to your liaison in the park with Melody
Watson. As to the other matter, have you any idea what
kind of containment and rehabilitation procedures I
would be entitled to pursue?'

As if a pail of icy water has been upended over my head, I'm no longer thinking of sex. 'Yes, ma'am.'

'It is in my power to have you committed to a comprehensive reform programme.'

I nod. Look at my lap. In a second, I renounce all my past sins and beg the Saviour to show mercy on this wretch of hers.

The Chaplain opens two files and arranges them under the white light of her desk lamp. Her fingernails are painted the colour of hard-shell plum candy. Perhaps it's already too late for me. I can't be helped. Maybe I'm damned.

'I can see nothing in your school or citizen records that demonstrate any tendency towards delinquency or sexual impairment. You come from a good home, and are an excellent student and a committed athlete.' She looks up at me. The sympathy in those grey eyes is fake because she wants me to confess something. 'So I am forced to draw my own conclusions. Something, or should I say someone, has had quite an effect on you recently.' The Chaplain stares right inside me. She gets underneath my burning face and tosses the rooms of my mind looking for evidence of Mrs Berry. 'Well?'

I shrug.

'Would you like to tell me about your Mentor?'

'She's cool.'

'Well, I'm sure she is, but "cool" is neither a relevant or proper response of a young man to his ideological companion. Is it?'

'No.'

The Chaplain looks at her long fingernails tracing circles over my open files. 'So what has she been teaching you?'

'All kinds of stuff. You know.'

'No, I'm afraid I don't know what kind of instruction would permit a young man to expose himself to a member of the clergy on the Day of Grace.'

I can't see straight; the heat from my face makes everything in the study shimmer.

Irritated, she sighs. 'How can I impress upon you the gravity of this matter? Have you any idea what is at stake? It's not going to go away. Perhaps you were hoping I would let the matter drop. If so, you are mistaken. Unless I am convinced otherwise, I am left with no choice but to suspect that you are a deviant and a possible threat to our community.'

She was using words that made my guts fill with a strawberry slurpy – the really cold ones that make your lips go blue. Once branded a deviant, a deviant you remain, like the two old guys who pack shopping at the supermarket checkout: Sandy and Hershey. Sometimes my dad chews the fat with them on Friday when he does the weekly grocery run. All the dads feel sorry for them. People say they were caught taking photos of women in changing rooms and stuff. They put in hidden cameras. For the rest of their lives they're not allowed near photographic equipment and have to pack bags at the Saviour Saver Store. I get an image in my mind of myself wearing a candy-striped apron while loading up the boots of family cars. I can't swallow the big lump in my throat. My jaw starts to tremble; if I try and speak, I'll probably cry.

She sees the terror in my face and smiles. 'I am not insensitive to your age and all of the difficulties and temptations that afflict young men. But my own sympathies are irrelevant if the sanctity and safety of our community is at risk.'

My voice is a squeak. I'm like that mouse in the cartoons, wearing a nappy and smashed flat in a trap. 'I won't screw up again. I'm sorry. I mean it.'

Under the desk she crosses her legs, leans back in her leather chair. Puts both hands over a shiny knee, smiles. 'I'm sure that now you've had time to reflect on your unacceptable behaviour, you feel remorse. I'm sure it is genuine too. But remorse can be overcome by stronger urges in vulnerable and impressionable young men.'

'I'll make amends for what I did.'

'Good. Your realisation that you must pay penance is encouraging.'

'I'll come to church more often.'

'And we will look forward to your attendance and participation in congregation. But I think we both know that a few half-hearted visits to church will be insufficient. Don't we? Your position is far more grave than that.'

I see the glee in her pointy pale face at having this power over me. I know she enjoys my discomfort and remorse; it excites her. I suddenly stop feeling sorry for myself. I stop feeling repentant. I feel like I did as a kid right after I'd cried myself dry and my stomach muscles hurt. I'm empty now, but quickly filling up with rage and disobedience.

'I believe that if you are honest with yourself, Franklin, you will admit that more stringent steps need to be taken.'

The boiling anger goes cool. 'How do you mean?' My voice could have come straight out of a flute. Her face flushes with pride and joy at my weak tone of voice. Despite changing the whole world to the way they like it, these women are never satisfied. I never thought that before, but I can see it now like it's writ large in neon. She takes a sip of coffee, speaks while swallowing. 'I see the problem as two-fold. You have been misguided by an individual in possession of a very sacred and responsible position. You know of whom I speak. And you have been additionally encouraged to slide into a moral torpor by some of your more immature interests.'

I can't move. Time pauses. All the little atoms of my being stop moving. Even everything in this room is holding its breath.

'And so, after careful consideration, it is my opinion that your current Mentoring cease as of today, until a more suitable candidate can be found to guide you into a more wholesome, responsible and useful adult role.'

'But –'

The Chaplain raises her hand for silence. Doesn't matter what I say; she has it all figured out anyway. 'And I think it vital for your moral and spiritual well-being that you distance yourself from this pop group of which you are so fond.'

Feel like I'm going to suffocate. Can't breathe because of all the inarticulate stuff that is trying to blast its way out, but has got stuck like hot potato indigestion behind my breastbone.

'In my experience, certain individuals and situations can foster an irresistible desire in the young to revel in transgression that will have serious consequences on that individual's future. A new degree of maturity and discipline is required ...' She goes on and on. Says other stuff that sounds like 'Blah, blah, blah' to me. Mrs Berry has never seemed so beautiful and exciting as she does at this moment, my band never more precious. And this priest whose hair smells of perm oil will take them away. I'm so angry I reckon I could have a seizure or a stroke. Some little tube in my head could just pop. One eye would fill with blood. No more sex, or rock 'n' roll (she even called the band a 'pop group'). Instead, I see my new future: wearing a tie and boring casual suit with a smile that aches on my face, while I listen to women in hats chat on the lawn at some church event. And all the time, the Chaplain will be smiling at me while I hold my wife's cardigan over one arm and nod appreciatively to what the women say.

'No.'

The Chaplain stops talking. 'No? Did you say no?' She pauses to take a deep breath. Something weird happens to her eyebrows and forehead and eyes that start to bulge from her determination to be right and to have her own way. Her voice is much deeper now. 'Let me outline your choices. You can accept my choice of a new Mentor, end your affiliation with pop groups, and engage on a strict programme of character redevelopment, or your parents will be notified of your recent behaviour and the very real danger you pose to our community. Reformatory is the next step.'

Behind her desk, the Chaplain goes blurry. When I blink the tears away, my eyes fill up again. 'I won't do it again. I wasn't thinking. I was drunk. I won't ever drink again.'

She softens her voice. Again her face is flushed and intense. 'I cannot rely on your word. You make promises now, but what will they be worth when your urges return? When you desperately, desperately want to regress with alcohol so you can pursue your carnal, animal desire?' Her eyes are shining with excitement.

She leans back, her lips part. I know she's breathing steady to relax herself. She feels delight at what she is putting me through and is restraining herself from tormenting me even more. I know it. 'You can go now. I expect you back here, same time next week. By then I expect you to have broken both relations with your Mentor and made steps to disengage yourself from this puerile fixation with pop music. And I will have organised a suitable corrective programme for you.'

I stand up, but my body is heavy, inert as metal, heavy metal. I turn to the door. Feel a tear go dry and gritty on my cheek.

'For a man of your obvious talents, we can surely find a new role for your creative, musical interests right here with an ensemble of the Saviour Fellowship. Was it the drums you play?'

Unable to hear another word, I shuffle to the door.

'Next Friday, Franklin. And I expect to hear some good news from you. There is much work to be done. Be grateful we haven't given up on you yet.'

Chapter Nine

'So it's over. You can't be my Mentor any more.' As I get to the end of telling Mrs Berry about all the things that happened at the Day of Grace and afterwards with the Chaplain, I put my face in my hands to hide all the shaking from her.

She showed no emotion while I spoke. But was listening and thinking real hard at the same time. Never seen her concentrate so much on what I had to say before.

When I finish, she laughs and lights another cigarette. I look up, my face one big mess of confusion and questions.

'Oh, she's good. That bitch is good.' Mrs Berry shakes her head in appreciation.

'What do you mean?'

'Past history. We've tangled before. She was watching you all night at the celebrations because she knows I'm your Mentor.'

'What do you mean? What? Tell me.'

'Another time, darling.' She takes another pull on her cigarette, speaks through the blue smoke that curls around her face. 'So the bitch thinks she can mess with my guy?' Under the diner table she strokes her foot up my leg and puts the tip of her spiky shoe in my lap. My hand goes to her ankle. I stroke her Achilles tendon and then slip my fingers around the sharp heel.

'Where were you at the celebrations? I needed you.'

'Don't be needy. I've shown you enough to look after yourself. You were a fool. Now I've taken that beautiful cock out of your pants, you just can't keep it in there, can you?' She blows smoke at the ceiling.

'You were supposed to be there.'

Her eyes are challenging. 'Why? I go where I please.' I look down at my seafood basket.

Her voice softens. I know she's smiling. 'Whatever tempted you to show her your lovely cock? A daring, ambitious move, but also incredibly stupid.' She narrows her eyes. 'What a curious boy you are.'

'I'm a dumb-ass and I've ruined everything.'

'Not necessarily. The game has changed, that's all. So tell me about the virgin. This slut called Melody.'

I blush. 'She's not a slut.'

'Oh, how sweet, darling. You're getting protective. We'll have to sort that out. Your kind can't afford to be so generous with emotions. But then you're new to this, still so charmingly innocent.'

I reckon she's jealous.

'And no, I'm not jealous of some swotty tramp who kisses like a camel.'

Surprised, I look at her. Can she read my mind or does she just read every flicker on my face? I try to keep it deadpan.

Mrs Berry watches me carefully with a sexy but condescending smile on her face. 'Don't try and be opaque. You're see-through.'

'What?'

'You'll learn. Now eat your crabs. You need the energy. I've got plans for later.'

'Are you crazy? We can't. This has to be the last time we can see each other like this.'

'Don't be craven.'

'I'm not.'

'Don't be petulant.'

Enough of this teasing. I go to stand up from the table.

'Sit down, Franklin,' she says in the most sensual voice.

I stay on my feet.

'The last man who walked out on me was dead before he reached the door. Sit down, darling.'

I swallow and wonder again if she's crazy.

'Yes, crazy enough to make your head spin. But not in the same way as that Chaplain bitch. Now eat your fucking prawns, darling.' She smiles so sweetly. Winks at me. I can't stop the grin that creeps over my face. She's so bad.

I pick up my fork and stuff it into a tomato. 'So what do we do?'

'We? I intend to do absolutely nothing. You got yourself into this mess, so you can get yourself out of it.'

'How? What can I do?'

'Time you stopped thinking like that. It's getting tiresome. You're not a kid any more. You're a man. You had to grow up fast, but you'll never be a kid again. I saw to that. You could have this whole town on its knees in no time at all if you wanted. But you may as well put the apron and rubber gloves on right now if you continue to be in awe of it. I know it's hard. You've been well produced. A gleaming, inoffensive, bowing, blushing man-mannequin perfect for some snotty bitch to walk all over till she's tired of your puppy-dog eyes and fucks the neighbours while you're doing the ironing.'

I can't stop laughing. 'No way.'

'Yes way, tiger. Think you're a tough guy? Prove it.'

'How?'

'Fuck her.'

I can't swallow the lobster between my cheeks. There is no saliva left in my mouth. I shake my head.

She nods her head. 'Go back Friday and lie to her. Tell her you've finished with me and left the band. Look

81

heartbroken. Feel heartbroken. Imagine if it was so and believe it. Convince her. But carry on doing what you need to do. Play with the band and fuck me after dinner. Be a bad man tonight, Franklin. And go hunting all week. Don't stifle your feelings. Let them flow, but never abandon all reason no matter how soft the breasts in your hand are, or how good the thighs of a housewife feel when you put her up against a refrigerator door.'

'But?'

'But nothing. Fuck with the Chaplain. And if she doesn't go for your story, then fuck her. Right in that fucking study at the Saviour Centre if you have to.'

Under the table, her leg has stretched out to find me again. 'Get it out,' she whispers, and then takes another drag on her cigarette.

Deftly, without looking down, I unbuckle my belt and unzip my jeans. Mrs Berry kicks off her high heels and puts her hot feet on either side of my cock. My head spins and I know my face has gone all dreamy. Using her toes and soles and the smooth tops of her feet, she rubs my cock hard. Even tickles under my balls with her painted toenails, which makes me moan and then sit forwards. Not once does she break eye contact with me. 'Don't come. Don't let yourself. I want that inside me. All of it. I want it to come out slowly all day tomorrow. I have meetings morning and afternoon.'

She puts the roof down and tells me to get in the back. There's an urgency to her words. I like it when she wants me so much.

Skirt pulled up to her waist, she sits across my naked lap on the back seat of her car. Looks down at me, bites her bottom lip and then slips me inside her sex. Moaning, her body goes tense. Then, slowly, she lowers her weight down to me. Pushing my buttocks up, I go all the way inside and make her suddenly inhale.

Both of my hands stroke up and down her thighs. Her stockings are so fine and match the colour of her skin; it's hard to see she's wearing any. But they're so soft and slippery in the palms of my hands. Suddenly, I want to swing her underneath me and thrust hard, but she holds my shoulders down against the seat and moves slowly, agonisingly, on and off my cock, rotating her hips when just the tip of me is inside her.

Undoing the three buttons of her blouse, I free her breasts. I can see them through the transparent brassiere cups; flesh-tinted and making her chest shine in the thin moonlight. Cupping, stroking, flicking her nipples, gently squeezing, I can't take my eyes off her breasts. My mouth waters for the taste of her skin, and for what runs, silent and hot and red beneath.

'Oh Franklin, I do miss your cock. I can't stop thinking about it at work.' She grinds herself into my lap and kisses my face.

'You know where it is. It's all yours. You know that.'

She smiles wickedly, and then starts pumping my lap hard. My feeling her breasts with firm hands makes her even more excited. 'Sometimes one must resist temptation.'

'Why? I want you all the time. Most days I can't think of anything else.'

'You know what to do.'

'But I love you.'

She frowns from the pleasure that almost hurts. She claws my chest. I put my hands against the seat to support my weight and really begin to thrust up hard. Moaning, she goes limp in my lap. Seizing her little waist and planting my feet hard against the floor, I pull her on and off my lap. Then I stand up, dizzy with love and lust. Her legs wrap around my waist. One of her spiky shoes falls off. The top of her body and her screwed-up face fall over the front seats. Holding her hips I thrust down and into her, making her whole body shake. She calls me a 'bastard'. I tell her she's a slut and come inside her. But hold the last contraction back for a split second. Some crazy notion makes me pull out and pump on to her tummy and garter belt. When she opens her eyes, she dips a finger into my come. Then she slips it between her lips.

She smiles. 'Now bite my ass. But don't take too much, you naughty, greedy boy.'

Dreamy, I lie on the back seat and look up at the stars. Can't ever remember being so high and so happy. Soon as one thought forms another splits from it and demands my attention. She sits opposite me, smoking. I kiss the sole of her silky foot. She smiles, but has that look on her face which lets me know she needs to be serious now the sharpest part of our need has been gratified. I like the pain in my shoulder where she cut me with her pretty mouth and licked me like a big cat that wanted salt. In my mouth, I savour the precious liquor I supped from a pale buttock.

'Other people are going to interfere. It always happens. But don't let them win. Whatever happens, remember who and what you really are. What I've made you. Promise me. Even if I'm not there, be strong. Be strong for me, Franklin.'

'You going away?'

She takes another drag on her cigarette, but doesn't say yes or no. 'There are things I can't do for you. There are things you must learn on your own. The hard way.'

'Like what? Just for once, can you be more specific?'

'Those of us who have what we have, who share a bond, must prove we can survive, alone. It's just the way it is. You will have lovers, Franklin. So many lovers. You are beautiful. I picked you at your peak. If you like, I preserved it for you. But in some ways you will always have to be alone.'

'But our bond? Nobody can take that away? We'll always have each other, right?'

She looks sad because of the hope in my voice I tried to hide. 'I made you like me, Franklin. Put myself in you and put you inside me. So we will always be together, even if we're not together.'

'But why can't we be?'

She looks away and sighs. 'Is it any accident that you are much stronger than you were before I became your Mentor? You can feel it every time you train. Is it normal that you now have to fuck like most people need to eat? And when you fuck you need to take something else from them? In time, you will be surprised that you know what people are really thinking, no matter what they say. Really know, and not just guess. I shared this with you. And now you have to deal with it on your own. That's just the way it works. You have to be strong, darling, in so many ways.

'You see, I really am your Mentor, Franklin, but not in the way this town thinks.'

Chapter Ten

After my morning chores, I drift through the afternoons in the malls and shopping arcades, watching the beautiful creatures at play: dabbing new scents on pale throats; rolling ankles before floor mirrors to admire their pretty feet in new shoes; stirring lattes with long spoons pinched between shiny fingertips; pirouetting in white gowns in front of a nodding stylist. But I am invisible to them. Away from me they walk – aloof and indifferent – into the marble distance. Not a shy smile returned nor a look of adoration acknowledged. I was there among them to break every code and rule and taboo. But it is no good. The task Mrs Berry has given me, to obey my instincts, to seduce and feed, but to maintain reason, is too much for me. It's weird without her around. Now I must hunt alone, I begin to believe I will starve. When will it ever happen again? When will the next encounter with a stranger occur?

I throw a coin into the fountain in Ladies Square and make a wish. Stretch out on the stone wall and lie down. The only other men here are pushing prams.

Melody Watson has been seen drifting in smaller and smaller circles in my neighbourhood, getting closer to my house, out walking her dog, hoping to be noticed by the boy who took her hand and led her into the woods.

Mrs Berry has forbidden me to make attachments: 'To go some way into making a bond when you're

86

young and inexperienced is the best way I know to make trouble. What I've given you is precious. Don't misuse it. Be especially careful of the women close to you. There are few women in this town who will be content with just one time. A jealous, desperate woman can be persistent. Can be reckless. And you have been indiscreet enough already. So find strangers.'

But that's all right for her to say. Cruising around out there, wherever she goes, in that car. While I'm going out of my mind with frustration and boredom, feeling weak and dizzy and desperate. And all the time, Melody is close and keen. Walking her dog, thinking of me. It would be so easy to ask her in while dad is out shopping. Quickly get my hands on those white breasts. I can see it so clearly. Feel her slippery thighs. I get short of breath thinking about it. To be inside her again, while drinking her most secret flavours inside me. I can still taste her: lipstick, soft girl skin, milky breath, salty blood. And the danger of her wanting me too, and dreaming of me inside her, just makes it harder to resist. No matter the consequences, I have begun to think that if Mrs Berry keeps disappearing and starving me for days, and if I can't find a lover without her help, I might not be able to resist Melody for much longer. And then I'll take her everywhere. Take her to the woods again, or take her quickly over the bonnet of a parked car, take her on the lawn, in the garage, anywhere, everywhere ... I can think about nothing but gorging myself. My cock thickens against my thigh; I grow short of breath.

'Franklin? Why, how nice to see you. What on earth are you doing in Ladies Square? Buying a gift for that glamorous Mrs Berry, I bet? She must have expensive tastes. She always looks so good, don't you think?'

I snap out of my dopey daze. It's not just the weakness at not having fed; the sunlight and the waterfall sounds of the fountain make me drowsy and dreamy. I look up, blink, squint and see the big silhouette of Mrs Mullins before me. 'Hi. I'm just . . . You know –'

She sits down beside me and puts her shopping bags by her feet. Fans at her face with one gloved hand. 'What a lovely day, but these sales and these shoes are killing me.' She's always puffing and blowing around town, reprimanding the young people in a friendly way, and nosing around other people's business. She and my dad don't get on. She's one of those people who aren't interested in listening to what anyone else has to say; they only like to talk at other people. 'So do tell me about Mrs Berry. We don't see so much of her at the club these days. But I hear she's been seeing a lot of you. Mmm?'

I swallow. Panic enough to be lost for words. Just raise my eyebrows and clear my throat.

'You know, I often thought I would be your Mentor. You know, just had a hunch. Not to say that Mrs Berry isn't doing a wonderful job. On the contrary, I'm sure she's so much fun to be with. Exciting. You'd probably enjoy yourself much more with someone more racy than sad old me.' She laughs. 'I was just surprised. I've Mentored so many young men. But I rarely get asked these days.' I look at her. Feel sorry for her. Feel bad for all the cruel things me and the band have said about having her for a Mentor. She's a nice lady, really. Just tries too hard. Is always saying the wrong thing and asking the wrong questions. She may not be hot and fast like Mrs Berry, or some of the other women we idolise, but as I watch her chatting away beside me on the little wall that circles the fountain, I think of how attractive she really is. Big and round and voluptuous and a bit mumsy in her attitude, but pretty about the eyes and she has a nice little mouth too. Plump and shiny-red with lipstick. Dressed up for shopping and lunch in Ladies Square, she's wearing more make-up than she would as the Manager of Youth Services for the Saviour Centre.

I like what the mascara does to her eyes – makes them long and dollish. Quite sweet really. And the foundation and rouge make her handsome face just a bit saucy. I smile. Man, am I starting to fancy old Mrs Mullins? Why the hell not? Suddenly I flush hot, then cold. My skin tingles and my cock stiffens inside my tight jeans. No way.

Don't even think about it. As if she could be turned by some punk with rapture in his eyes. This is Mrs Mullins. Harmless, gossipy, big-hips Mullins, who runs Junior Rangers and Junior Business Girl out at the Youth Centre. Still, it's been five days since Mrs Berry took me for a ride. If nothing else I want to push my luck. Maybe flirt with her. That could take the edge off my cravings which, if I'm honest, must be running out of control if I'm even considering this.

'You look real nice today, ma'am.'

She looks at me, looks away. Blushes. Smiles. 'Oh, don't be silly.'

'I mean it. You look real glamorous. I like your dress.' And I'm not joking; it's black and has gold buttons all the way up the front, so you undo it like a coat. She has a big bust too and it's pushing to come over the top. I can see about one centimetre of her bra. It's black and sheer with a lacy design. In my mind I think of the heavy softness hanging inside that black lace. Nipples big as pink saucers you could drink sugared milk from.

'Well, thank you, Franklin.' She blushes again and sits a little straighter. Pushes her lips forwards, suddenly self-conscious but not uncomfortable. I look at her legs. Plump, but real shapely in black high heels. And I like the way her little painted toenails can be seen through the peep-toe shoes. Around her ankle, something glints. She has a golden ankle chain under her sheer flesh hosiery. Kind of naughty; I didn't expect that. I clench my cock and widen my thighs to relieve the pressure a little.

'You should be careful what you say to us old gals. We might get the wrong idea.' She chuckles in a cheeky way and nudges me in the ribs. 'And Mrs Berry might get jealous.'

'What's not said is not known.' I look into her eyes and smile innocently. Slowly, I rest the finger of one hand against the side of her knee. It feels tight and slippery in her stocking. She doesn't seem to notice. She giggles and fans at her face again. 'My, my, what has she been teaching you? I'm sure there will be plenty of pretty young girls out to court you for a husband once you finish college.'

I shrug. 'Who wants a girl when there are so many beautiful women in this town?'

Mrs Mullins shrieks with laughter and dabs at one eye with a tissue. She likes the attention sure enough, even if it's from a young punk who has just finished high school. She doesn't get much. Her husband is a bit embarrassed of her. Stays in the garden, keeps out of her way; I can sense this. But she's not thinking indecent thoughts about me. Not yet. As if by accident, I stroke her knee with the back of my fingers. She sniffs and giggles some more, but doesn't seem to notice. I stroke it again; up, then down. This startles her. The knee is moved away. She pretends it never happened.

'Well, this won't do. I better get on. I hear there's a sale at Beaton's and Pankhurst.' She starts to gather her bags with those chubby, white, mumsy hands, thick with gold rings and glossy with lacquered nails. I imagine them stuffing my cock into her greedy mouth and feel a bit dizzy.

'Mrs Mullins,' I say, softly.

'Yes, dear?'

I look deep into her eyes and smile. She smiles back, confidently, eager to help as always.

'I'm not such a big kid any more.'

'I know, dear. You've turned into a fine young man. We're all very proud of you on the athletics committee.'

'Thanks. But I was wondering if I could . . . Well, talk to you in confidence. There's something I need to say.'

She looks concerned. Moves her face closer to mine. I can smell her perfume and lipstick. This is how she would look underneath me. 'Is it serious?' she asks.

'Afraid so.'

She looks around. 'It's OK. No one will hear. It's safe. And you know you can trust me.'

'I know. I think you're great. If there is one person we can rely on in this town it's you, ma'am. Everyone thinks so.'

'Do they?' She can't resist saying that; her face beams; she really suspects she is a laughing stock.

'Oh yeah. You just have this way of talking to us. And understanding our feelings.'

'Well, I try.' She blushes again. I widen my eyes and look at her like she's my lover and I adore her.

I notice she inhales, sharply, and parts her lips, but doesn't move away or break her stare from mine. 'But this isn't about kids' stuff. Or teenage problems. Can I talk to you as a man? A young one, sure, but still a man?'

'Of course, Franklin. Of course you can.'

'It's kinda hard to say, but . . .'

'Tell me.'

'Well, as a man I think of you as a woman. I have done for a long time.'

She looks flustered. 'I don't understand.'

'I've had a crush on you for ages.'

She shakes her head. Thinks about laughing. Then looks at me sternly; she thinks I'm making fun of her.

'I'm not fooling around or trying to make a fool out of you. I just think you're . . . You're so sexy, ma'am.'

Her mouth opens in shock, but I won't let her break from my stare.

'I needed to tell you. Even if it makes you mad, or you go and tell my folks, I don't care. I just needed to come clean about how I feel about you. So, it's just as

91

well you're not my Mentor, because I think I would have disgraced myself by now.'

'Oh, my poor darling,' she whispers. 'But you must be mistaken. I mean, how could I? How could you? Well, it just seems preposterous. I'm twice your age and you're such a handsome young man.'

'Things don't always turn out the way they should or the way people think they should. I just know how good you look and how I feel a bit dizzy sometimes when I see you around. Especially like today, when you're dressed up and everything and looking so fine. I go a little crazy and just don't know what to do with myself. But I know what I'd like to be doing.'

Her voice is a little breathless now. 'Who else knows of your feelings? Your friends?'

'No way. I keep these things to myself.'

'Good.'

'But I wanted you to know. I guess some people give you a hard time. Especially some of the women who are always organising stuff in this town. I've seen the way they speak to you. They disrespect you. But if only they knew how foxy I find you, well . . .'

She places a hand on her bust without knowing she's done it. Bites the side of her mouth. 'Perhaps you shouldn't say any more.'

'Perhaps I should. Somewhere private.' And into her eyes I stare with all my desire and need and youth and let her know that if she goes someplace quiet and safe with me, it will bring her pleasure, and it will make her feel young again, and more beautiful than she's felt since her Day of Grace Prom Night, all those years back. 'We should spend some time together and not think about anybody or anything else. I just want to make you feel good. And no one will ever know. It can be our secret, ma'am. Let me please you.'

She seems to sway a little before my eyes. Her face is red and her eyes are frantic, like she can't escape from

92

something she is almost certainly going to do but will regret. I can see the struggle inside her: the conflict between boring, mumsy Mrs Mullins, who the other women sneer at, and another character inside she keeps hidden. An identity that would put a lot of people into shock.

'No. I'd better not. Well, no. What if? No, no, we really should stop.'

Too late, ma'am. You drove him up to the Saviour Youth Camp by the lake. You unlocked a cabin and stepped inside to the dusty darkness with a young man. A young man whose lap you kept looking at in the car. When he closed the door you were secretly glad that it was too late to go back or to change your mind. You let him steer you over to the stripped bed, in the corner, looking so empty with the wire frame and bare mattress. You murmured and shook your head and protested when he knelt before you and slid his hands up your big, shapely legs. Right up inside your skirt so he could marvel and enjoy the width of your thighs, stretching those pantyhose until they turned invisible. And you bit your fingers but didn't push him away or come to your senses when he unbuttoned your dress-coat. Even when he was holding your big breasts, one in each hand, and just staring with wonder at the size of your rounded flesh in their lacy, see-through hammock, you never stopped him. And surely it was just a matter of time before he unbuckled himself and let you see what you had done to his sex. All that strutting around in high heels, swinging those big hips and pouting those cherry lips, can you blame him for being so hard and veiny and eager to plant himself in a part of you that has lain fallow for too long? So why didn't you stop him when he placed your white, manicured hand on his youthful meat? Why did you finger it and

*stroke it and coo at it like it was a kitten in a basket?
And did he force you to sit on that creaking wire bed
and to eat him like candy?*

*Stuffing all of that beef into your plump, watery
mouth in one go. Relishing the taste and the thickness
between your respectable housewife cheeks. Bobbing
your head up and down and making those little girlish
noises of surprise through your petite nose. Gobbling
him down like a hungry queen at a feast. So let her eat
cake.*

*And still complaining and muttering as you stood up
and lithely swivelled around and bent over. Getting your
panties and pantyhose down to your dimpled knees in
one smooth motion. Despite all the 'No, no, no. Better
not,' and 'We should stop this now. Before it's too late,'
it was you that offered your buttocks to his eager wet
spear, and then encouraged him to push it between your
damp pink lips. So who can blame him for thrusting so
hard and so deep into the woman who wears the khaki
Ranger outfit every Sunday, and who perches glasses on
the end of her girly nose when she takes Young Business
Girls' Club out to the skyscraper tower of black glass
downtown?*

*And only then did you stop making such a fuss.
Amidst the groans and creaks of the bed, this was a time
of no reason or logic or facts or rules. And you went at
it like an animal with him in that gloomy cabin.
Completely lost yourself and opened yourself to as
much of that length as possible. Pushed your body back
into his slamming groin and said terrible things at the
unswept floor. In there with the cobwebs and dust
rabbits, you were empowered by the passion and
firmness of the young man. Asked him to be rough with
you, 'if you like'. Even shouted and shrieked with
delight as he paused at his thrustings to take his belt off.*

*His leather turned your buttocks pink, then red, after
ten good lashes. You wanted the pleasure but you*

*wanted to hurt for being pleasured too. He made your
seat sting, he made your voice croak and skin shiver and
head spin when you came on that endlessly pushing,
thrusting cock. On and on and on it went through you,
never pausing, like some machine, leading you up to
another climax, and then another. And you couldn't
get away with your underwear strangling your knees
together and your fingers hooked on that bare mattress.*

*Well, you've come this far, so you might as well ask
for his cream in your hungry, sucking mouth too. Open
and demanding in a face he finds handsome and lusty.
No sooner had he withdrawn from your engorged sex,
than you managed to turn and sit and gather that
swollen purple head between your lips. So nimble on
your feet for a big woman. And even though you should
never have been in there with so young a man, the
transgression never stopped you from sucking and
devouring every ounce of his fresh seed. Pumping its
length with a hot hand like it was a towel you were
wringing out. Such big eyes you have, ma'am.*

Chapter Eleven

'Dude, what's up?'

'Nothing.' I stand out front of my house and watch Davey's dad drive Davey and Brad away after our Thursday night band rehearsal. Glancing up and down the street, I see there's nothing unusual happening; no cars I don't recognise. Maybe I'm just being paranoid; my meeting with the Chaplain is scheduled for tomorrow morning. How could she know whether my 'pop group' is still together or not? As Mrs Berry said, I just have to lie and make it stick; be convincing. Need to stand up on my own, now things have changed so much. But Gretchen can tell something is up with me.

'That's BS, man. You been coming up with so many songs and ideas that have been, like, blowing our minds, but outside of practice we don't see squat of you. This is the summer break, man! The last one. We should be living it up. So what the hell are you doing every day?'

'I got track practice and shit like that.'

'Sure you do.'

'Stuff to help my dad with too.'

'Yeah, right.'

'I have.'

'Quit stalling. Something is going on. Ever since you got a Mentor, you've changed. You can't fool me. I've known you since first grade.'

I sigh. Look up at the wide blue sky without taking much notice of what's going on up there. 'Things can't always stay the same, buddy. Some stuff changes.'

'But not that fast. I knew there was something up with her. I knew it.'

'Leave her alone,' I snap back. I'm starting to get real sick of people hassling me about Mrs Berry. 'She's totally cool.'

Gretchen looks at me, irritated. 'No one says she's not. But you can't blame your friends for being curious, that's all. She's the hottest thing in this neighbourhood.'

'So everyone keeps telling me.' I can't keep the sarcasm out of my voice.

Gretchen tilts his head at an angle. 'Don't tell me. No. Don't tell me you've gone and fallen for her? Your Mentor? For the sake of Our Saviour. And what's this I been hearing about Melody Watson?'

'Dude, just drop it. It's got nothing to do with you, or Brad, or Davey, or anyone else.'

'Fine.' Gretchen's pissed with me. I wish I could tell my best friend something, but I've made enough mistakes being impulsive. And now people are talking about Melody Watson? That I didn't know. And it sure didn't come from me. It makes me feel even more edgy and sick with nerves. Now I'm worrying about what I did with Mrs Mullins too. It's this biting thing Mrs Berry showed me; it gets people hooked on you.

'Man, sometimes I don't even know who you are any more.' Gretchen walks off, carrying his guitar case.

'Gretch! Gretch?' I call out, but he just keeps walking.

When I go into the house mom and dad are talking in tense whispers. When they see me come in, they stop talking and stare at me. I pretend I haven't noticed, try to sneak up the stairs.

'Franklin,' my mom says. 'A word please, darling.'

The blood feels like it's stopped moving inside me. My scalp prickles, makes me shiver. I have no idea what my parents are going to ask me. Could be about anything: Mrs Berry, or worse. I turn around and trot into the kitchen. Try and make out I'm totally unflustered.

'Love, you never told us that you and Mrs Watson's daughter – is it Melody? – were so close.'

I go stiff all over and can't swallow. The ticking of the kitchen clock gets real loud. Dad is frowning; mom is smiling, but puzzled. 'I know her, sure.'

'You don't have to be shy. You can tell us about your friends.' The way she says 'friends' is loaded like a shotgun.

'I know I can. I do,' I say, doing my best to keep the blushing back while looking real innocent.

'Well, it took us by surprise, that's all.'

'What did?' My voice isn't much more than a croak.

'How close you two are. I can't ever remember you mentioning her before.'

I can barely breathe, let alone speak. 'She's cool. We've hung out.'

My mom is trying not to giggle, but dad isn't finding this funny. 'More than just hang out, it would seem. Much more,' he says.

Mute with fear, I lean against a wall, trying to make it casual, but I need the support.

My dad folds his arms. 'Otherwise, why would Mrs Watson invite your mother and I over for dinner? To make a courtship proposal on behalf of her daughter. This Melody I've never even heard you mention before.'

'Huh?'

'That's right,' he says, his eyebrow raised. 'To discuss the possibility of an engagement.'

Chapter Twelve

'It's not been easy, ma'am.'

'No, I don't suppose it has.' Her staring, interrogating eyes are already making me shift about on the chair in her study. Maybe that's why she has short hair; to make her face look more severe. Most of the Chaplains are the same; smart, elegant, but hard-faced; you would never push your luck with them. Everyone knows they run the show in this town.

'I've been with my band for three years.'

'But you explained to the others that you have a very good reason for disbanding?'

I nod, not able to make another lie crawl out of my mouth.

'You are sure you made it perfectly clear to them?'

I put on my best face of sulky disappointment, look at my lap and nod my head again.

'I see. And what about your Mentor?'

'Told her too, ma'am.'

'What exactly did you tell Mrs Berry?'

'That, you know, we weren't suited and stuff. That I'd done some stupid and immature things.'

'Indeed. So when did you tell her?'

'After I left here. Last Friday.'

She nods her head, thoughtful, but her face doesn't give much away, although I sense she's trying hard to control her temper. I avoid looking into her eyes.

'And what about Melody Watson?'

'Haven't seen her.'

'You've been avoiding her?'

I nod.

'So your seduction of her was just a passing fancy? You manipulated her into satisfying your most base male urges and now you want nothing more to do with the poor girl? The kind of behaviour we buried a long time ago in our town. Something we certainly won't be welcoming back. Look at me when I'm talking to you.'

I raise my head. 'I stayed away from her so it doesn't happen again. You know, I was avoiding temptation. Things like that.'

'Things like that. I see. I know all about young men and things like that. Temptation makes a man lie and cheat and betray the trust of others. Was it a wonder we put a stop to it?' I don't like her tone one bit and her staring eyes are burning my face red with frostbite.

There is a long silence like she's waiting for me to say some more. 'Is there anything else you'd like to share with me this morning?' She opens the brown paper file she has between her hands and looks down.

At this hint of a conclusion, I vigorously shake my head from side to side. 'No, ma'am.' I stand up and take my denim jacket off the back of the chair, terrified of making a sound.

'Sit down,' she says, without looking at me.

'Ma'am?'

She raises her voice but still doesn't look up. 'Sit down.'

I retake my seat. The Chaplain continues to read the file. Under the table, she crosses her legs. They make a raspy sound like women's legs do when they're wearing nylons. I squash the inappropriate thought. Like with Mrs Mullins, these days I can find something sexy about every woman I see. It gives me pleasure, but a great deal of worry too. It's like whatever I'm not supposed to think, I think.

The Chaplain looks at me. 'I'd like you to look at some pictures, Franklin.'

'Ma'am?' I can't keep the tremor out of my voice.

'Start with these. Take a good look and tell me what you think.' She turns the file around and pushes it across the desk towards me. I notice her fingernails are painted red like a fire engine. I push another inappropriate thought away.

I look down and swallow. At first it's difficult to even recognise myself in the photograph. But Mrs Berry I identify straight away. Sitting across from me in a diner, she's smoking a cigarette; I'm talking. The photo was taken from outside the diner. 'Yeah. Last Friday night. We had dinner.' My voice is tiny, like it's coming from a distance.

'When you told her you would no longer require her services as a Mentor?' I say nothing. 'Look at the next one.' I do this and am confronted by a black and white image of Mrs Berry straddling my lap in the back of her car. Her fingers are gripping the back seat and her head is thrown back. Both of my hands can be seen feeling her breasts; her bra is so sheer it's hard to tell she's even wearing one. Everything looks so clear I can almost smell her perfume. It's weird seeing yourself doing it. The next four photos feature the same scene. Only our positions have changed. On the last one I am kissing her foot; she is smoking. I would like to keep these.

I look up at the Chaplain. My bottom lip is starting to quiver and my eyes don't know where to go. 'Keep looking,' she says. Her face is so white.

I see Gretchen, Brad and Davey walking down the drive of my house. They are all holding their instrument cases. Except for Davey; he leaves his drum kit in the garage, but is carrying black vinyl cymbal bags. I can see the band were photographed twice, after each rehearsal this week. I suddenly want to laugh hysterically because I know I'm totally fucked. I clear my

101

throat. 'These things take time,' I say, and grin because I'm trying not to.

'Do not open your mouth again unless I ask you a question. I will not communicate with liars. Look at the other pictures.'

And there I am with Mrs Mullins, chatting by the fountain in Ladies Square. Followed by a snapshot of the two of us leaving. We look weird together. Then there are snapshots of us entering the cabin and leaving sometime later. Her hair is mussed up. I close the file and pretend to wipe at my nose. I try to suppress a giggle and make a snorting sound.

The Chaplain stands up so quick her chair falls over and smacks the wall. 'How dare you mock Our Saviour in a consecrated house!' She slaps a hand against the desk and I nearly jump right out of my seat. 'You are a liar! A despicable, remorseless liar! You are a degenerate! A filthy pervert pig!' Her whole body is shaking and I'm so shocked I can't swallow the lump in my throat.

Then, real calm, she corrects the position of the chair and sits down. Sniffs. 'I apologise,' she says.

Shaking my head, I say, 'I can't believe you followed me. Took photos.'

She fixes me with a look that makes me shrink all over until my boots feel loose on my feet. 'If the behaviour of a citizen is a threat to the well-being of our community, any action that leads to his apprehension is justified. And surveillance was justified after what I witnessed on our holy Day of Grace. I've also taken the liberty of calling Mrs Berry at work and requesting she meet us here this morning.' I stop breathing. My vision goes a bit blurry. 'Unfortunately, she could not be reached.'

I swallow hard. 'My parents?'

'Know nothing, yet.' Suddenly I feel grateful to the Chaplain. Want to get down on my knees and thank her. 'And the amount of information they receive will

102

be entirely dependent upon your co-operation.' She sits back in her chair, raises her chin and folds her hands in her lap. Crosses her legs. I look down, then back up. I deserve everything I get. Maybe I should be given the needle and spend the rest of my life in an orange boiler suit weeding a flower bed in Saviour Park. 'You put me in a very difficult situation.'

I look at the desk, wish I was blindfold – anything to avoid those hard metal eyes.

'I cannot give you another chance. You are sick and hopeless and a danger to yourself and others. We must pursue a different course of action. I pray Our Saviour will guide each of us on the difficult journey ahead.' She clears her throat, wets her lips. 'Before and during the Graceful Revolution, my holy order was assigned with the task of re-educating men and women. You will not be aware of this, and I hadn't even been born. However, procedures involving the restraint and correction of a whole variety of sexual deviants were employed. The practices and techniques of my forebears have been, shall we say, handed down. And not solely in the spirit of tradition. A select few of us have been made privy to the craft of our blessed predecessors by virtue of their effectiveness in reconstructing the male animal.' She pauses to take a breath. The colour has returned to her cheeks. 'It is my intention to begin an immediate programme of rehabilitation with you. A specific tuition that will remain strictly confidential and private. It may interest you to know that this is not the first time I have been called upon to take such action. Now, I would like you to take a look at another set of pictures.' She unlocks one of her desk drawers. Removes what looks like a black leather photograph album and places it, gently, in front of me. I notice a new energy in her eyes, similar to the excitement and anger and satisfaction I saw there when she confronted me behind the marquee tent at the Day of Grace celebrations. More than anything else, more than the spying and the evil way she got me to lie while knowing the truth all along, this look in her face makes me hate her.

'Don't you dare. Don't you dare look at me like that, my lad. Just do as you're told and look at the pictures.'

Pretty soon my sulky hateful glare has dissolved from my face and been replaced by the icy stiffness of shock. I can tell these photos have been taken ages ago because of the hairstyles on the men. But that doesn't lessen the horror I feel.

The pictures remind me of the photo strips in the old manuals in the sports science library at high school: men in white leotards and crazy lace-up boots showing you, frame by frame, how to do gymnastics and how to throw a discus. Only the men in the Chaplain's book are mostly being tied up with white ropes. A frosty-looking woman in a black uniform demonstrates how to tie up a man's wrists and ankles, how to secure a strait-jacket, fix him upside down from a ceiling hook, stretch him into a star shape with ropes and ground pegs, and how to knot his body into all kinds of strange positions so he can't move at all. And with that rubber ball strapped between his teeth, he can't call for help either. But these pictures were just like an introduction to the other stuff in the Chaplain's album.

I don't like the look of the metal head-brace one bit. Nor how this one guy in his white shorts and vest is tied down over a vaulting horse with a black sack over his head, just like the dead cowboy a woman sheriff shot full of holes in a movie I saw.

Other pages show a woman how to attach these big rubber pants and handcuffs to a prisoner, so he can't touch his balls or anything down there. He has to pee through a tube. 'This is sick,' I can't help myself saying.

The Chaplain smiles, but not in a nice way. 'That is precisely the sort of contentious comment I expect from an individual in your situation. Someone so ignorant of self-discipline that it must be imposed. You see, fortunately for us today, the deviant men of history were never quite the same again after suffering these corrective methods.' I note she relishes the word 'suffering' like it's a lemon bonbon in her mouth. These methods weren't designed to reform characters but to break them down into snivels and tears and fears. Any fool can see that. Since I've been with Mrs Berry I've learned many things, like how to know what people are thinking and why they really do stuff. And I know that the Chaplain's plans for me aren't just about protecting the sanctity of her precious community. In just the same way that Mrs Berry gets pleasure from me whipping her with my belt, this Chaplain gets the same kick from the pain and remorse and guilt and humiliation of young men like me. And knowing this makes me feel stronger and makes me a whole lot more interested in this moral guardian of my community.

'You've left me with no choice, Franklin. If you hadn't involved valued members of my congregation in your sordid and deviant behaviour, I'd have been happy to send you straight to the male reformatory. And you would qualify as an adult entrant. But as you've dragged Melody Watson and Mrs Mullins into disgrace, you've made it personal. And you shall deal with me in person, each and every week, perhaps even twice a week, until I am satisfied you are a changed man. Because, you see, Ms Watson – an intelligent and accomplished girl, but sadly an impressionable and vulnerable young woman also – has developed an unhealthy fixation with you. She now seems determined to pursue you as a marital companion. The thought, quite frankly, makes me sick. But, as you have sullied her for more suitable candidates, I believe I must take it upon myself to help you return to sanity and reason and decency. For both of your sakes. It would be irresponsible of me to allow this communion the breath of life, or indeed any future arrangement to continue, without the absolute certainty that you have reformed. I will not allow a degenerate to wander freely and prey upon my flock.'

I can't move or speak. While she's going on at me, panic and fear have been swirling around and shaking me up. Now I'm just stunned. I look at her fierce eyes and painted, determined face, so flushed and quivering with excitement. She's drunk on power. When the women in charge of us get like this, there's nothing you can do. Resistance just makes it worse. They can put you away. Get you the needle. I often wonder why women like my mom or Mrs Mullins are never in charge. Well, now I know. The kind and caring women are considered weak and just get pushed aside, so the bitches, the beautiful bitches, can run wild all over us with their spiky shoes. I've written a song about this. How the greedy, cruel and power-crazy have taken over. And they're not accountable to anyone. And now, weirdly, so many men like being crushed under their heels because that makes life so much easier. And giving in and being humiliated is something our sexuality cannot resist. We have to go along with it to be granted favours. We hate it; we love it. I know in a heartbeat that I have to leave this town, this state. Maybe Mrs Berry, in her mysterious way, has been saying this from the start.

But for now, whatever crazy, degenerate urge led me to seduce Melody Watson and Mrs Mullins, and to use the body of a married adventuress in a motel room, and to chase a strange business woman through the lingerie department, I can identify inside me now; speeding up my heartbeat and thickening my cock. This Chaplain has strange tastes and I believe her holy position is a cover for her own 'urges'. And I want to know who women like her really are. I crave the hidden desires of all women. I want to know them. Experience them. Not just some well-behaved girl from the suburbs for me, who I can cook and clean for – it would never be enough – I need more. Especially those at the top. Mrs Berry opened the trapdoor on my darkness and now it won't sink back underground. So give me them all: the mothers, the daughters, the neighbours and the priests. I am sin and this preacher wants to send me to hell. So let's go, bitch.

The Chaplain removes her gold watch and drops it inside her desk drawer with the album. 'And if you speak a word of what happens between us to a single soul, I'll send you to a place where they'll put the beast inside you to sleep, for ever. Now, follow me.'

I wonder how many of the priests and staff at the Saviour Centre know about this room. Are lots of them in on it? Is it a place they take men so Chaplains can work off their frustrations from the long journey that is celibacy?

Doesn't look like it's changed much from the days when those photos were taken. And I can smell the sweat of men in here, as if it's gotten into the painted bricks of the walls and under the dark wood of the floor. The place has no windows or ventilation. Nowhere to look in or get out.

'Don't look so glum, my lad. We won't be using all of the apparatus on your first visit. We shall have to start slowly. However, there is much work to be done, so by the end of your programme, I'm sure you will be quite familiar with every device we have to offer. So take a good look at them. Know them, respect them, admire them. They are your new Mentors. They are here for your benefit.'

With the big cube in the corner, made by wooden beams and metal joints, it's hard to tell where a body would go. There are so many hooks and leather belts and canvas straps hanging here and there. The floor inside is pocked by lots of little dents. These must have been made by women's shoes, over the years. The wooden supports and beams are a dark-brown colour, as if they're greasy or still damp from use. It's an evil-looking contraption. When put to use I imagine it making the creaking sounds of an old sailing ship. Hysteria bubbles inside my tummy.

There is a gym horse in here too, beside the cube. The leather cushion on top is worn thin and stained. Metal rings are fixed into the chipped wooden base. There are some wooden bars screwed into the wall too, like in a gym. And there are some nasty-looking boxes, like big coffins against another wall.

The Chaplain uses a big iron key to unlock a cupboard with long oaken doors. Over her shoulder I get a glimpse of lots of wooden things hanging from brass hooks. Some are thin, some look like canoe paddles.

'Take everything off except for your underwear. Socks too. Fold your clothes and put them in a corner.' She turns around holding something close to her body. She almost looks embarrassed, like she's sharing a secret with a new friend and scared they might laugh. 'It is necessary to use these. To put them on you.' She's short of breath with excitement too; she likes being down here in the smelly shadows with these weird things.

She walks across to me quickly. 'Put your arms out.' I do as she says. She puts the metal cuffs on real tight and then tugs the thin leash that is attached to the short chain between the rings. My chest goes tight; it's like I can't get enough air. I want to scream. 'Too tight,' I say. 'It hurts. I can't move my hands.'

'You won't need to,' she says in a raspy whisper. Her eyes are full of glee. 'You won't be able to do anything. You will be absolutely still. You shall have to trust me. And I want you to listen very carefully to everything I say to you. I'll make sure you're receptive, don't worry about that, but you must remember everything I tell you during the lesson. Understand?'

'Yes, ma'am.' My legs are starting to tremble and I can't stop shivering. She notices this and smiles. Part of me wants to pull at the cuffs and struggle and scream, because pretty soon I'm going to be in pain. Any fool can see that. The look in her eyes is getting all intense and serious, which is starting to make her face seem like a mask for what's really underneath. But there is something about this situation that is preventing me from resisting. Maybe it is my upbringing. For my entire life until recently, I have been absolutely respectful and obedient to older women. I've just let them make all the decisions for me. So, by instinct, I'm just obeying their will. Or it could be my own sick curiosity and my need to recklessly throw myself into intimate situations with women, no matter the consequences, that is playing a hand also. A crazy part of me just wants to be tied up and beaten by this hard little priest with petite feet and red fingernails. She's got my heart thumping and my cock swelling. This mature, respectable lady, with her compact body in a smart suit and her short, neat hair, the sensible court shoes and shiny hose, now wants to put a horse's bit between my teeth. 'Open your mouth.' Her voice has gone real deep.

The leather straps of the head-piece go over my scalp and around the sides of my head. It pulls my hair. I wince. She ignores me. Her little fingernails are busy buckling and pulling straps hard until the whole thing goes tight on my head. It feels heavy and smells bad. I feel silly. 'I don't like this,' I mumble, like a kid with his mouth full of potato.

'Makes you feel stupid, eh? Like a big dummy. Like a dumb animal that can think of nothing but eating and copulating.' She moves her face close to mine. Our noses nearly touch. I can see the fine lines around her eyes and the freckles under the make-up on her cheekbones. 'When the hurting starts, my lad, you'll be glad of it. And later tonight, when you're lying on your front,

109

you'll thank me for this. It'll do you the world of good.'
Her compact breasts brush against my ribs and chest. I
can't help the erection that pushes out my boxers into
her warm belly. She doesn't notice straight away, but
after fidgeting in front of me to make the final adjust-
ments, she looks down to see the hard thing that is
poking at her. Stares at it. The skin on her face goes
tight. She grits her teeth. Sticks her chin out. 'Have you
no decency, you devil?'

I blush and try to apologise, but can only make idiot
slurping sounds. 'Is the corruption so deep inside you
that you cannot control yourself in a house of god?' She
pauses to take a breath. 'Well, let me tell you something,
you're only making it worse for yourself.' She pushes
the rubber right into my back teeth, and steps away.
Instinctively, I try to raise my hands to pull it out of my
mouth, but she holds the leash tight so my clumsy
tied-up arms just waft around in front of my face.

I am pulled across to the vaulting horse. I think of the
man in the picture, on his belly in his underwear,
strapped over the saddle, while the woman in the black
uniform stands behind him holding a cane: the kind of
stick that whips the air and leaves a sting you can feel
a week later.

Tugging and pushing, she gets me on to the saddle of
the wooden horse that I am to ride through a blizzard
of tears. Pulls my legs down either side and cuffs them
to the metal rings. Yanks my arms over the front and
belts them down so tight, I can barely flex my shoulders.

She leaves me lying on the horse. Walks back to the
cupboard. I turn my head and see her selecting a cane.
She takes her time. Thrashes a few through the air real
hard. The skin on my back shivers. Then she unhooks
a black plastic apron from the cupboard and ties it
around her waist. Flexes her fingers. Rotates her wrists.
Takes the light-brown cane off the hook, the one she

tested first. Comes back across to me and stands where I cannot see her at the bottom of the horse.

I panic. Let out a moan. Try and shout, 'No. Enough. Sorry. No. Please.' But all I do is make gurgling baby sounds.

'Now listen carefully,' she says, in a quiet, serious voice. 'The next time you look at a woman and feel your filthy desires taking hold of you, before you even think about smiling at her or talking to her, I want you to remember this saddle. I want you to remember that you could not get off it. That you could not move. And I want you to think long and hard about what happens when I put you in this saddle. Now bite down hard!'

After the first blow, I spit and curse and try to writhe, but the straps cut into my skin so I stop moving. It's like being struck by lightning and the crackling electricity has nowhere to earth. Just stays inside you and screams. But the second switch makes me roar and curse. When the cane lands for a third time, I nearly pull the horse to pieces.

Can't see a thing. My face is soaked with tears. I try and count in the strokes, like I do with a drum beat before kicking in with guitar or vocals, but she's making up her own time so I don't know when the next blow is coming. Off beats.

Three more quick strokes come down hard with a sound like an egg breaking on a tiled floor. They kill my struggles with a pure white pain that streaks my buttocks and electrocutes all of my bones down to the marrow. I don't struggle after the next four strokes; just let the hurting come in through the back door. Feel faint and dizzy and hot. Never felt so tired, not even after breaking the school 1,500-hundred metres record. It's like my body has gone thermal with morphine too, sending a calming warmth to the pain.

'Every time you touch yourself, my lad, remember the pain. The damned suffer for ever, my lad. For ever. Save yourself.' I hear her heels tick-tack-tick-tack back to the cupboard. I feel a bit sleepy. My chin runs with spit. All I can taste is rubber and hot nose breath. A tingle and glow settles over my punished ass, but there is a deeper throb down inside the muscle that makes the surface sting.

She returns to the foot of the horse, and stands where I can't see her. I expect more pain; wonder if I can take any more. But there are no more swishes or stings that make you go deaf. Just the sound of her breathing – real fast girlish breathing – and the rustle of clothes. I'm confused. What the hell is she doing? It goes on for a few minutes, then she clears her throat and walks back to the cupboard.

I turn my head to watch. As she walks, she pats down the front of her skirt, then gets a cloth and spray bottle from a shelf inside the cupboard. This time she walks to the head of the horse, lifts my chin up and wipes the cloth over my face. Her knuckles are white and cold, her face stiff with contempt. I can tell she's trying real hard to control herself, probably so she doesn't do too much damage all in one go.

Carefully, she unbuckles my wrists and ankles, then barks at me, 'Dismount.' Shaky on my feet, I stand up before her. She walks around behind me. 'Push your shorts down at the back. Keep the front covered.' I do as she says, but glance over my shoulder to see what she's doing back there.

'Face front!'

Gentle hands then hold the back of my thighs. I wince when I feel her breath on my wounds. She must have her face real close to them, no doubt admiring her work. 'You'll live,' she says. 'But you'll have to toughen up fast. This was nothing more than an introduction to what awaits unless you straighten out real quick. And believe me, you'll know how to behave when I'm finished down here.' She stands up. 'Cover yourself.'

Slowly, ever so slowly, I pull my shorts up, careful not to touch any skin.

'Now, I suggest you go home and soak yourself in the bath. Better get used to lying on your front too. I want you fit for next Friday.'

I bow my head and let her unbuckle the head-piece. Rubbing my scalp and cheeks where the straps cut grooves, I watch her lovingly spray the mask with a bottle and carefully wipe it with a clean cloth. It's like the contraption reminds her of the good times. She notices me staring and snaps, 'Get dressed.'

I guess I'm still in some kind of shock. This is the first time in my privileged and protected life that I can recall anyone disliking me. And she really does despise me. I don't know why for sure, but I'm afraid of her; I flinch every time she looks at me. I hate myself for being afraid and hate her for making me so helpless. But my feelings are all mixed up too; I can identify another emotion down there. I think it's desire that makes me panic and feel ashamed. Some stupid, stubborn, crazy part of me wants to please her. And I want her to like me.

The Chaplain closes the door to the basement room and uses three different keys to lock it. Moving slowly and feeling a bit stiff every time I lift a knee, I follow her out of the basement level. Not sure why, but my cock is hard. I watch her buttocks and admire her ankles. I briefly imagine her writhing beneath me, her painted mouth biting at the air with pleasure. When I reach the top steps, the stripes on my bottom get lively again. The vision clears.

Back inside her office, she takes a seat. I remain standing. 'You will limit further contact with Mrs Berry to basic civility. What I mean by that is, if she calls, refuse to see her. If you pass her in the street, be polite, but you must never, ever be alone together again. Am I understood?'

'Yes, ma'am.'

'The same rule applies to Mrs Mullins and Melody Watson. This has to stop now. For your sake. And there will be no more music with your group for the time being. If, in the future, you have proven yourself to be responsible, we may consider a resumption of your interest in rock bands. Until that time, there will be no more rehearsals. And remember, I am watching and listening, all of the time. Now, is there anything you don't understand?'

I shake my head.

She smiles. 'Good. And not a word to another soul about this morning. If you defy my wishes, I'll send you straight to a reform programme. I'll see you here next Friday.' She looks down at her diary, as if nothing out of the ordinary has taken place.

I take off, but don't move as fast as I used to. Too relieved it's over to be angry. Guess that's the start of being broken down. This is what happens to men who step out of line. Same shit happened to Isaac and those guys packing groceries at the Saviour Mart. This is why my dad worries so much. Why he wants me to be like him; married to some girl like Melody Watson, looking after a house and bringing up kids. There is no choice. It's that or a service-industry job, or reform school and the drugs they give you to take away your sex drive.

Outside the Saviour Centre, I stare at the sky, then at the horizon. There's a lot of places to go out there. I turn around and look up at the marble face of the Saviour on the steeple – such a beauty, such an angel. I'll be your fool for a day, but not for a lifetime. Bitch.

The Chaplain might have made me weep bitter tears, but if she thinks I'm going to change, she's mistaken. I'm like Mrs Berry now. And I think you know that, holy woman. What just happened was for your amusement, before you take further steps. You underestimate me. And in a way, you're just the same as me. Denial makes you crazy.

Chapter Thirteen

Standing in the dark, sheltered by the trees, away from the streetlight, I wait for her. First thing I hear of her in the peaceful night is the rhythm of her heels, tapping towards my shadows. Close my eyes and raise my nose. Catch a breeze; find her scent. There it is. Thin but sufficient to remind me of a sweet princess's bedroom, where she prepared her softness from drawers full of fine, fine things. For me.

Melody walks into view. Pauses at the top of the street. Looks about.

None of the parked cars are occupied. There are no pedestrians. Amongst the leafy branches and smells of sleeping earth, my tummy fizzes with nerves. 'Melody,' I sing out. 'Melody.'

She starts and looks in my direction. Her little dog strains on its leash. Yaps twice. 'Hector,' she says, and pulls him to heel. He looks up, guilty, confused. Then she looks at the trees where I stand. 'Franklin? What are you doing in there?'

I take a step forwards, but do not entirely leave my hiding place. 'Waiting for you,' I say, softly, my mouth filling with saliva.

'Are you ashamed of being seen with me, then?'

'No one can see us together.'

She walks closer. 'Why have you been avoiding me? I haven't seen you since . . . that night.'

'Had my reasons, babe.'

'What are you talking about? Come out of there.'

'Sshhh. Keep it down. I'm being watched.'

'What?'

'Trust me. Meet me by the baseball diamond on St Agnes. In the dugout. OK?'

'Why?'

'I'll tell you there.' Then I vanish, back through the trees, and run down a track behind some gardens, knowing she will go to the baseball diamond.

Mrs Berry has vanished. I've not seen her car on the drive since last Thursday – on the night before my meeting with the Chaplain. Not even my mom knows where she's gone. I have a hunch her disappearance has got something to do with the trouble I'm in. You can never tell with Mrs Berry though. Maybe it's even a test to see how I cope on my own.

Which isn't very well.

The sting and the marks from the Chaplain's cane faded pretty quickly. Even stopped hurting by the time I got home. My healing felt perfectly natural, but I know those marks should still be there. She hit me good and hard with that stick – even lost her mind for a time. Mrs Berry is strong in me; in my heart and in my veins we are bonded.

Shame the Chaplain never managed to whack the urge to seduce out of me. I've barely been able to see straight these last six days since the last time I loved and fed. Tried to lay low, but the dizziness and hot flushes and bad, bad dreams came on real quick. Then I started to get the shakes. Last night, stomach cramps and nightmares so clear they still seem real kept me up all night save for two hours around dawn. Lovely dawn when the girls wake up and begin to make themselves look real nice for work, for school, for us? So I knew it was time to make a call.

Seems like I can go about four days without a fix. Whatever secret thing Mrs Berry has given me, I guess

116

I'm still at the baby stage. Go crazy and want to bawl and holler if I'm not getting my nutrients from shaven flesh that smells of soaps and scents and is full of the hot, salty stuff. Man, I'm getting the shiver and shakes just thinking about a taste. And now I got to slake this thirst without her help.

Reminds me of a programme I once saw on the Wonder Channel about this mother lion who stops hunting for her cubs, so they can start killing for themselves. A porcupine and a skunk were too much for them. But eventually they get themselves a little squealy bush pig. Mrs Berry is that lioness and I'm just getting bit, scratched and going hungry while trying to get on the back of something soft and good to eat that squeals.

In the dark of the dugout I smile to myself. In the distance, I hear the chain-link gate open and then close. Real soft, I send out a whistle. One note. Hector comes scampering up to me. 'You gonna have to keep watch, little man, while me and your mama go at it.' He blinks twice and then shakes his furry face.

'Franklin? Franklin? Where are you?' she says in her West-side princess voice that gets me all short of breath. Tried to kid myself today that I only called her up so I could put these courtship proposals on ice. Her family are very important in this town and I'm sure my dad will be rubbing his hands. But when you got music in your heart, nothing else will do. Most days I dream of a long road, and it's getting clearer.

'Melody, I'm down here.'

She's got herself all jittery with excitement. 'This is crazy, Franklin. Why can't I just come over for tea like a normal girlfriend?'

In the back of the dugout, I wince at her mention of the girlfriend status, but then what I see of her outfit takes my mind off future troubles. She has unbuttoned her coat and is wearing a thin summery dress, cut low, that hugs every curve to the knee. Her legs are shiny in

117

stockings and her heels make her walk real nice. 'You look great,' I say.

She blushes, smiles. 'Thanks. It's new.'

I pat the bench beside me.

She sits down. 'I've been so mad at you, Franklin. I don't hear a word in two weeks and now we have to meet in secret.' She looks around. 'On a baseball diamond. It's not very romantic.'

'Ssh,' I whisper, screwing up my eyes to check out the outfield and bleachers. 'I'm in trouble, Melody. So I had to cool it. You know, keep a low profile.'

'What have you done?'

'What have we done, you mean.'

'No!'

I nod. 'A Chaplain saw us that night. And heard everything too.'

'Which one? Mummy knows all –'

I cut her off. 'You're fine. She thinks the world of you and wants to keep you out of it. But she's not so keen on me. She's kept her mouth shut because of you, but she's forbidden me to be alone with any woman.'

Melody giggles.

I look at her, raise an eyebrow. Melody is another one of those girls who stops at nothing to get what she wants. That's why she's the best at everything at school. I got to go real easy. 'She's freaking out over this courtship deal.'

Melody stops smiling and looks down at the pointy toes of her shoes on the dark cement floor. 'I wanted to talk to you about that, but you were avoiding me. Are you mad?'

'No. Surprised is all.'

She takes her coat off and folds it on the bench.

I touch the hair by her ear. 'We hardly know each other.'

'We know enough. What happened between us was magic. Destiny. So much passion. So much intensity. It only comes once in a lifetime. You got inside my head.

118

My heart. I've been thinking of nothing else since the Day of Grace.' She squeezes her hands together. 'Which I know I shouldn't say, in case you think I'm too pushy.' She turns and looks at me. 'Don't you feel the same?' There is a tremble in her voice and her face seems ready to collapse.

I clear my throat. 'It was great. I think you're great too. Real pretty and everything.'

'But?'

'Can't we go a bit slower?'

'Why wait?'

'It's not something to rush into.'

'But if you know you're right for each other. If, if, if something magical happens when you're together, then you have to follow your heart.' Then her face darkens and her eyes go narrow. 'I don't want some other girl putting a bid in for you. I just know it will happen if I wait. And I know what I want.'

'I don't doubt it.'

'What's that supposed to mean? Franklin, you seduced me!'

'I know. I know. Ssh –'

'Don't you shush me,' she says, but drops her voice to a whisper. 'You fucked me. You started something. And now you're trying to wriggle out of it. I just knew it.' She stands up to go. 'I won't let you make a fool out of me. You'll be very sorry if you try.'

I jump up and snatch her arms, before she can get her coat on. Pull her into my chest. Hold her still. Instinctively, she gasps at the preposterousness of a man putting his hands on a woman. I look down at that pretty, sulky face. 'Don't talk about me like I'm some object,' I say, 'that gets bargained over by women. I'm not a piece of meat. No one owns me.'

She struggles to get free. 'We'll see about that.' The dog growls. Its little barrel-body tenses and its hackles rise.

Don't know what tempts me to do it. Maybe it's her tummy pressed into my cock; her perfume getting inside my head; her sullen, pouty mouth; her will to own me like that little dog on the leash; maybe the Chaplain's crazy influence plays a part, but I get real mad and frustrated and aroused at the same time. I twist her around, bend her over. Slip one hand on the back of her head and quickly slap her silky buttocks with my strongest arm. 'You behave like a spoilt brat and this happens.'

'How dare you!'

'I dare, all right.' I slap her hard, my arm moves real quick five times, in and out. Tight with little panties and a thin dress stretched over her buttocks like the skin of a snare drum, the spanking makes a dull, splatting sound that echoes in the dugout. My cock stirs, lies in my shorts like a fat python that's just swallowed a deer.

She sniffs, says, 'Ow, that hurt me,' in a tearful voice. Boys get spanked in school, but girls? Never. Not even if they're really bad as kids.

'Probably the first time you ever been spanked, huh? Won't be the last time either, if you keep this up.'

'Do you know who my mother is?' she says through her sniffles. Then kicks a leg at me.

'Sure I do.' I must be insane to give her another four good ones across the plumpish rump. 'And I guess she's real bossy, just like you. Now, you gonna stop cussing and fussing and carrying on, or do I have to take this big old belt off?'

She sniffs a bit but stays still like she's sitting for a portrait to go on some wall in her mommy's big house. I let her up. She stares at me like I just walked down the ramp of a flying saucer. She shakes her head. 'You're a bad man, Franklin.'

'Got that right, peaches. Now let's be nice. I'm in trouble deep, Melody, and I don't need you breaking my balls over some engagement. I need you to be cool. Real cool, OK?'

120

She sniffs back a tear and wipes at her eyes. She nods. 'Do you still like me?' she says in a little-girl-lost-in-the-woods voice that makes my cock want to start weeping tears of its own.

'Been going crazy just to stay away from you since that night in the woods.' Which is not a lie, but I want to kick myself, with spurs on my boots, for saying it. 'And I've been tempted to hook up with you too, but it would have been stupid.'

She touches at her smudged mascara. 'What was I supposed to think?'

'I don't blame you for anything. But let's just be right here and now and stop thinking about what was, or about what is going to happen next. It's good to see you again. And one of the reasons I spanked you was because you get me so horny.'

I see a new smile forming. 'Really?'

'Oh, yeah. You're a princess.' I look deep into her eyes. Step forwards and raise her chin. Kiss her lips. Slip my tongue inside her mouth and suck at her until she nearly goes blue. Then I'm kissing her neck and she's panting for breath while her whole body is shivering. I cup her buttocks and press my hardness into her tummy.

'Ouch,' she says. 'You hurt me there. Be careful.'

I place my hands on her breasts instead. Moving my hands around real gentle, I feel their weight and shape and softness. No bra. 'You're a bad girl, Melody,' I whisper. Her eyelids close halfway and her body feels limp like it's surrendered. I bite at her neck, taste the skin and move my hands up and down her curves. Trace a finger around her garter belt. 'Are girls allowed to wear these?'

'Thought you would have guessed by now that I'm not a girl. I'm a woman.'

I think of her sex, no doubt damp by now, and act immediately on an impulse that makes me feel so good

I get dizzy. Sinking to my knees, I slip my hands on to her strong calves. Then push her skirt upwards with my wrists while my hands stroke her legs, following the silkiness until it becomes naked flesh. I pull her panties to the side and bury my face in her fragrant fur, lick and tease her lips with my mouth. Clawing the back of my scalp, she starts to totter on her high heels. Melody has a soapy, salty taste without the stronger smell of Mrs Berry or Mrs Mullins. I knock the sniffing dog away.

Replacing my tongue with one, two, then three fingers inside her, I stand up and smother her mouth with another kiss. Can't remember wanting a woman so much, but then I think that every time. 'On the grass,' she says, breathless. 'Fuck me on the grass.' I take my hand from her sex and lift her off her feet. Carry her out of the dugout and lay her gently on the fresh grass beside the white foul line of the diamond. I like to take a girl while she's still dressed. Then it doesn't feel so planned and they must be really into you too if they're not insisting on a bed or something. And Melody seems to share my taste for being bad under the stars. 'Fuck me, Franklin. Fuck me like before.'

'You liked it? Mmm? You need it now?'

'You have no idea,' she says as I unlash my belt. Kick my jeans and boots free, then place her ankles on my shoulders. Kiss her insteps and lick her spiky heels. 'I wore them to get you going,' she says with a smile that is not at all saintly.

'It worked.' I hold my cock between her thighs and furrow the head up and down the front of her sex. In the thin light I can see the pinkish blush on her buttock cheeks from the spanking.

'Don't tease me. Don't. Don't be like that, Franklin. Just fill me.'

'Oh, baby. You talking like that makes me crazy.'

'Just as well you can't read my mind. I had a dream that you went in my ass.'

I take a moment and shake the swoon away. There is no way, no way at all, that you can know what a woman really thinks about sex. All you can be certain of is that you'll never know the full story. Even if they tell you stuff, there will always be more. You just get clues. This I can sense as I slip inside Melody Watson. Hold her legs by the calf muscles and begin to push a little harder each time inside her pussy until she makes a croaky sound and sucks at two fingers. 'Imagine how this would feel in your ass,' I say.

'Bastard,' she says in the middle of a lot of panting.

Seems like being perfect and over-achieving all the time has opened a little space inside this girl for misbehaviour. 'Oh, yeah,' I say. 'Real deep. It would make you squeal.' After wetting my little finger I reach down and tickle her tight ring. She starts this yearning, groaning sound from deep inside her tummy. I slide the finger inside and her body jolts, her limbs lock. Now she doesn't care what she looks like or sounds like, she's just writhing her head around in the grass. 'Can you feel how wet I am?' she whispers up to me.

'Next time I'm going in there.' I move my finger around inside her hot bottom. 'And I'm going to go deep with this.' I thrust my cock hard into her sex. She makes a snorting sound. I remove the finger and hold her legs behind the knee. Then take my pleasure fast and at depth, prolonging her escape from being Miss Melody-goody-two-shoes-Watson at the same time.

Changing position, I stand up and pull her to her feet. Take her from behind so hard her whole body shakes. Pull her back firmly so her buttocks give me a lovely squashing sensation against my groin. Can you see me, holy woman? I want to shout out. Nothing can stop me. This is my new life. I live for this and the taste of a woman's sweet flesh.

Lying behind her, again on the ground, I hold one of her ankles in the air to give me the room to thrust into

123

her from behind while whispering bad things from a bad man into her tiny ear. Her face is wet with sweat and I can feel the damp of perspiration under her clothes. I see the luminous hands of my watch and realise I've been inside her for nearly an hour. She looks exhausted and mostly has her eyes closed. Eventually, she asks me to, 'Come. Come inside me, darling.'

Holding her breasts, I roll her on to her tummy and mount her from behind. Stroking her to another little mumbling, murmuring, moaning climax, before I fall into my own swoops and release one week of frustration and need into Melody.

We lie still for a while afterwards. No one speaks. I lick at her neck. Make her shiver. She smiles. 'Bite me again,' she whispers. 'It makes us closer.'

I drink the wine of the privileged world, of lawn tennis and garden marquees, of antiques and holiday homes, and functions and the best of everything. It tastes good. And under the moon and stars of this big unexplored world that I will make my own, I realise that only a few weeks before this night, I was a virgin and destined to never taste a woman until I was at least twenty-one on my wedding night. I wish you could see me now, holy woman. Wish you could take a good look for I am always hungry.

Chapter Fourteen

'So how have you coped since the last time we met?' the Chaplain asks, sitting forwards in the chair, arms folded on the desk. She's done something different with her make-up; her lips are painted a dark red and her eyes are tinted a charcoal colour, but the rest of her face is pale, which makes these colours seem more noticeable. For some reason her cosmetics unsettle me and I can't stop staring. I swallow the dry lump of fear and nerves from my throat. 'OK.'

Looking at me like I'm some silly kid she's about to lose her temper with, she says, 'OK? Well, go on. I don't have all morning. I've made time in my schedule especially for you, Franklin. Tell me about what you've done. Or, more to the point, what you haven't done.'

'I haven't seen Mrs Berry.'

She smiles, but it isn't warm, it's mocking. 'I know you haven't. She's out of town.'

'Haven't been with the band either.'

'Speak up! Don't just sit there mumbling and sulking.'

I repeat myself but am unable to keep the surly tone out of my voice.

She nods. 'Good. I can confirm that. Go on.'

I shrug. She frowns; leans back in her chair and sways from side to side. Crosses her legs. 'So there is nothing more you have to tell me?' I shake my head. The Chaplain sighs. Stands up and walks around her desk. I glance down and take in the high-heeled shoes and black nylons. Never seen the Chaplain so dressed up before. Some of the others dress like this all the time, but men don't dare look. Maybe she has a meeting later.

The Chaplain stands behind my chair and places her cold hands on my shoulders. She bends over so her face is close to the side of my head and I'm drowning in the smell of her perfume and thick lipstick. Seeps up my nose and into my mouth. Makes my heart beat fast and takes all the strength out of my arms and legs. 'You wouldn't be holding anything back from me, would you, Franklin? Do I have to remind you about what happened last Friday? Mmm?'

'No, ma'am.'

'I see.' Her lips brush my ear. My spine tingles and my tummy flops over. 'So can you explain your whereabouts on Wednesday evening?'

Feels like my whole body is frozen. If she shouts, I'll shatter. I try and speak but nothing but a mumble trips out of my mouth. Clear my throat and say, 'Home.'

'Home? Did you say home? Home?' She mimics my flat voice. Tightens her grip on my shoulders so I can feel her red nails through my T-shirt. 'You remember what I said last time? About how I have no patience with liars? And that I can see and hear everything you do?'

My backside begins to burn with ghost stripes. 'Yes, ma'am.' I close my eyes to put myself in the dark; the plain white walls and electric light are blinding me. At any moment I could break from this chair and run. I took a risk. Knew this could happen, but it still doesn't make the consequences any easier to deal with.

Against my cheek her breath is warm, becoming wet. Quiet, but mean, she whispers, 'Where were you on Wednesday night?'

'I went out to walk. Clear my head.'

'You were alone?'

Does she know I met Melody? Is she just tormenting me and ratcheting up her temper? Or were her spies unable to track me? I was discreet. I stayed hidden. But did they see Melody and follow her? 'If I did anything, you would know.'

She goes quiet for a time, but keeps her face close. When she finally speaks, she says, 'You haven't changed, my lad. I know you met a woman that night. And I know what you did to her. So I think it's time that you and I took a walk downstairs.'

'Whatever you want,' I say, starting to get mad at this bully, but also at myself for getting aroused with her so close. I peek down at her slim legs and shiny black shoes, recall her hot breath on my wounds, her cold fingers on my thighs as she inspected me like a beast in a field after beating me. I clench the muscles in my cock. It's going to hurt like hell, but part of me wants to be taken downstairs, so she can touch me some more, even if it's mostly with a stick.

Through pain and humiliation she aims to reduce me and demonstrate her superiority. How can I allow this? Why do I not object? Why am I so hard between the thighs?

Pointed toes kick my ankles apart so she can put my feet where she needs them. Busy fingers buckle leather straps around each ankle, so I am tied into one side of the wooden frame. Gripped by the wrists, my arms are pulled above my head where she cuffs them to the polished wooden uprights. She carefully climbs down from the little wooden steps. Watching her intense face and the trim little body in an elegant suit, as she goes to work, excites me in a way that truly scares me.

With a quick glance, then a double-take, she sees the swelling in my white shorts. Says nothing but her sharp, pale face seems to darken and her features thicken with an emotion I can't read. But I think it's anger. Into my mouth goes the hard rubber gag, big as a squash ball. Straps go around my head and pull my hair like a diving face-mask does when your hair is still dry. Then she kneels behind me and I feel her fingernails inside the waistband of my underwear. Gently, she pulls my shorts away from my buttocks. Looks at my tensed-up bottom for a while, then takes them down further. 'Have you been to a doctor?' she asks, and I can hear the confusion in her voice. Seeing no scars has rattled her. I shake my head. She stands up and walks around to my front. Seizes me by the ears and stares into my eyes. 'You are lying. No one heals so fast. It's not possible. What have you done?'

Keep looking into my eyes, ma'am. Girls seem to like what they find there. Gently, I press my groin forwards and brush her womb with my thick erection while holding her stare and trying to transmit my desire into her. She is a priest and is celibate; the only time she touches men is with a stick. But I want her to know that she can have me – all of me. She can find another use for my body.

As her lips part and her eyes widen, her face drifts closer – she does not remove her tummy from the rock inside my shorts. Suddenly my whole body floods with the heat of hope. I feel giddy. To seduce the Chaplain, as Mrs Berry instructed? To achieve the impossible?

'Is that for me?' she whispers, and then pulls the gag from my mouth.

I take a deep breath. 'Yes, ma'am. I can't help it.'

She gives me a wicked smile. 'Even me? A poor old Chaplain?'

'Especially you.'

'Why?'

'You're very handsome, ma'am. And strong. I like that.'

She nods, still smiling. 'Stronger than you realise, my lad. I could change your whole world, Franklin. Just like that.' She clicks her fingers in the air beside my ear. 'I can beat you whenever I wish. Send you to a reformatory. But still, you want me?' I nod. 'You desire me so much?'

'Yes, ma'am.'

'You adore me?'

'Oh, yes, ma'am.' I stare at her glossy lips and imagine the taste.

She slides her fingers on to my cheeks and stands on her tip-toes, so that my erection is rubbed by her stomach. Her lips are nearly touching mine. I stare deep; deeper than I have ever looked into a woman's eyes, and I will her to join her mouth to mine. 'You want to do to me what you did to that woman on Wednesday night. Melody?'

I can hardly move my tongue to form the word. The muscles in my cock pulse against her body. 'Yes.'

'You'd be hard with me. Thorough? Mmm? Like you were with her?'

'Yes. Yes, ma'am.' I lean forwards and try to touch my lips to hers.

She smiles, pulls back. 'You want to be inside a woman of God.'

'I want to serve you. Please you.'

'Is sin so exquisite that you would risk everything to please me?'

'I am weak, ma'am. For you.'

She closes her eyes and breathes on my face. 'He's in your bones. Your blood. I can see him in your eyes and hear him in your voice.' Suddenly her eyes flash open, then narrow. Her face pales and her lips quiver. The fingers on my cheeks close and begin to squeeze hard. I cry out, try to pull free but cannot. Through the stinging tears in my eyes, I can see her handsome, white face, the gritted teeth. 'You wish to turn a servant of Our Saviour

129

into a whore. To make a Chaplain lie down with you.' With one hand she grips my erection through my shorts. 'In my life only two men have ever tried such a feat. So corrupt were they that even now they hang in chains.'

Staring at her, with eyes full of hate and desire, I realise I have been trapped again. Lured into confession to confirm all of her worst suspicions about the deviant loose in her flock. I start to tremble. Find it hard to breathe. She squeezes my cock until it hurts, like she wants to destroy it with her cold virgin hands. 'You mark my words, you devil. The day when you can display yourself and indulge your lust is over. Over. Do you hear?' Releasing my cock, she stuffs the ball gag back between my jaws and steps away, her chest rising and falling.

Turning on her heel, she marches towards the long wooden cupboard. The doors are unlocked, opened on squeaky hinges. Things are unhooked and taken out. Razored through the dense air to cut through the heat of man's need and desire and frustration and fear. I was wrong to try and tempt her today, because she is already tempted by me, and others. But her desires are all knotted and twisted and painful inside. Her need for a man has become a need to restrain and scar the flesh. The intensity with which she would have fucked me must come out another way. I had better prepare myself. As I clench my fists and flex my shoulders, the whole frame creaks around me.

'Try and break free while you still have the strength, for I will be hard with the flesh that nurtures the filth inside you. I will make your lying, sinful mouth sing until it is choked with repentance. You will beg me to stop, boy. And then we'll start over again, and again, until the beast is gone.' My shorts are yanked down to the top of my thighs. 'Let's see how quickly you heal this time.'

The slap of wood against my buttocks turns to streak lightning that crackles and spits through all of my nerves, until the sound and the pain are one. I am on fire. I even burn in my ears and inside all of my toes. Don't have enough flesh to hold so much pain. I whimper and writhe and then scream in a hail of blows that never stop falling.

'We'll see how quick you are to push your disgusting meat in a woman's face. In her body. Deep in her body. On top of her in the trees. Thrusting at her. Your hands on her flesh. Your mouth on her flesh.' Her voice has gone deep; she is talking to herself and to me and swings the cane at the end of every sentence.

With the last of my resolve I try and bend away from the spears of agony that fall across my shoulders, back, buttocks, thighs. But it's no use. My strength is evaporating from the welts that grow from my skin, until I have no strength. Hanging from the cuffs, I just want to sit down now. No, lie down on something soft. My cock goes limp. I am brought down in this world in a way I never knew possible. Broken down by a little bitch in high-heeled shoes.

My head has dropped forwards before the stick stops falling. Close my eyes and grit my teeth. Try and throw my thoughts to any place that isn't here with all the burning and stinging. I think of Mrs Berry; she just appears in my mind. She looks good, all dressed in black, and is smiling at me. I smile back at her.

The stick stops falling. And in the hot, damp air I can hear the Chaplain taking short, quick breaths. Almost sounds like she's panting. I open an eyelid into a slit and peek under one armpit. What I see takes my mind off the pain for a while.

With her shiny shoes spread apart, legs polished by fine stockings, I see far more of her body below the waist than any man ever should. As the front of her skirt is held in one white fist and raised to her waist, I

131

watch her other arm move in little jerks as it rubs the cane against her naked sex. The stick that has just cut up my body is now rubbing against her shaven intimacy, and moving in tense little circles. Her eyes have rolled white and her red lips move quickly, muttering, 'God is a woman. Devil is a man,' over and over. I thought she was too strong for me and for the power Mrs Berry has bitten into my body. But I can see now this is not the case. She uses that stick like a sword to keep us apart, but her defence is slipping and now she has turned that weapon on herself. And in my pain on this rack, and through the exhaustion that comes with such a flogging, I swear that I will have her. I will come to you, holy woman, and I will defrock you and take you. Put so much sin inside you. Even if it means the end of me, I will do it. We both know this. It's just a matter of time, that's all.

Chapter Fifteen

'So what's on your mind? It's not like anyone has a clue these days.' Gretchen is finding my attitude hard to take, but hasn't given up on me; he's just pissed because I haven't told him everything that's going down like I usually do. But this stuff is different; can he handle it?

I wince and change my position on the wall out the front of his house. The Chaplain was right about me not healing so quickly this time. But I wonder about how her soul has healed, after giving in to her own little temptation. 'Dude, what I said about stuff changing was no lie. It's why I've had to put the band on hold for a while.'

'That's your decision. Not ours. And I don't want to hear any more shit about having the flu. That was bogus.'

I nod. 'I'm sorry.'

'Rehearsal is the only thing I look forward to.'

'I know. But I've got myself in some real trouble.' When I pause to think about the fix I'm in, and how I start to tell my best friend about it all, I'm filled with a kind of fatigue that makes me groan out loud. Another letter arrived from Melody Watson this morning. That's one every day since that night last Wednesday at the baseball field, and her parents are serious about the courtship deal. Mine are asking me every day about what I think. Mrs Mullins heard that I was sick and brought round some fruit and soup, which like totally threw my mom, especially as the good Mrs Mullins was all dressed up nice and barely able to walk on these red, ultra high-heeled shoes. I stayed up in my room, hands over the face, praying it would all go away and everything could go back to the way it was before Mrs Berry took me to my Initiation dinner. And where the hell is she? No one knows. I need her. I miss her.

'Is it bad? I mean, it must be for you to miss band practice.' Gretchen is giving me a chance. I can tell by his voice that he is giving me a chance.

'Real bad. You ready for this?' Can't bear to look at him, but I tell him pretty much everything: that Mrs Berry and I are having an affair (while leaving out the part about the biting) which gave me a taste for sex. Kind of opened the gate for all the forbidden, unacceptable stuff that guys suffer from, which led me to fuck Melody Watson and two other women I met downtown (though I don't mention Mrs Mullins: that can wait). Only, I tell him, I was caught by a Chaplain, who is now threatening me with reform programmes if I'm ever alone with a woman again or carry on pursuing the corrupting influence of heavy metal music in my 'pop group'. I finish by telling Gretchen that Melody wants to marry me, and that I have to meet her mother later. 'That's pretty much the size of it, dude.'

Gretchen looks at me with his mouth open. Then he grins, because it must be a wind-up; some big practical joke I'm laying on him. But he doesn't grin for long, because he can tell by the look in my eyes that I'm telling the truth. 'For the sake of Our Saviour,' he whispers. 'That's radical. Totally off the radar. What were you thinking?'

'Not much. And this is between us. You know that?'

He nods. 'My Mentor showed me how to lay a table last night. And you get your cock sucked. It just ain't fair.'

Pretty soon we're both laughing until we're crying. Neither of us can talk for ages. Every time we open our mouths to say something, we start laughing again. Man, it feels good to just let go. Seems like ages since I've had anything to laugh about. I exhaust myself until my back starts to hurt.

A father walks past with his two little daughters; both of them are crying. He looks at us and rolls his eyes. 'Laugh it up, boys. You got all this to look forward to,' he says in passing.

'Not me, man,' I say, real quiet. Gretchen hears me.

'So you and Melody. I mean, she's real pretty, I guess, but she's not the type I thought you would go for. And no offence, dude, but what does she see in you?'

I shake my head – the despair is back like a dark, rainy sky inside my head. 'Forget about Melody. I ain't marrying Melody Watson. Or anyone in this town.'

'What you saying, buddy?'

'I'm going to run.' He goes a bit pale. 'Got no choice, Gretch. I don't want any of this. It's been kind to us, sure. We've never had a real worry to deal with in our lives, but it's not for me.'

'Everyone says that, Franky. Me more than most. But you have to get past that, because there is no alternative. The other states are fucked, man. Like totally fucked up. Like anything could happen at any time. You wouldn't survive out there, man. It's the wild west. Just like those people out there wouldn't last a minute here. You're a product of this system, man, and you have to deal with it. At least we ain't getting shot or divorced and stuff.'

'That's bullshit. That's the line we've been fed from birth. But Mrs Berry has shown me things.'

'I bet she has.'

'Not just that way. She's clever, man. It's hard to explain. She's crazy. She's wild. But cool with it. She's done a lot of things, dude. And I'm like her. She's broken me out.'

'How far did Isaac get? Huh? And where is he now? Think about it. You want to go that way? Wear an orange boiler suit and shovel shit all day, pumped up on meds?'

'No. I want to play music. That's what I'm going to do. Get down south and start doing this for real. Time to get out of the garage, buddy. And time to stop making cakes, unless they're full of hashish.'

'Ssh. Man, keep your voice down. Our Saviour, if someone hears you.'

'With the Chaplain on to me, I have to go. Before Finishing College starts, I'm long gone. If I stay, I'll be weeding flower beds with Isaac. No doubt about that in my mind.'

'You serious?'

I nod. 'And I want you to come with me.'

Chapter Sixteen

'Of course, Franklin, this has all come as something of a surprise to me, and no doubt to your parents as well.'

'Yes, ma'am.' I walk beside Melody's mother, down the long perfect lawn of her house, towards the orangery and the stream. The Watsons don't just have a garden, they have grounds. I feel all delicate inside and am wary about opening my mouth. Scared too about breaking something, like a glass or some social code I've never paid too much attention to until now. Like staring at your girlfriend's mother in an inappropriate way. I mean, this is a woman you would never dare to cross, let alone upset by checking out the way her white lacy bra can be seen from a certain angle if you look inside her silky blouse. And I'm doing my level best to stop admiring her legs. They have a great shape when she's teetering on those high-heeled sandals with the little white straps over her toes and around her ankles. Expensive feet; pedicured and paraffin-wrapped every week, and never dressed up in anything but the finest stockings and most expensive hand-made heels. Even the way she smells is exclusive – this is not a perfume I've ever smelled before – and her face is like a sculpture. A beautiful mask crowned with blonde hair. Bet she looks like this every day and doesn't weigh one pound too much. Not a bad mother-in-law to end up with, in terms of eye candy, but just about the worst nightmare you could imagine in every other way. She has one kid, and that's Melody.

'As you probably know, my daughter is very head-strong.' She laughs in a forced way. 'Some say she takes after her mother.' I smile until it aches on my face. 'But I doubt any man could meet a more exceptional young woman. She's bright, talented, accomplished, and has only just begun to realise her potential. She is, as you may have heard, a rising star in our country.'

'Yeah, I know. She's something else,' I mumble.

The mother frowns. Looks like she has something that tastes bad in her mouth. 'So I hope you do not take offence to my mystification about her desire for this union.'

'No,' I say, taking offence. *Mystification* – ain't no mystery to me that your precious daughter wants it in the ass, ma'am.

'But the heart often follows a different course to the head, wouldn't you say?'

'Sure seems that way, ma'am.'

'Though I appreciate all of your achievements on the athletics field, I was surprised with my daughter's wishes.' Man, I want to slap this bitch across the ass. I'm pissed with her looking down that thin little nose at me. 'I thought she would pursue a more, and I mean no disrespect, a more cerebral companion.' She smiles and will no doubt be recounting this little chit-chat to the ladies at the Country Club this afternoon. 'I will make myself absolutely clear from the outset: I thoroughly disapproved of her choice. In fact, I was a trifle horrified by it all. But –' she places her elegant white hand on my forearm which makes me go all rigid '– the more I thought about Melody's wish, and I won't say our discussions were easy, I began to consider its merits. Don't worry –' the hand on my arm again as if to steady me '– I haven't given up all hope on you yet.

138

'I began to believe that a union between a very clever and well-bred woman, who is just bound to be running all kinds of things before long –' she throws her head back and makes this snorting, horsy laugh '– and a dependable man whose charms and abilities are more earthy, may not be such a bad mix. He becomes her oak. May not say too much, but she can rely on him to be there through all the excitement and frisson of her professional life and in her role in society. It's not easy for a woman at the top, Franklin. And it has been said, there will always be a place at her side for a man. The right man, of course.

'I make no bones about it, Franklin, Melody is quite demanding. Any man she chose for a partner would have his hands full, that's for sure.' *But maybe not in the way you think, ma'am.* 'And she would need a lot of support from her companion, Franklin. It would be a full-time job. What I am asking, why I have asked you here, is to find out if you will always, and I mean always, be there for her.' She stops walking and turns to face me under the privet arch some gardener has made.

Colours from all kinds of flowers I have no names for are exploding all around me. Divided up by grass so green it hurts to look at. The sun is shining down on it all, and always shines down here because they make it shine on them. They make everything work for them. And I'd be some joker in a suit, sipping a martini, or playing golf and entertaining her guests. Someone quite useless but always around. It wouldn't work and not for a minute does it tempt me. It's just another big prison, a comfortable one, but a cage all the same. And in a heartbeat, I'd be trying to fuck all her friends and even her mother at the wedding that would be held on this big lawn, with society photographers snapping shots from every angle at the million-dollar dress she's wearing.

'You know, ma'am,' I say, looking right into her eyes,

'I appreciate your concerns, I really do. I'm not from this end of town for one thing.'

'I never meant to suggest –'

'And some family from the bridge club or polo club must have a son who would be far more suitable for Melody. I don't doubt it for a minute. All this stuff you guys have is real nice, but I think I'm rich in other ways. I have my friends and my band and the track, which has all kept me just dandy so far. And I think Melody is a beauty, I do. Don't care so much about what she's good at. She's a sweet girl, that's what really counts. And if she looks half as good as her mother does when she gets older, then I'd be a happy man. And she has a lot of spirit that maybe gets a bit tangled up in other things. I don't know. But I think we should all sleep on this for a while longer.'

This woman doesn't lose control much, but she blushes a little. Looks surprised, like she's underestimated me. 'I see. That was well put. You boys from the suburbs are straight talkers. I've heard that. Melody certainly wouldn't be able to walk all over you. Perhaps that's the attraction.' She looks me up and down. 'Amongst other things.'

I keep staring deep, not really knowing what I'm trying to do, but I hold her stare. Don't let the prissy, sexy snob look away once. 'We have our uses,' I whisper.

Her breath whistles out of her nose. She raises one eyebrow. 'I bet.'

'We can walk between any two lines you care to draw on the ground, ma'am. But there is always a little something else, a little wild part of us that I think can be amusing for you girls uptown.'

'Yes,' she says, in a vague, dreamy kind of voice. Everything stops moving in the garden. Even the butterflies seem to land and close their wings. 'Yes.'

'And a lot of women need more than a maid, ma'am.

140

They like to change things back to the way they used to be, just for a while anyway, if you know what I mean.'

'I'm sure I do,' she mutters, and titters, rubbing the top of her thigh with the long fingers of one hand; red varnish catching the sunlight like the bonnet of a sports car.

'And young women like all kinds of things, at different times. They change their minds. So this combination you were talking about, between a more "earthy" man and a successful woman, might be better suited to a situation when the woman is older than the man. You know, like a private arrangement.' I'm absolutely convinced I shouldn't be saying any of this, but I just can't help myself. The edge of it all, the excitement that makes my guts fizz and my blood fill with adrenaline and my thoughts glaze over with the promise of all kinds of situations that should never be, is like an addiction to me now.

And if this extra sense I seem to have is right, then just for a moment, Mrs Watson has forgotten all about her position and status and is getting carried away by an excitement of her own, that is not so different from mine. 'Yes. Though I doubt many young men have such feelings for their seniors.'

'You'd be surprised, ma'am.' I take a step closer to her. She trembles.

'Have you? Are you one of those men I've heard about?'

'Those men?'

'Who . . . Who have done things . . .' She cannot even speak of such things – doesn't have the words – but she thinks of them all the time, in pictures.

'Bad men?'

She nods.

I widen the scope of my vision briefly and make sure no one is watching. Melody has gone out with her friends to leave me and her mother alone for the afternoon. Mrs Berry was supposed to be here too, but she still can't be reached. As far as I know, other than the two male servants I saw in the house, it's just me and mother here. I reach out with shaky hands, and hold her by the hips. Move my face closer to that perfectly redesigned face. Against her tummy, she can feel me swell and press. 'It's best that bad men do things in private with more experienced women who know their own minds, is what I'm suggesting, ma'am. It's the best role for a bad man, and there is no shame involved for an important woman who needs a certain kind of attention now and then.'

'You've done this before?'

I nod. Then take her mouth with my own.

Like her daughter she kisses real clumsy like she's not used to doing it. And under her thin clothes her body is trembling. It's like having a delicate little bird creature fluttering in my hands as I hold her against my body so she can hardly breathe. I swallow her tongue and lips.

She breaks away. 'Not here.' Her voice sounds thick, drunk. 'Don't do this to me here. I know another place where you can ruin me,' she says, her face full of a fear of herself as much as me.

Unsteady on her feet, she walks away from me, between two long avenues of roses. I follow, watching her buttocks, so tight in the skirt, and her legs so shiny in the sunlight, and all the time thinking of her slim shape wrapped around me. I want to eat her alive.

'Here,' she says, standing with her back to a tree beside the stream. 'If you must do this to me, then do it here. No one can see us. I promise I won't scream.'

Gently, I kiss her throat and run my hands, lightly, over her breasts – too young, too pert, too tight for a respectable mother – and then caress her hips. Slip my knee between her legs. She shivers, knowing that her legs will soon be wide open and what's between given

142

over to the prowling beast that lives in this man. 'You won't hurt me,' she says in a tiny voice.

'No, ma'am. But you're so sexy, I could really get carried away down here.'

'Oh, God, what am I doing?' she says to herself and closes her eyes. I slip to my knees and reach around to unzip her skirt. She just leans back against the tree, her eyes shut tight, as I slip her skirt and satin slip down her legs. Never seen such pretty underwear. I shake my head and can't stand straight because of the hardness in my jeans. Feel like I could just blow at any minute. I clench the muscles in my cock and let the craziness pass. It leaves me light in the head. Her panties are like a man's boxer shorts but made from a creamy satin. Suspenders pass under each leg and fasten to stockings fine as cobwebs that you can hardly see on her legs. I run my hands all over and around her legs. Then slip my fingers on to the flesh of her thighs, up and then into her panties. Gasping, she bites the forefinger of one hand. 'Franklin, no. We can't.'

I look at her, hold her frightened stare, and then make her eyes go all dreamy again. 'Just a taste, ma'am. I just have to have a little taste of you. I can't stop. Now that I've seen how good you look underneath.'

Through the slippery material of her panties I lap and suckle and kiss at her sex. Pull the wet patch deep into my mouth and exhaust it of taste. She makes this kind of sobbing, hiccuping sound through the hands that cover her nose and mouth. There is no objection as I slide her panties down to her shoes. I never break eye contact, just nod, and she steps out of her underwear.

I stand up and put my hands on the tree, on either side of her head. She makes a tiny snuffle of disappointment because my mouth is no longer feeding between her slim thighs. I whisper to her. 'Don't worry. No one will ever know. This is just something that has to

143

happen between me and you. We both felt it back there. You can't deny it.'

'Make it quick,' she hisses and then thrusts her mouth against mine. Licking, biting, wetting my whole chin, clawing at my chest with her long nails, she goes at me like a wild thing. I don't even recognise her face any more. I unbuckle my pants, knowing this is the right moment to get inside her. But no sooner is my cock free of my underwear and belt, when Mrs Watson makes this deep grumbling sound that shocks me a little, because I would never have expected it to come from her. She falls against me, grits her teeth, looks at me with crazy eyes and then slips down my body to my cock. Devours it. Stuffs it into her smudged mouth and holds the barrel with her ghosty fingers. Makes real smacking and sucking sounds all over the swollen head. Stretches her whole jaw to the limit, to stuff as much of me as possible into her mouth and throat. Clings on to my cock like it's a tree root growing from the side of a cliff that she needs to hold to stop herself falling. Pulls me down on top of her. Wriggles around on the grass in her blouse, jacket, stockings and high heels, just sucking and clutching at my cock. Pumps it with her hands, like she's dying of thirst and hunger at the same time, and all the while making this deep, growly cat noise in her throat.

Oh, man, I want to say, if I marry your daughter, I'm afraid we'd make a habit of this. But I hold back, not wanting to remind her of the situation and whose cock she is sucking like it's a toffee apple. Instead, I keep quiet, go into a press-up position and gently fuck her whole head. As I move my cock up and down, she moves with it, like her mouth is fastened to me with rivets. 'Oh, ma'am. I'm going to come. I have to pull out.'

She makes a pleading, whining noise through her nose and clutches at my buttocks with her fingernails. I get on to my knees, pulling her whole weight between my legs. But still she won't let loose my cock. I pry her fingers off my ass cheeks where she's left scratches and marks, then pull my wet cock from her puffy lips. She gasps for breath. Not wasting a moment, I kneel between her legs, seize her by the bony hips and pull her body across the grass towards my crotch. 'Oh, God,' she says. Then twists her head to the side and makes a gargling sound. I slap her feet on my shoulders and hold her legs tight behind the knees. Her stockings are full of ladders from where she's been rolling on the floor. Fisting my cock, I press it forwards and into her sex.

A loud, keening moan that sounds like a forest creature caught in a trap rushes out of her mouth. I slowly slip the rest of my length inside her and she goes absolutely silent, but her mouth and eyes are wide open like she's been frozen in the middle of a scream. Her whole body is stiff and her hands are clenched into little white fists. Slowly, I withdraw and thrust, enjoying the sight of this rich, respectable lady beneath me, skewered on my cock and risking everything she holds dear in this world for the touch of a man on the banks of a stream.

'That good, ma'am?'

She nods. Her wide wild eyes fixed on me. *Please*, she mouths at me.

'You want me to stop?' I say, not at all sure of what she's going to do next.

'Please,' she says again, but this time it's a thin whisper I can hear. 'Fuck me.'

And to hear that word slip from her expensive, exclusive, first-class mouth just makes me shiver to my core. Leaning over her, so her feet reach right down to her cheeks, I begin to thrust and ram my whole body against hers, slipping and stretching my cock right through her sex to the back of her womb. She makes the groaning and gargling sounds, but occasionally goes silent and absolutely still except for these little shakes as

145

she rises to the peak of her pleasure. Most of the time, I could be forgiven for thinking she's in some kind of pain, but her fingers are dug into me so I can hardly move.

Holding her ankles, I spread her legs wide apart and begin to take longer, deeper strokes at a slower pace. She rolls her head around and snaps the grass with her fingers. 'You're so beautiful,' I tell her. 'So, so beautiful. But you're such a slut, ma'am.'

After I say that, she pushes and pumps her thin body on and off my groin and thrashes her head about in the grass. 'I'm a slut,' she spits out, insulting herself but exalting herself at the same time.

'Oh, yeah. Such a slut. A slut who eats young cocks and likes it hard in the grass.'

'Yes! Yes!' she hissy shouts at me. 'Fuck her. Fuck the slut!'

And I do, so hard we move all over the grass and the buttons on her blouse snap away. And when I nearly pass out from the force of my climax and my ejaculation into her that just seems to keep streaming out of me, she is clinging to the trunk of the tree with her fingernails and showing me the whites of her eyes.

She lies there, panting softly, and giggling to herself like a naughty girl with a stolen cigarette, while I kiss and lap at her throat. Find my spot. Feel the goodness pooling under the softest skin that smells of soap. And bite. Then quickly purse my lips over the incision and suck her life into my mouth.

I stop quickly. Her taste is like sherry. Old, refined, almost bitter-sweet tasting. Something you only sip because it can get you real high, real quick. I lick at the wound. Clean it. Close it.

Looks like she's gone to sleep. Her eyelids flutter. She's smiling.

This time I keep my composure. Look around. Listen out for every snap of twig or rustle of cloth against a hedge. Nothing. I stand up and buckle myself back together. Knock the grass from my knees. Straighten my jacket and tie.

Kneeling down, I slip Mrs Watson's shoes off and then roll the ripped stockings off her legs. Tuck them inside my trouser pocket and then help her into her slip and skirt. The panties I keep also. Eventually she sits up and pats at her hair. Shakes herself awake and smiles. 'Well. I never expected that. Are you hungry, Franklin?'

I smile at her. 'Yes, ma'am.'

Stands up and zips her skirt back into place. Then leans on me while she tucks her feet back into her shoes. We kiss one last time, with tongues, then I follow her out of the garden, smiling. I remember what Mrs Berry said about the most unlikely situations and most unlikely people. And how you have to keep your cool and not take too much. I'm learning. At last.

Chapter Seventeen

'Who's there?' she calls out from the other side of the door. Through the frosted glass, I can see the hazy shape of the Chaplain; thin and black with a white oval of face.

I breathe in; it's too late to run; I must go through with this; time to stop waiting for things to happen. 'It's Franklin, ma'am.'

The door opens so quickly, I take a step back in the porch. The Chaplain glares at me. Breathing hard, my face all white and doing its best to quiver like jello, I smile. 'Ma'am.' She is still wearing her black suit and heels, as if she never changes from these clothes or her role as guardian. Looking past me, she checks the street. 'You alone?' She is suspicious, but not of me. The adrenaline coursing through my blood has made my instincts keen; my new and mysterious sense tells me that when the Chaplain thinks of me she thinks of Mrs Berry at the same time. 'Yes, ma'am.'

One hand on the edge of the door, the other curled around the door frame, she raises her chin, looks me up and down. 'What are you doing here?'

'I needed to see you.'

'You have an appointment with me Friday morning. Can't it wait until then?'

I shake my head. 'Didn't know where else to go.'

She steps aside, not taking her cold eyes off me for a second. 'Quickly then.' Before she closes the door behind me, she peeks out at the street again; wary, unsure, but her curiosity about my visit is stronger.

Standing beside the coat-stand in the hall, I look around the big old Colonial hall and the stairs leading up to the next floor, protected by a banister. Everything is made of wood, free of dust, polished and very old; just what I imagined it would be as I threw my imagination into this place from outside, across the street. The air smells of cleaning fluid, perfume, flowers. A man comes here to clean. I can sense him. He spends a lot of time on his hands and knees, or working bent over. She likes to watch him.

'It's late. What do you want?' She stands beside me, her arms folded under her compact breasts that always look solid under her blouses. I put on my best sheepish expression – which is not hard as I'm so nervous – and look down at my boots. 'You told me to think of you. To remember the instruction classes, if I ever had . . .'

'Spit it out, boy.'

'If I ever had certain thoughts. Bad thoughts. About women.' I swallow. 'Well, they've been really bad, ma'am. So I came.'

Her pale face is tight with a surprise she's trying hard not to show. This she didn't expect. Then she blinks twice, forcefully, and regains her composure. 'I see. Then you better follow me.' I follow her click-clacking high heels across the wooden floor of the hallway and into the room she must have been using when I rang the bell. Never seen so many books. All of the bookcases covering the walls are full. She walks across the big circular rug to the two leather chairs on either side of the fireplace. On the mantle I can see lots of framed photographs. Some look real old, but I don't get a close look at them. She points to the chair on the left. 'Sit down.' Beside her chair is an open bottle of wine and a tall glass, half full of red wine. She was sitting in here alone with her thoughts, drinking wine; just as I knew she would be. But I don't have the time to dwell on another of these weird coincidences, or premonitions, I keep getting whenever I daydream about someone, or deliberately use my imagination on them. I'm distracted when the Chaplain sits down.

Sinking into her chair, which now reminds me of a big man with broad shoulders who has a girl sitting on his lap, she crosses her legs with a raspy sound. I quickly look at her excellent legs. The light from the tall lamp behind her chair makes her nylon legs go all shimmery and her black high heels look like polished glass. I want so much to look up her skirt; I think of a cane held in a little white hand with crimson nail polish on the fingertips, pushing, pushing, pushing between milky thighs at a sex with no floss. When I look up, she's watching me with a mean look on her face. Around her neck, she wears the gold circle of the Saviour church. It glints at me from its bed of breast, wrapped in a black silk blouse. She sinks deeper into her chair, so the top half of her body falls into shadow while her feet and legs stay shiny in yellow electric light. 'You are a curious young man, Franklin. What am I to make of you?'

'Ma'am?'

She takes a sip of her wine. Concentrates to keep up the superior tone in her voice because she finds it difficult to talk about what happened between us. 'After the last time we met, I would have thought I would be the last person on earth you would go to, in a moment of weakness.'

I reflect on what she says, watch her drink more of the wine. 'Me too. But you understand me, ma'am. You're probably the only person I could tell. It's crazy.'

She stays quiet, just watches me with her bright, cold eyes from the darkness of her chair. The Chaplain's not mad at me for calling; instead, she thinks this is some kind of triumph. 'What about your Mentor?'

'She's not around.' I don't understand her fixation with Mrs Berry, but I remember Mrs Berry saying something that suggested they knew each other. Until now I always guessed it was because Mrs Berry is very sexual and a threat to the order of things. Now, I think there is something else going down between them.

The Chaplain smiles, knowingly, gloating. 'No, she's not around. Funny, that. When you need her most, Mrs Berry has a habit of vanishing. After she's had her fun, that is.'

I don't take the bait. Immediately jump to her defence. 'She goes away on business.'

'Oh indeed. Indeed she does. Goes to all kind of places for her business.'

My heart starts to beat against my temples again. It was my intention to turn up and act all nervous and vulnerable and innocent. Now it's not a hard role to play. This woman is full of so much darkness she makes the little hairs on my body stand on end. 'Was it wrong for me to come here?'

'That depends entirely on the nature of your transgression, Franklin.' She pronounces 'transgression' slowly, then washes the word away with another mouthful of wine.

I look right into those hard eyes, glinting back there in the dark. 'I can't help myself, ma'am. I've tried hard. It's driving me crazy.'

'You're an addict, Franklin. This is precisely what becomes of those who succumb to temptation. Why they need treatment.' Again, the word 'treatment' is relished by her pouting, red mouth. 'So are these indecent thoughts you have come to confess? Or is it something worse?' Slowly, she rotates her foot in the spiky shoe, then hangs it from her toes, bobs the shoe up and down. For some reason this makes me sweat and

151

my cock starts to thicken, like this innocent action is another sign she's transmitted to me to let me know how desirable she is.

'Yes. I mean, it's both.'

'How often have you been having these unacceptable thoughts?'

'All the time, ma'am. But only about certain women.'

She might be leaning back into that big soft chair with a glass of wine, but I sense the tension in her body. She can't hide her discomfort from me, or the other emotion that's plaguing her. I think it's apprehension; not just at what I'm going to say, but at how she will react to it. It's like she doesn't trust herself. 'Who?'

'Older women, ma'am.'

She takes a moment to steady herself, to moisten her suddenly dry mouth. 'But ... Melody Watson is your age.'

'An exception, ma'am.'

She clears her throat. 'Have you met many older women who are, shall we say, open to your advances?'

I nod. 'Plenty, ma'am. But it's not just me making the advances.'

I hear her breath pulled in. She has to deepen her voice to control it. 'Who are they?'

'Besides Mrs Berry and Mrs Mullins, the others were strangers. Never saw them again.'

The foot stops moving, but the fingertips of one hand press into the leather cushion of the armrest. 'Where did you meet them?' she asks, in a thin voice.

I shrug. 'Around. All kinds of places. Malls. Downtown mostly. It's not hard, ma'am. There seem to be plenty of women who want to do all kinds of stuff. Weird stuff too that I never even knew about. Most men don't.'

Rigid with a rage that's dangerous if it boils up inside her and goes over the rim of her control, but also compelled to know every sordid detail, she keeps up the questions, just like I hoped she would. 'Weird?' But that's all she can get out of her mouth.

I pout all of the wide-eyed innocence and youth and sweetness I can into my face. 'They mostly want me to be in control. "Assertive", one lady said. Another told me to be "rough". And they don't always want me to . . . It's hard to even talk about, ma'am.'

'Tell me.'

'They sometimes ask me to . . . To go inside them, ma'am, but not in the usual way a man goes into a woman.'

'Mouth?' The word is a husky whisper. Everything in the room has gone still. If the fire was going I bet it would stop with a hiss. This dark, complicated woman seems to have sucked all of the life and motion out of this place and into herself.

I nod. 'And in another place too.'

'No.'

'It's like the worst thing they can do and that's why they like it so much. It's all been a big shock, ma'am. I've been going a bit crazy with all this on my mind. It's like there was nothing that ever prepared me for it.'

The Chaplain changes her position in the chair. Takes another big sip from her wine glass. Regains some control over her voice, but not much. 'You were right to come to me with this. All of what you have described disgusts me. It is a sacrilege against all of the values that have rebuilt our world in a better image. The holy image of Our Saviour.'

'Yes, ma'am.'

'You have been led astray by a very disturbed and dangerous woman. Others have contributed to your downfall. Unfortunately, it has always been the case that men are weak before certain sinful things. Only marriage can civilise a man. It is why I have been so hard on you. You understand why?'

'Yes. Well, kind of, ma'am. But . . .'

'What?'

'Men are mostly the ones who follow the rules, ma'am. All the ones I know do. I'm the exception, ma'am. It seems to be the women who –'

'Silence!' Everything made from glass in the room rattles in its frame or on its perch. I fight hard to stop the icicles in her voice from puncturing and bursting all of my confidence and resolve to go through with this crazy plan. When she drinks from her glass, I take a quick moment to admire her long, glossy shins and spiky heeled feet, to rediscover my purpose.

'Sorry, ma'am. I thought you wanted me to confess.'

'You speak of things you know little about.'

'I guess so. It just seems all upside down to me at the moment. You see, I've changed too, ma'am. Especially since I started seeing you.'

Her quick, birdy head cocks at an angle. 'What do you mean? What are you saying?' There is a little slur in her words.

'I know I've been bad. With other women. I'm not making excuses. I've tempted myself and let myself be tempted too. Been wild. Been crazy. Like a spoilt kid. Been a deviant, like you said, ma'am. But there's no point in punishing me any more, ma'am.'

'That's for me to decide. And after what you have just told me, I would say there is every reason to continue with a strict schedule of correction.' She leans forwards and pours another glass of wine. Her hands seem unsteady. When she dips her face into the lamplight her eyes are drunk like my mom's are most weekends. Some of her poise has gone too. Her knees open too much for a Chaplain. I lean back a little and look up the shiny valley of her thighs. I just get a glimpse of a white welt at the top of one leg and know for sure she's wearing stockings and not pantyhose, like I'm sure Chaplains are supposed to. I lean forwards when she sits back in her chair and crosses her legs.

154

'But I like it, ma'am.'

Wine spills from the glass into her lap. As she dabs at the mess, a shoe falls off her foot. Man, she's a mess, but a real handsome one. Something dark red or maybe black seems to grow up through my body and flex its muscles under my skin. Its eyes go a bit narrow inside mine and its jaws zing with power and saliva. There is usually no going back when I get like this. I let it take over.

When she looks up at me, her mouth is open like she's trying to talk but has run out of words. She takes a breath, tries to regain the upper hand. 'What are you saying? Don't be ridiculous. What do you mean, boy?'

'Well, it kind of works, ma'am. I've stopped having thoughts about other women. You sure whupped that out of me. But I think of you instead. All the time.'

'You're lying. Twisting. Stop it right now.'

'All day, ma'am. All night too. Even though you hurt me, I can't stop thinking about you.' I shake my head, as if in exasperation at myself; let flow all of my desire and passion and sincerity into my eyes and face. Hold her stare, don't let her break free in embarrassment or rage. This is the moment. Why I have come here. 'You're beautiful, ma'am. And real smart too. I can't help my feelings for you. My impure thoughts about you are so strong, ma'am, they blind me.'

She shakes her head, face white and lips quivering. Bites at her bottom lip. Nearly tears through the armrest with her red claws. 'It's . . . It's a childish fixation. A transference.' Her voice sounds skittery and frantic.

'I'm a man. Not a child. And in my sleep I hear the sound of your heels on the floor of the basement, ma'am. I hear you walking to that cupboard.'

'No.'

'It wakes the beast in me, ma'am. Then in my head I can see your eyes and pretty hair and the real smart but

155

sexy way you always dress. And even if you whup me good in my dreams, I'm glad just to be there, alone, with you. You said I needed a strong woman, ma'am. A new Mentor. Well, you were right, and I've found her.'

I'm pretty sure from the shock waves that are crashing through her tipsy head that no one has ever said anything like this to her before. And now she's trying to calm down and stop all the spinning and confusion that's going on: the impulse to lash out and razor my body into red tiger stripes; notions to be gentle and understanding and to send me on my way; impulses to keep me here . . . Yes, part of her – the most hidden and the darkest part of her soul – is thinking of taking advantage. The drink has helped it to come gushing out and now it's making her feel light-headed. Her neck and cheeks are flushed with wine and the feelings no priest can ever allow to be seen.

I slip off my chair on to my knees. I plead with her. 'It's best I stay away from you, ma'am. Or I'll disgrace myself. You've seen how excited I get near you.'

She holds her breath. Goes rigid.

I inch closer, slowly, across the rug. Keep my imploring, burning eyes on her pale, stricken face. She tries to look away, but cannot. Hurriedly, she takes a swig of wine. Shrinks into the darkness of her chair. 'Ma'am, I just can't help myself. It's not a crush.' I sallow and blush. 'I adore you.'

I pick up her fallen high heel. Cradle it in my hands as if I'm lucky to be given permission to handle such a precious item. Watching her, I raise it to my lips and kiss the spiky toe of her shoe. 'I want to please you, ma'am. All I want is to serve you and make you happy. I want you to like me, ma'am.'

'Enough.' Her voice is a hissy whisper. 'Enough of this. Have you no decency? No self-control?' There is no strength in her words, no conviction; she's just reciting what she thinks she should say – this woman of Our

Saviour, drunk and watching a keen young man kissing her shoe like it belongs to the Saviour herself.

I move as if to put the shoe back on her foot. She gasps, leans forwards in her chair at the thought of my making contact with her body. The intense, dangerous look in her eyes stings my whole body. I place the shoe on the floor. Look at her, pout my lips in defiance. 'I can't resist you, ma'am. I don't care any more.' I cup her slippery little heel in my hands again, and bend down to kiss her toes. Through her nylons I can see her red toenail varnish.

'No,' she says, goes to pull her foot away, but I tighten my grip. Bow my head again and kiss the top of her silky foot. Keep kissing up to her ankle. Then close my eyes in rapture and begin to rub my stubbly cheeks against the top of her foot. Nuzzle my nose between her toes, then raise her foot and deeply kiss her instep and the sole of her foot. When I glance at her face, I can see the flush of excitement tinting her cheeks, glazing her eyes – the pupils big as cherries – the teeth gritted to both fight desire and to revel in temptation at the same time. 'I am a wretch, ma'am. Just like Our Saviour wrote about men. It's all true. I am a wretch who defiles a woman of Our Saviour with every thought and wish.' I slide my hands up and on to her calf muscle. Stroke and caress her leg, ripple then smooth her nylons over her shaven skin. Kiss at her shins. Trap her legs against the chair. Pull her other shoe off to make her look smaller, diminished in a more feminine, vulnerable way without those black spikes. Stroke her knees, then kiss their taut, shiny surfaces while sliding the palms of my hands up and down the rear of her calves, feeling them grow warm from the friction between my uninvited hands and her sheer hose.

I feel a hand on the top of my head. Cold fingers slide through my hair. Claws register on my scalp. 'You want to please me? Mmm? Serve me, you say?'

'Yes. Yes. Yes,' I say, still covering her shapely knees with kisses and carefully slipping a few fingers up inside the hem of her pencil skirt, seeking a wider surface area of transparent silkiness that will lead me to my eventual goal.

Suddenly, the hand in my hair clenches. I release her legs, cry out. My eyes sting with tears. Somewhere above me, I hear her laugh; drunk, reckless laughter. 'My pretty little wretch. My pathetic little sinner. You regard the pain I cause you as affection.' Her voice has gone deep; the same tone from the basement. Now she's lost to her own passions and darkness and I am her passenger. I welcome the journey. 'The shame I inflict upon you is a joy. Every harsh word a promise. Each slap a kiss.' She laughs some. 'Am I right?'

'Yes,' I cry through my tears as she twists my head this way and that, flexing her polished claws. She holds me away from her body, like I've been hauled out of a swamp and stink real bad.

She stands up, smiling and laughing to herself. 'So what should I do with my ardent little admirer? Eh? Indulge him? Acknowledge his praise? Many of the whores in this town seem fond of him. Opening their sluttish bodies to his disgusting needs. What should I do with him who showers my feet with kisses, but dips his disgusting prick into the assholes of whores?' That I didn't expect. I look into her bloodshot eyes. She has gone wild. Never knew a Chaplain knew such words. 'Oh, that took you by surprise. You thought some silly old spinster Chaplain knows nothing of the flesh, or its temptations, its ways, its struggle to pollute all that is decent and holy? You are the devil's worm, my boy. And you will know thy place, my sweet.' She releases my hair, leans over me and yanks my T-shirt up and over my head. Then pushes me on to my back with her little, slippery feet. Kneels beside me and unbuckles my jeans. Her breath coming fast, full of fumes and the sweet scent of lipstick. Tugs my jeans down my legs and stands up to pull them from my ankles, taking my socks with them. She rolls me on to my front and stands with her feet on either side of my ribcage. I feel her fingers pressing at my skin, at the places where the scars should be. 'What are you, mmm? You belong to me, child, not the devil. And you will bear my brand.' She slaps at my buttocks and then rips my shorts down my legs, off my feet, and casts them away. 'You wanted to be naked with me, my little amour. Well, now you are.'

I look over my shoulder and watch her reclaim her high heels. Unsteady on her feet, holding on to the chair for balance, she tucks her feet inside her stilettos and then teeters across to me as I lie naked and splayed on the rug.

Hands on hips, she raises her right leg and then plants her shoe on my back, near my shoulders. I feel the cold point of the heel press down through skin, fat and muscle. I tense my spine in preparation as she applies all of her weight through the smooth leather sole and steps on to my body. The second heel digs into my back. My breath goes shallow. It's like she wants to flatten temptation by pressing my body into the ground; humbling me by trespassing across my indecent body.

But I can sense the fight inside this woman who has brought me to heel. Twisted by dreams of young male flesh, tormented by thoughts of a surrender to a man's lust, she keeps temptation close, but not too close; keeps it at the end of a spiked heel or whipping stick. But how long can you last, ma'am? Drink has loosened her foundations like an earth tremor under a wooden house. And few men would persist as I have done, even offering themselves as slaves. It's as if she craves the improper attention and is thrilled by her resistance, like it's some kind of vigorous exercise. And by taking one of Mrs Berry's boys down to that basement, ma'am, you really have put yourself in danger.

Muscles and skin slide under her wobbly soles. Injected by her tipped heels, I feel her slowly teeter to my lower back. She snatches at the mantel for support. Her breath is ragged. 'How can a man desire a woman who walks across his flesh, mmm? A woman who flogs him like a beast? Is the attraction so strong? Even now, do you desire me?'

'Even more, ma'am.'

She steps off my back and retreats back to her wine glass. When I roll on to my side, my face beaming with adoration, she sees my cock straining between my thighs, pointing at her. In some kind of shock, she stares at it; can't take her eyes from the blasphemy on her rug. Young, clean, fresh, eager, offering itself to the high priestess and her drunken, vicious pleasures. She wants to destroy me; she wants to be loved by me. 'Come to me, ma'am. Let me please you.' I focus my stare on her flitting, nervous eyes. I promise passion, intimacy, lust, devilish excitement. 'Just once, ma'am. Let me ease your burden.'

The hard lines of her compact figure, tight inside the tailored restraints of her suit, begin to tremble. The hand on the mantel turns white as it squeezes wood. She shakes her head, raises her chin.

'Come to me, ma'am. We need each other.'

She pushes herself away from the wall. Slowly, unsteadily kneels beside me. Like a snake in the woodpile, I don't let something so good to eat look away. Her chest is rising and falling fast. Eyes are wide open. Pupils big as olives. I slip a hand up and down my cock. 'It's all yours now, ma'am. All yours,' I say with a tremor in my voice.

She grits her teeth, but reaches out a hand. I collect the hand and bring it into my groin. Place it upon my cock. Her eyes roll back and she releases a sigh that I know feels good as it comes out. Cool fingertips and hard nails explore me. My girth is circled by a damp palm, held like a club. She holds the tip of her tongue between her teeth.

Reaching up, real slow, I slip one hand inside her jacket. Cup a breast. Chaplain Skinner gasps, bites her bottom lip, closes her eyes. 'Oh, God.' I caress the small swell of breast through the silky blouse. Then the other. I unbutton her blouse. Her face goes pale. I change my position and notice she is reluctant to release my cock. Kneeling before her, I push her jacket off her shoulders and then pull it free of her shaking hands. As I begin to remove her blouse, our faces are close. Our eyes lock. All differences between age and status are forgotten in a moment. She seizes my face with both hands and pushes her mouth on to mine. Tonguing, biting, sucking at my pretty devil face – all the time making this frantic gaspy sound.

My fumbling fingers unclasp her bra and unleash two lamb-soft mounds into my hands. Holding a breast in either hand, I massage the skin and tweak her nipples. Pull my face back a little to calm the attack of her hungry mouth, and then take control of her lips. Surround her mouth, hold her still, slip my tongue deep inside to be welcomed by her own which lashes with enthusiasm.

Breaking from her mouth and leaving her panting, I dip my face to feast on her breasts. Lapping her nipples, swirling them around my mouth, pressing her flesh with my fingers, I can sense her delight at having a man's hands on her most guarded, naked flesh. So often has she imagined this.

Leaving her chest so thoroughly pleasured and shiny with saliva, I move my mouth to her neck. Bite, kiss and nuzzle her fragrant skin. Nervously, but then in a grasping, desperate way, her nails go at my chest, shoulders, then around to my back. Pulling me against her, wanting a warm but harder male shape crushed against her topless body. 'Show me what you did to

161

them. Show me how they take their pleasure,' she whispers, her voice breaking. She sucks in her breath, keeps her eyes closed, licks her lips. 'Show me what you made them do. So that I may know the devil.'

I stand before her and press the swollen bulb of my cock against her holy lips. She trembles, her eyes flutter open in alarm at how big it feels on her petite face. Stares up the barrel of brute, animal excitement. Her eyes flit up to mine. Grits her teeth. I cup my hand behind her head. 'Suck me,' I say, like I'm giving an order.

She moans, then opens her mouth and swallows the end of me. Strangling my shaft with her white fingers, she sucks and laps at my erection. Then rubs it against her cheeks while looking me right in the eye, which nearly makes me come. 'Is it good?'

'The best.'

Pulls my foreskin back and slides her tongue around the purple curves. Becomes momentarily shy. 'I'm only doing this to know sin. You know that.'

'Yes, ma'am.'

'It has nothing to do with love, or emotions. It's about understanding the poor devils who stray.'

'Absolutely. But it means I'll have to go inside you, ma'am. Deep inside you so you can know the pleasures they crave from strange men.'

She shivers when I say this. 'You want me to feel like the whores you lay on the ground?' she hisses at me, shuffling her hand up and down my cock.

I nod. 'Oh, yeah. I want you to feel the devil inside you.'

She closes her eyes for a moment. Her hand pumps my stiff muscle even faster. Arching my back, I moan. 'Not too much, ma'am. Unless you want me to come real soon.'

Flushing with pride at the effect her attentions are having on me, she gives me an evil smile. 'But you'd like that. Mmm? Pumping it out all over my face and breasts, like I'm a whore being baptised in hell?' Oh boy: I go all swoony and weak. She looks at me the way women look at me when they've gone past this point of no return, behind their husbands' backs. Then she swallows my cock again and puts her whole body into the worship of swollen male sin like Mrs Watson did.

Noisy suckings and murmuring that comes with the rapture of sin. Red fingernails indent my buttocks. A sharp tongue flicks the seamed underside of my cock. A thin arrogant nose buries itself into my balls, inhales. It's like she's gorging herself.

'I want to be inside you, ma'am.'

Sucking at me, she watches me with one scornful, challenging eye and sees the intensity in my face, the eagerness turning to a desperation to penetrate. With a slow pout of her lips, she releases my cock from her hot mouth. 'You need it? Mmm? Need to put yourself inside my body?'

'So much, it's driving me crazy. Ma'am, I want to fuck you like a devil.'

Her eyes narrow. She shows me her teeth. 'Not in my bed. But on the floor. Here. The way whores do it.'

'Yes.'

'Lie on your back. Close your eyes. Don't open them.'

I lie down on the rug, arms at my sides, feet slightly apart. Hear her heels click-clack across the floor, followed by the sound of a zipper. I can't resist it and slit my eyes to see her pushing her skirt down her legs. My cock muscles clench, have never been harder. Then she removes her slip with a hiss. Standing, dressed in her shiny flesh stockings, white garter belt and high heels, she watches me from a few feet away. Parts her legs and slips three fingers on to her shaven sex. Begins to massage herself while staring at my erection. 'Keep your eyes closed,' she warns in a deep, breathy voice. I have to swallow the lump in my throat to say, 'Yes, ma'am.'

Angles her head, screws up her face, the fingers ever circling, kneading. Soon, I will be inside her. Have already been in her mouth. Have put my hands on her body. Did I ever believe it was possible? Mrs Berry said anything was possible. With this gift she has given me, I want to live for ever and try everything.

Unsteady on her heels, breathing hard, the Chaplain walks across to me. Stands astride my body. Stares down at the straining erection between her ankles. Lowers her body into a squat. The golden emblem of Our Saviour swings over her pretty breasts. Grips my cock and points it between her legs. Nudges it against her lips. I breathe in, hold my breath. Slowly, I begin to stroke her thighs. The silky film of her stockings is tight over her shaven legs.

There is a sudden intake of breath from her at the same time I feel the end of my cock press against skin that soon gives way with what feels like a tear. Her body goes rigid and she bites her hand. The fluid warmth of vagina surrounds the head of my cock. Chaplain Skinner moans. Spreads her fingers wide across my tummy, slides herself down my length. Right to the base, where she pauses and gasps like she's in pain. I seize her hips, steady her, then help to move her weight around and along my cock.

'That good?' she pants at me.

'Like a dream come true.'

Now that she pumps and rocks and rubs her sex over mine and against my groin with her eyes closed, I sense she is reliving past excesses behind those painted eyelids. I am not the first. It's like she cannot bear to actually see herself indulge in yet another disgrace, so she has put herself in the dark. But the dark is where the ghosts live. Now it is my turn to be shocked, to be in awe.

She has been good for so long; so prim, so correct, so disciplined, keeping her desires and her urges repressed. Has taken to restraint and canes to take the edge off her

164

needs. Blames anyone but herself when she knows all flesh is weak, especially holy flesh. And in my mind, as we share this forbidden communion of body, I share the memories that inflict the most shame, most guilt and the most electrifying pleasure on her. Flashing out of the red abyss inside my head, I see her sitting on an office chair, legs open, skirt raised as another young man – so slim, so tanned – pushes an incredibly long cock into her sex. Then, on a tartan blanket in a silent, sun-bathed meadow she is again disgraced, face down, buttocks raised as a Saviour Scout rams himself deep inside her, holding her garter belt like the reins of a horse. On and on they come. Appearing and then vanishing like mirages. Sucking a cock that protrudes from dark trousers in the aisle of a library. Then dressed in a mask and some kind of leather skirt that is pushed around her waist, as she kneels with her face down in a dark place where people watch from the sides as a muscular man throws himself into her body from behind. It is this image that arouses her more than any other; the memory she recalls the moment before she reaches the peak of her slow climb to intense, blinding pleasure. It excites me; I feel betrayed; it excites me more.

The Chaplain's body trembles. She claws my body until I wince. Bounces up and down so her sex slaps against my groin. Holding her trim waist I pull her up and down to prolong her ecstasy, to force her further into the pleasurable despair of succumbing to temptation. She is lost inside herself, wordless, adrift, damned again.

Without resistance, I then swing her small shape beneath me on the rug. Place her spiky feet upon my shoulders. And thrust deep to reach my own paralysing conclusion. I look down at her wanton face – lipstick smudged by a young sinner's lips, eye-liner melting from the heat of her own eager participation, legs raised and parted, breasts still flushed from a thorough fondling.

'Don't come in me,' she rasps. 'Pull out.'

I kiss one of her shiny ankles and then release a scalding flood through the centre of my cock. Hold her body still until every drop has been expelled inside her holy womb. 'Did you? Inside me?' she asks. I lower myself over her body and kiss her lips. Smother her face with adoring lips, before I place my mouth over her neck. 'What are you doing?' she murmurs. 'That hurts. You'll leave a mark. Don't.' Then a sigh, then silence, and I close my eyes to drink.

Drunk with triumph and satisfaction and the mineral richness I found beneath her skin, I carry her limp body up the wooden stairs. Open a few doors with my foot, until I find her bedroom. Arrange her on the bed, kiss her forehead. Then cover her body with a duvet. But not before I remove her stockings, deciding to keep them.

I look out the window of her room at the quiet street. Time I moved on. Tonight I made sure there is no going back.

Part 2

Chapter Eighteen

This is a strange institution. It's nothing like the reformatory they frightened us with in boys' school. It reminds me of a hotel with cameras in every room. There is no privacy. A little glass eye above the door watches me whenever I'm lying on the bed reading or staring into space, or sitting at the desk doing the assignments. Not a bad room despite the camera.

From my window I can see the gardens and tennis courts. If I didn't feel so lousy I would use the gym and swimming pool down the corridor, during the Special Periods when the other *clients* aren't around: I can't fraternise with the other men yet. Been here for ten days and it's been ten days since I've been with a woman. As a high-risk offender, I can't leave the facility. Only women here are the doctors with the smiling, unkind faces. They watch me at all times with suspicious eyes.

Abstinence has given me the sweats, chills and real bad dreams. Worse than ever before. Most of the time I lie around in this room in a kind of half sleep. Sometimes I dream of Mrs Berry; she sits on the edge of the bed, legs crossed, smoking cigarettes from the long red packet. Or she stands by the window staring into the distance while I roll and mumble on the bed. When I wake up with a cry, she's never here. For the first month I'm not allowed any visitors either. Mrs

Berry vanished weeks ago, but I have a hunch she's coming back. She has to. My skin tingles like it did before our dates back at the beginning of the Mentoring.

And inside the brace, my cock swells and feels good like she's stroking it with one of her fine hands. The brace reminds me of a jock-strap; it is locked on to your waist so you can't touch yourself. It's open at the back and there is a tube to piss through. The carers fitted it when I first got here. So even if I could get a woman inside my room, there is nothing I could do with her. Every man wears one at the start of rehabilitation, but they never take them off the real bad-asses. The ankle bracelet stays on for life, so the Security and Welfare Department can keep track of all the deviants.

Strangely, thoughts of the future don't bother me. Unless I am free to roam and seduce and take what I need, there won't be a future. This I know. And when you're lying around feeling sick and tired all day, you don't think about your disgrace, or what your parents must be thinking, or what happens to you next, because you just think about being sick and tired. Keeping my head straight takes up most of my energy.

There is a knock at the door. That will be the two carers with the big arms who wear white suits and shoes, come to take me to therapy. I have therapy with Doctor Nichols every day. Group sessions will come later, the carers said, like it is something to look forward to. Pretty soon, unless I can escape from here, they will be checking me into the hospital wing.

I dream of the cool skin of my doctor's throat.

During a secret rehearsal with my band, the police came for me. Two days after I went to visit the Chaplain at her home.

We were in the basement of Gretchen's house, using acoustic guitars and drum pads. Brad and Davey never gave me a hard time about cancelling the other rehearsals; even though they knew something was going down with me and had heard rumours about Melody Watson. Gretchen had told them nothing.

We played the new songs and worked out how to finish *In Her Service*. I came up with lyrics and a riff for another song, a bluesy power-ballad called *Sinner in the Red Motel*. All the guys loved it, and the horsing around and pipe-dreaming about doing a tour was back. After what happened between me and the Chaplain, I guessed if I kept a low profile she would cut me some slack with the band, especially now we were so intimate and all. Thought I could keep her sweet, like I'd done with Melody; long enough until I got some cash together and thought of a plan to get me and Gretchen across the border. The other guys too if they wanted to come. Can't hang around much longer, I thought; with the Watsons on one side and the Chaplain on the other, things could go crazy at any time. But shit happened much sooner than I expected.

Must have been the Chaplain who called the cops. Maybe she woke up the next morning and went crazy with guilt and remorse; maybe she was just crazy all along. Who else would have had me committed to a reformatory?

While me and the band were chopping through a rendition of *Paradise City*, Gretchen's dad came into the basement. His face was real pale. In a calm voice, he said, 'Franklin, will you come upstairs please? There is someone here who would like to see you.'

I knew right away it was serious. Brad and Davey just gaped at me with fish faces. Saying nothing, I packed up my guitar and followed Gretchen's dad up the stairs. 'Just do what they say, Franky,' he whispered, so the others couldn't hear. 'Don't go being a smart mouth with these people.' He used to be in trouble all the time with his drinking, until they gave him the booze-hound treatment that makes you puke if you even smell liquor. At the top of the stairs I turned and looked down at Gretchen. He winked at me and mouthed the words, 'See you soon, buddy.' Which made me feel good until I saw the three detectives standing in the hallway. All female officers in plain clothes. I've heard they're mean as snakes. Once, downtown, I saw the police spray some guys with gas for demonstrating about the end of the bars.

Outside there were three police cars in addition to the cars belonging to the detectives. Guess they thought I might run, being a track champion and all. They put the cuffs on me in the hall and took me out to the cars. Lots of kids in the street were staring. Some women watched from doorways: still in their chic suits after work, holding glasses of wine and staring at me. And I saw some dads in aprons, peeking out from behind curtains.

The detective with the red hair and seamed stockings sat in the back of an unmarked car with me. As we drove off, she said my parents had been notified. They drove me outside town to the Twin Cedars Reform Facility. The police handed me over to the carers and Doctor Nichols. I was processed – stripped and photographed and given the one-piece suit with rubber flip-flops – then tied down in my bed for the first night.

This whole place smells like vanilla. Never been anywhere so quiet. Regret and fear does that.

'Tell me about the biting.' Stretched out on the table in the dark room, I listen to the doctor's voice; she sits behind me, rustling. Stood against the wall out of sight is her colleague; a pretty blonde woman who gave me the injections. I am brought here every day by the same two carers, so that beautiful women can prick me with needles, make me sleepy and ask me questions. Feels like going to sleep and talking from inside the dreams that are instantly created by their voices. *Biting*: makes

170

me think of the Chaplain's soft skin, stretching like a web from neck to clavicle.

The drugs make me feel good. For a while they take away the aches in my joints and the fatigue in my muscles that come from not biting. 'Why do you bite the women?' she asks again.

'They like it,' I say, thinking of the faraway look in the Chaplain's eyes; the trembling and the sighing that came out of her.

'Why do they like being bitten?' Her voice is soft and she speaks real nice. Sound of her voice makes me think of her fresh red lips and her glasses with the black frames and how good her blue eyes look behind the thin, clear lenses. There is a streak of white in her black hair. With my eyes closed I can see her sitting on the chair behind me; black suit, long legs crossed, red fingernails holding the fountain pen that scratches away on the clipboard. 'Makes them feel good.'

'By biting them? Do they not feel pain?'

'Not in a bad way.' My words are slurred. I concentrate on keeping them whole and firm in my mouth. 'Some of them want to feel more. More than they usually do.'

'But why is it so important to bite?'

'Come close, doctor, and I'll show you.' The air in the dark place thickens with the discomfort of the two scientists. I hear the court shoes of the anaesthetist walk across the room to the doctor behind me.

'What's happening?' the doctor whispers to her colleague. 'He still seems to be conscious.'

'I don't know,' she whispers back. 'He seems to have a resistance to K5.' They don't think I can hear them, but I can hear every delicious smack of lip, flick of tongue, rasp of leg, swish of skirt lining. I can even hear what they're thinking. This K5 just makes my new senses even stronger.

'Can't you give him any more?'

'Yes, if you want him to slip into a coma. His pulse has dropped lower than I've ever seen, but he's still half-conscious. I can't risk it.'

'OK. Let's do our best.' She turns her attention back to me. 'Franklin, I want you to think about your experience with the Chaplain. I want you to think again about the bite you gave her. I want you to concentrate.'

'I already told you about this.'

'I know, but I'm still not clear as to why you had to bite her.'

'It's part of loving. Like a kiss, that's all. A special kiss. It made us closer.'

'Did she try and stop you?'

'No. It only hurt her for a little bit. But it was so good she wouldn't let go of me.'

Both women wet their lips. They feel a bit hot in here. 'Do you enjoy the biting? Do you enjoy inflicting pain?'

'Only if they like to be spanked, or strapped with my belt. Then it's good to see a woman so excited. Women who want me to handle them. To be assertive. I've not met many who just want to sit down in the conception positions. Why is that, doctor?'

'It's not for me to say. That's up to you.'

Oh, doctor, if only it was up to me. If only I could look into your eyes. By bringing me in here and locking me away like a wild animal, you are making me sick. You give me no choice; I must reach out to you again, like I did yesterday and the day before. You are strong, but I feel we're getting closer. So now I will slip across the velvety smoothness of the air between us and slip inside your clever mind. Can you see that? An image of me between your long thighs. Don't resist. See my hands on your breasts and my tongue curling around your nipples. Feel my hard enamel brushing your throat, so close to giving you a pleasure you have never experienced before. Think of pleasure, doctor. Our two warm bodies pressed together. Me, deep inside you. This man

172

is not like the other patients, he's special. You know it. Looks like an angel and seems to pleasure women in no ordinary way. Like a devil with sharp teeth. Best method to understand him is to give yourself away. That's it, think of it. Take him. Take your pleasure like the others did. He's not dangerous; he is here to please you. To serve your wishes.

Her pen stops scratching on the clipboard. Her mind drifts for a while. She shows me things that make me smile, that make me hard inside the brace. Then she regains control of herself. Is angry at herself. Angry at me. 'Are you not taking revenge on women for being in control? For knowing better? For being stronger than men are?' Somewhere in the darkness, against a wall, the doctor's colleague frowns.

'No. Women are exciting. I like them being so powerful. But they're so full of mystery too. They always surprise me. You would too, doctor. It's hard being in charge all the time. Being responsible for us. Sometimes a woman needs to let go. To just give in to passion. It's why they come to me.' And it's why you should come to me when it is safe. Come to me, doctor. Soon as you can. Save me.

This doctor feels hot and restless and cannot concentrate on the interview. Instead, her thoughts keep drifting back to her memories of being fucked backwards, and really hard too. Over her desk, against the wall in a darkened side street where the cameras don't peek, just before going on stage at a conference, in her hotel suite. She's feeling light-headed now. Wonders if my simple view of the world has any validity. I mean, there was that first time in the back of her car, at night, when she let that strange man fuck her ass so hard. When he pulled out and ran off, she turned around and saw his come on the back of her legs, so white against her black stockings. And ever since that night, she has looked for the same feeling, the same intense escape.

And when she can't find it, she goes to bed with the big plastic toy between her thighs; the one she keeps locked away in a bedside cabinet. I concentrate on this part of her and tell her that these are the pleasures of my world. Think only of the steadily building pleasures that come from the fake cock and your memories, that lead you to the jolt and shiver of your climax in bed.

'Don't you want to save yourself?' Her voice is unsteady. Her colleague is stiff with embarrassment.

'Loving a woman saves me. Passion saves me. You would risk everything for it, doctor, if you knew how good it is.' And I want you to take that risk, my dear doctor. So tall and straight and clever and elegant, so professional with so much belief in the Saviour System, but boiling underneath with wildness and shadows. Wanting to feel strong fingers on your hips, or pulling your buttocks apart; dreaming of thick cocks pushing deep inside you. But never inside your sex. Never! Only in your ass where the fireworks are launched. Even now I can sense the tingling around your little ring and the dampness between your legs. Sometimes you leave that toy inside yourself for hours. Close the curtains in the afternoon. Take off your clothes and replace them with the sluttish underwear you like to wear because it makes you feel sexy and bad and no one knows that you wear it on your long, pale body. See-through black underwear and the stockings with the seams you've never worn outside your apartment, because it is unfitting for a professional woman of psychiatric medicine to wear such things. A woman who works in a facility for deviant men, like me. The thrilling, electrifying shame of it all. But into the transparent panties with the slit at the back you go, and up your legs you roll the black smoke of nylon before you unlock the bedside drawer and curl up under the hot sheets. You suck the toy slippery before pressing it inside yourself. And this is what you have already decided to do this afternoon on your lunch

174

break. To go back to your condo to spend some time in the dark.

All of this you have shown me. Like Mrs Berry, I can see these things hidden inside other people. It's the biting, doctor. I'll never admit it to you, doctor, but it's the biting that allows me to see such forbidden things inside the dreams of women.

'Think he's gone to sleep,' the anaesthetist says. 'Brain activity has suddenly dropped.'

'That's enough for today, anyway.'

The anaesthetist leaves the room. The doctor uncrosses her legs and stands up. Watches me. Wonders about who or what I am.

'How can I sleep, doctor?' I say. She gasps and steps away from the table. 'When you make me think of so many bad things?'

'What do you mean?' she says, breathless with fright.

'Same every time, ma'am. When you ask me these questions about sex, all I can think of is you bent over. Biting your knuckles. And me –'

'Stop!'

'And me behind you. It's always quick, hard, deep. I'm sorry, but the injections make me say everything I'm thinking, ma'am. I can't help it.' She feels guilty now. 'I see you in a side street. In an office. In your car. Always bent over, always so excited. So excited you cry sometimes. Especially in the car. That was the best.'

Remorse and pity for me turns to shock, outrage. 'No.'

'The first time for you. It was so quick, so easy, so unexpected. I wish it had been me.'

'Stop. Stop it.'

'But it can't be right. You're a doctor. Am I going crazy? Every time I have these visions, I find out they're true.'

She rings the bell to summon the carers.

* * *

175

'Must be his age.' Behind me, as I walk unassisted to my room, I can hear my escort of two carers muttering to each other. 'Least it makes the job easier. We usually carry them out of therapy.' Then their voices drop even lower to a whisper that I can still hear if I concentrate on the sound. 'What's he in for? Anyone know yet?

'Category A offences. That's all I know. Files are sealed. Doctor's eyes only. Must be bad.'

'But he's only a kid.'

'You get them in here now and again. Difficult age. All those hormones. Hard to toe the line. And the girls play them up.'

'But he must have done something real bad. Doctor was all shaken up after his session. Better keep a close eye on this one. Think he'll get the needle?'

'Wouldn't be surprised.'

My eyes are open but I am dreaming. Can't remember falling asleep, but I must have done. Could have been like this for hours. Hard to say. Guess I could snap out of the trance at any time, but it feels like I'm supposed to be waiting for something, someone. Staring at the door of my room I've been seeing other things in front of it.

It's like all the women I have loved I still have a connection to. I see the Chaplain in a plain white room. There are two long doors that open on to a balcony. From there she can see the Saviour Mountains. She stands on the balcony and looks at the sky, but is thinking about me, that's why I can see her. On the bed in her room, a young man is lying face down, like he's sleeping. He's exhausted and can't move a muscle and can't stand the sheets touching his back or buttocks. She's been going at him for hours with a stick. He is kept in this place with the view of the mountains to pleasure important women. They can do what they want with him. She has tried to get me and what I did with her out of her soul by caning other young men. But I'm still inside her.

I start to feel excited and warm with joy. The scene changes. I could cry with relief when I see Mrs Berry sitting in a dark booth, in a bar. Smoking, she sits alone with a martini glass in front of her on the dark wood of the table. She has eaten the olive already. Sucked it with her red lips and then eaten it. The screens around the booth are made from little squares of red glass. The bench seat is upholstered in cherry-red leatherette. Doesn't look like a place in our town, or even our territory, unless it's a private club for women. She looks right at me and smiles. Doesn't say a word – her lips don't even move – but I can hear her voice inside my head.

'Turn my back for a minute and you head straight for trouble. Been running around with all those good girls who know where you live. Dangerous habit, Franklin. At least you found out who the bad girls really are.' She smiles. 'Mrs Watson? I'm surprised at you. And our mutual friend, the Chaplain?' She smiles. 'I knew you had the hots for her. Just can't leave the important women alone, can you? You little tramp.' She winks. 'Suppose if you can take a priest you can take anyone. Can't think of two women, though, who are more likely to put you behind bars. Oh, they had a good time all right. But that's the problem. So maybe we need to work on your after-service. There's more to this than fucking bad girls.' She lifts up a book of matches I can see real clear: DADDY O'HANCOCKS is printed on the side. She lights the cigarette. 'You must hang on, Franklin. I'm coming soon. But I've a little business to take care of first, out of town. Be careful who you kiss.' Mrs Berry leaves some money on the table, stands up and leaves the booth. Then I'm looking at the door of my room again. This time I'm awake. I get up to take a piss.

Feel like I should be in shock, or even amazed by these dreams, but it feels natural, necessary. It was like

177

Mrs Berry was actually in the room with me. Maybe it's all the drugs they've been injecting me with. One day soon there might be something in the needle that takes it all away. Just the thought of it makes me go all cold and I hold on to the towel rail to force the fear away. Got to keep my head straight. Got to get out of here real soon.

Just as I'm patting my face down with cold water, I hear footsteps in the corridor outside. They stop near my door, which unlocks with a beep and whirr. I kill the lights in the bathroom and stand inside the door. Maybe it's the carers come to give me the needle. Everything stops moving inside my body. Little hairs on my forearms and the back of my neck stand up. The door opens. Someone steps through real quick and closes it behind them.

I stay out of sight. Even though I see good in the dark these days, my sense of smell is even sharper. I know that perfume. Almost like candy. It's the scent of my doctor, sneaking into my room in the early hours of the morning. Most of the fear goes but I don't relax. Maybe this is how they administer the final treatment.

With the blinds drawn, she can't see much and edges her way across the room towards my bed, fingers spread out like feelers so she doesn't crash into anything. Near the bed, she feels the covers and moves her hands up to the pillows. She hisses my name. Becomes suddenly worried when she realises the bed is empty. Stands up straight, looks around, sees nothing.

'You wanted me, doctor?' I say, real quiet, from the bathroom door.

'Where are you?' she asks, her voice trembling. Turns to the sound of my voice, but I slip into the room on silent bare feet and stand close to her.

'You read my mind, didn't you?' she asks the dark where I am not standing.

'You inspire me.'

Gasping, she turns about and throws her hands out to seize me. I step away. 'You knew what I was thinking. It's a part of it, isn't it?'

'Part of what, doctor?'

'The biting. Like the last one. He was the same.'

I cock my head at an angle and step forwards. 'Isaac?'

'You knew him. You are the same. That's why they were watching you and your friends.'

'What happened to Isaac?'

She stays quiet. 'It was not my decision. He was not my patient.'

'Sounds like you bit him back.' I stretch myself out there, into the controlled air of this comfortable white cage where men are sealed away for trying to be men. I get no sense of Isaac. Just my memories of him; as silent and worried as his long face, the way it was before they took him away. 'He's not around any more, is he?' I stare at the pale luminance of the doctor's face. Look for the answers. Isaac got sick and real thin in this place and they never knew why. Never knew why the medication affected him that way until it was too late.

'That's confidential.'

'Like this visit out of hours? You shouldn't be here, doctor. I'm a real bad hombre, or haven't you heard?'

'The cameras are down for one hour,' she says, breathless. 'All my interviews are recorded and will be studied. But I had to know. Off the record. What you are. Before they make the same mistakes.'

Something dimly shines on her legs. Even though I know my old friend is dead, the urge in me to live and love is still strong. I tell myself to mourn Isaac later. A voice inside me whispers about opportunity and how it might have presented itself, unexpectedly, in the middle of the night. When I step closer to the doctor, I can see the tight leather boots on her legs, responsible for the shine. 'My guess is you have some way to go to make up for what you did to Isaac.'

'What did you have in mind?'

'Get me out of here.'

'Impossible.'

'I'll go the same way as him, unless . . .'

'Unless you can bite?' She can barely get the words out.

'Smart lady. Who sent me here?'

'You know I can't tell you.'

I step forwards and grab her by the elbows. 'You're not much good to me then, are you?'

'I can be.' She swallows. Tries to find my eyes in the dark.

'Thoughts are one thing. Actions are another. Isn't that what you all believe? Isn't that your excuse?'

'Sometimes we go too far.'

I can sense her trembling with all kinds of emotion: anger at herself for coming, guilt for Isaac, and a frustration that makes her almost want to harm others and then herself. 'Seems like there is too much vengeance in this town.'

'It's not vengeance.'

'Then what the hell is this place? Most of these guys haven't done anything bad.'

'That's not for you to decide. You're eighteen. Every boy thinks he can change the world at eighteen. We must have standards. The rest of the world is falling to pieces.'

I shrug. 'I'm not such a boy any more. And that's why you're here.'

'I knew you were sick. I wanted to help. You're different, like he was. I want to understand.'

'There is only one way you can heal me, doctor.'

There is a long silence between us. 'Do it.' Her voice is so thin and her body is trembling so hard, but the secret part of her nature is taking over and demanding she sacrifice herself – her professionalism, her career, her status, her reputation – everything for one intense

180

moment of total surrender. She wants to be punished, she wants to make amends, she wants to be loved. Hard.

I find her lips with my own and crush her body against me. She goes limp but resists my kisses like a clumsy girl during courtship. Keeps her lips closed but her eyes wide open. But after I kiss her neck and make her sniffle and moan and beg that I don't hurt her too much, I soon find her eager tongue inside my young mouth.

'Be quick,' she says, breathing hard, breaking away from the kiss. 'You must be quick. The cameras.'

I don't need to be told. My needs take over. I move this tall lady back towards the bed, turn her around. Briefly smile into the dark; this doctor has probably saved my life, which is what doctors are supposed to do, but not by these methods. I bend her over so fast and then push her on to the bed. She makes a girlish squeal of surprise, which is always nice to hear from a powerful woman, so rarely undone. I kneel behind her and run my hands over the smooth leather of her boots. Then caress the thin nylon that clings to the soft skin of her legs. Push her skirt up to her waist.

She likes to be bad in the dark. Fists the bedclothes. Closes her eyes and moans to herself. I pull the flimsy black panties down to her knees. Caress and squeeze her buttocks; astonished that a woman's flesh is in my hands again. 'Use this,' she says, and passes something back to me. 'Put it all over your penis.' It's a metal tube that feels cold. I quickly uncap the salve and press a dollop of cold, tingly gel into my palms. But as soon as I pull down my shorts I notice the thickness of the brace about my middle. 'The brace. The damn brace.'

'Wait. Wait,' she says, scrabbling at her ID about her neck. Using the electronic key, she presses the touch pad. I hear a beep and feel the device go slack about my hips. I step out of the brace and my shorts and kick them away, across the floor. Cool, conditioned air rushes in to embrace my imprisoned sex. The doctor kneels on the bed, widens her legs. 'Hurry.'

Covering my length with the cold gel, oiling from tip to base, I exhale to calm my nerves. It always feels too good to be true. I slide my hands on to her waist. Over her garter belt and then press the head of my cock between her white cheeks. 'I should make you suck me first. Like a slut.'

'I would. I would do it. But there isn't time. Just push it in me.' As the slippery head of my cock nuzzles against her ring, she presses her face into the bed-clothes. 'Use me. Just push it in. Use me up.'

Slowly, I swirl and circle my cock against her little pinkish valve. Then press and feel her asshole stretch wide around my thickness. She makes a deep groaning sound from the bottom of her stomach. The taut ring of muscle suddenly softens and I feel myself slide inwards. I hold still until she wriggles around on the bed, trying to ride backwards and take more of me in. I push again. Make her claw the sheets. Then stop. Then press the rest of myself inside until my floss is compressed against the skin of her squashed buttocks. The doctor makes a choking sound. I notice she has slipped a hand between her thighs and on to her sex. Her fingers become busy. I withdraw and push. Pull back and push. Keep going until I have a smooth, merciless rhythm that keeps time with her chesty groans.

'Hard. Hard. Harder.'

I begin to thrust deep, and then grind her body into the mattress. Collapsed face-down on the bed, she slaps a hand against the wall. Riding her back I dig deep, spear her until I cannot sink any deeper, withdraw, slam myself in again.

She bends her neck back. 'Bite me.'

'You want to know what it's like? Mmm?'

'Yesss.'

'I'm close to the warmth of your blood. I just have to

taste you. You know it. Taste you while I'm deep inside your ass.'

'Yes.'

My eyes change – I can feel my pupils grow into big black saucers and my mouth fills with saliva. Delicious gum pain comes, and a tingly cock that wants to chug its thick cream inside her grasping, greedy ass. Every molecule in my body thrills with electric shivering delight. With my hungry mouth, I find the right place on the back of her neck. Press her down into the bed with my body weight for the moment of struggle, before she seems to deflate with a satisfied sigh when my teeth go in. Still pumping her soft backside – more slowly now, but still at depth – I draw her salty morphine into my throat. As if to replenish what I have taken from her, I pump my seedy vitality deep inside her stretched rectum.

Hope I'm not taking too much. All I can hear is the rushing inside my ears. It's like my gullet and stomach have become guzzling pumps to acquire the vigorous life of another. I force myself to stop, to break my teeth free before lapping at the smudged place to seal it clean.

I withdraw and lie beside her. She does not move on my prison bed, only murmurs in her dream-time.

Chapter Nineteen

Next time I take therapy, the anaesthetist is not present. Carers don't take me to the usual place either, but to another level of the facility where Doctor Nichols has an office. Overlooking the golf-links, where men in white suits hit little balls; it has big windows with silver blinds, soft couches, a little bar and a beautiful big desk made from red wood. The carpet is so thick and deep, it's like walking through long grass.

When the carers shut me inside, the doctor is sitting behind her desk and another client is polishing the glass of the coffee table. 'Good morning, Franklin,' she says, without smiling. Then clicks her fingers and the cleaner scuttles off. As he brushes past me, I receive a quick mental impression of women's shoes; many pairs that he used to spend hours holding and staring at. They didn't belong to his wife either. Whenever my dad got uppity, my mom used to joke about these institutions being good ways of getting rid of unwanted husbands.

'Please take a seat,' the doctor says.

I sit on the leather couch closest to the windows. Although this doctor came to me in the night, let me love her and told me she was sorry about Isaac, I find it hard to believe and trust anyone with authority in this town. She's nervous about something today and is trying to hide it. It's not the sex or biting either. I think she's suspicious of how many of her thoughts I can hear.

She comes around the desk and across the room to join me. Looks real nice in a black suit and white blouse. Skirt stops above her knees. Stockings are black and her heels are real high. If I'm not mistaken, she had her hair and nails taken care of this morning; probably by one of the guys in a salon downtown. 'I decided to continue your therapy in more comfortable surroundings.'

She brought me here because it's off the record and the therapy drugs don't work on me. 'Nice place.'

'Thank you. Before the Graceful Revolution it belonged to the state governor. He had taste.' Sitting down opposite me, she crosses her long legs. Doesn't mind the moment I take to admire them. 'You are a very special young man, Franklin. And conventional treatment, although effective in the majority of cases, is not suited to your specific needs. So –' she raises her eyebrows and stretches out her long white fingers with the scarlet nails '– we shall have to pursue more unconventional methods.' I listen to what she's saying but hear what she really means. She tells me she has a personal interest in my case and a unique responsibility for my well-being. But she's mainly thinking about Isaac: he was like me, he was brought here, and he died here. But who made him like me? Where does it start? It wasn't his Mentor; she turned him in to the cops. And my Mentor cannot be found for questioning, though she's convinced Mrs Berry was responsible for Isaac, and my condition. 'In fact, it's very fortunate that I recognised your particular symptoms in time. Had another doctor been assigned your case, we both know it would have had serious implications for your health.'

I nod. 'Thanks.'

She smiles, but her mouth is a bit tight. She's trying really hard to keep control of her thoughts. Speaks a bit more slowly. She's getting to what she wants, which is the reason I'm not drugged on a table in the dark. 'Your

185

illness could be seen as something of a gift. But in the wrong hands? To seduce and indulge one's cravings at will? To enjoy privileged insights into another's thoughts, without years of training? You can see my problem, Franklin. Those individuals with such an affliction would obviously require careful supervision in a society like ours.'

'You don't say.' Which is why we have to keep moving; why Mrs Berry never stays in one place for long. State of Our Saviour is nothing but a bolt-hole for her, a place where she raises cash for something I don't know about yet. And this doctor wants me to change her too. To pass on the 'affliction'. She's trying hard to keep her mind focused, but her greed for power and control is simmering away too fiercely to remain hidden from me. My 'illness' is best reserved for women like her. Men cannot be trusted; they cannot be allowed to roam free looking for a good time, and a little taste of a woman. We need to be saved from ourselves. But if women like the doctor had my gift, they would be unstoppable. The thought makes her stomach fizz and flop. Superwomen of the Saviour.

'Which means we must also protect you from well-intentioned, but somewhat misguided factions in our society. It would be their mandate to have you destroyed. Do you know what a mandate is, Franklin?'

'Sure do, ma'am.'

'So it is in your best interests to remain in the secure wing for the time being. Until you and I are a little more familiar with your condition.'

So the church wants me too, wants me put down like a sick pet, but I'm all yours now, yours to keep. The Chaplain has made a mistake; she was sure I'd get the needle right away for biting a priest. 'Sounds like you reckon it's not such a bad condition to have.'

Don't like the look in her pretty blue eyes after saying that. My head suddenly fills with what feels like cold, black water. Truth hurts, doctor, don't it? The smile has gone completely now and her voice has dropped to the same tone as the Chaplain's before she flies into a rage. 'Your life can be made very comfortable for you here. Safe.' She forces a smile. 'Your particular needs can be indulged also. With discretion. If you follow. But it will require your complete co-operation.' She slowly un-crosses her long legs. 'It's important you and I become close. That we build a relationship.' She looks uncomfortable, is in utter disbelief that she has actually said such a thing to an inmate of a facility for sexual deviants. 'And I can make sure, in time, that you are provided with variety.'

So I'm never getting out, good doctor. And if I do what you say, I will be imprisoned in luxury and used as a kind of stud horse to breed my condition into you and women like you. That's the thinking. Only Mrs Berry always told me not to take too much from the same woman, nor to go with girls who can find me again. Which has been my undoing up to this point. This condition is not for sharing. Not unless you're sure. Of what? Still don't know why Mrs Berry bonded with me in this way. But there was a reason. One that I don't know yet. But this condition is not for spreading around like confetti. It only works between certain people. Goes real wrong in some. Makes them insane and cruel. But as far as I know, and this doctor knows, there has only ever been me and Isaac in this town. But who turned him? Mrs Berry, she's sure.

'I don't think I'm being unreasonable. Do you?'

Well, ma'am, screwing hot, high-steppin' chicks in Saviour Town while all my responsibilities are removed and my needs catered for, sounds like a real sweet deal. But it just don't work like that. With the bite comes devotion, then obsession. I only have to think of Melody Watson walking her dog, Mrs Mullins bringing soup and the Chaplain caning young men in a mountain retreat to know a bite leads to an attachment that lasts a long time and makes people do crazy things. So I can't see this experiment working. Can just see me and a lot of important ladies getting torn apart. But I guess I better play along with it until I can get out. 'You've been very kind, doctor.'

Smiling again. Up on her feet and moving with long easy strides to her desk. 'It's not easy for me to come at night. It's better we meet here in future.' Leaning with her bottom against her desk and hands spread wide, she looks at me with seductive eyes. I'm ready for you now, they say to me. Come to me now before my next meeting. 'Do you know what I'm thinking right now, Franklin?'

I nod. Few days ago this would have felt like every wish in the world granted at the same time. But the fact that I'm just a lab monkey in a nappy who lives in a scientist's cage, who is being manipulated by a clever, beautiful bitch into fulfilling her needs, makes me kind of sore. Makes me mad mostly because being in her service gets me so horny; this brace feels four sizes too small. Women in this town will always be one step ahead of me; their heels are too high and their eyes are too clever. Mrs Berry said I had to grow up fast. Should have listened instead of drooling over her legs.

I approach the desk and smile at my new keeper. Doctor Nichols is pleased with herself: she's beautiful, totally in control of the situation, practically owns me, feels she's on the verge of a breakthrough in harnessing my freaky abilities, and is about to enjoy the kind of intimacy she dreams about most nights. But if she is the winner and I'm just an animal that performs on command, then why is my cock so hard?

She rolls one foot around, hangs a shoe off her toes. 'Well?'

I stare into her eyes; let her fill up with my heat and hunger. 'You like being beautiful. And sexy. You like young men being totally into you and desperate to fuck you.' She's shocked at the 'fuck' word. 'Someone who can be assertive for a while and let you escape from it all. But someone who knows his place soon as you've had your fun.'

'My, my, are we getting bitter, Franklin? Sounds like sour grapes to me. Most men would –'

'Most men would like to have ideas of their own.' I begin to unzip my suit. Her suspicion clashes with excitement. But she likes tension with sex. Likes to be the plaything for a while. Leaning towards her, I go to kiss her shiny lips. And move away when she opens her mouth. Her eyes go narrow. 'Don't fuck with me, you little tease. You're lucky to even be here.'

'That so? Well, I can't do much in a brace. Gets real uncomfortable when I'm horny.'

'That's the idea,' she says through clenched teeth, but quickly releases the clasps of my brace, using her ID card like a television remote. 'Get it off. Quick.'

I kick the brace and my crumpled suit away and stand naked before her. One of her long hands wastes no time in wrapping itself around my cock. She feels a pride in ownership – a brief, hot, maddening desire for complete possession. Bites the tip of her tongue between her front teeth. *In here he's all mine. No other bitch can get near him. That Chaplain should have thought things through. No use turning up here and expecting instant access to my client. No use giving me all that 'Do you know who I am' nonsense. You gave him away, bitch. And he belongs here, with me.*

Stroking my cock with gentle fingers, she leans forwards and begins to lick my chin and lips. Her pupils are big as black marbles and her breathing is short, quick. Inside the jacket of her suit go my hands. I help myself to her small breasts. 'You've been fucked in here before, doctor. Twice.' Doesn't like the intrusion; her eyes go narrow and mean, but she's desperate to acquire

189

the same ability. 'I like that,' I say, while massaging her chest through her bra. 'Real clever, foxy doctor likes to go at it like a slut over her desk. Just the idea would keep a guy in this town going forever.'

'Don't play with me.'

'Think you've been working here too long. Thinking about sex all day. Working with desperate, rejected men. So who is the guy who did it to you in here? An inmate?'

Embarrassed, angry, aroused, she wants to slap me. 'You tell me. You can see the images.'

I kiss her neck. A gasp escapes from her mouth; her body locks. Reaching behind her, I unzip her skirt. I receive a few images of my doctor lying face down on the rug, still fully dressed with her underwear around her knees while a hairy, muscular shape slammed its groin against her pale buttocks. She can't help but think of it, considering her present situation. 'Get out of that skirt. But don't take anything else off.'

'Giving orders, are we?'

'When my cock is this hard and I have a slut in my hands? Yes. There might be a few more too, so get used to it.'

'You're a bad, bad boy, Franklin. How did it happen? Who turned you into such a bastard?' She wants to be handled, stripped, called a slut; it's making her heart do a drum-roll around her ribcage and her legs feel like water.

'You want me to fuck you in the ass again? Mmm?' I whisper into the silky black hair over her ear.

'Watch yourself.'

'Deep. Hard. Right in the nasty place. And then I'm going to come all over the backs of your beautiful legs. Like the guy in your car. Some stranger who rammed your tight ass and then chucked his come all over your pretty stockings.'

Her claws sink into my shoulders. She screws up her eyes, pants 'Bastard' again at me.

190

'And it's going to happen again. Right now. Right here in your office. A place where hundreds of men dream of taking you.'

She sighs and rubs her sex against my thigh. Grinds her hips into me. I glance down at her; absorb the sight so it can haunt me forever: eyes closed, lipstick glossy, panties sheer but slit at the back, stockings long and clipped right under her buttocks to a purple and black garter belt. 'Now?'

'Do it.'

'Take your shoes off. You're too tall.' She kicks the heels off her long, sexy feet.

'Use the gel.'

'Better had. I'm really thick today.'

She rummages and clatters frantically inside her clutch bag for the little tube of lubricant. Despite my excitement and my need, I am fussed by one sobering notion: there is no way at all I am ever getting out of the reformatory. Each time we make love, another lock is fitted to my cage.

'Make sure you bite me. Bite me real hard.'

Sure I will, ma'am. But I won't take much today, I'm afraid. Just a taste to take the edge off for a few more days. Bite you good, four maybe five times, and you're just like me and that can't happen. You'd be a monster.

'Leave me bitten and used. Call me names,' she whispers in a voice both thick with desire but hoarse with shame.

Throwing her hair around and clawing at the desk, she's finding that special place again that thrills her and hurts her at the same time in such a way she just can't leave it alone. I slip my hand between her silky nylon thighs and tickle her sex; so wet now the thin fabric of her panties clings to her hairless lips. In my other hand, I hold the wooden ruler she never saw me slip off the desk.

'You like to dress up like a slut.'

191

'Yes.'

'You need this?'

'Get on with it. Fuck me.'

'I want to see your cheeks blush first. Want to hear my doctor squeal.' Slip my fingers into her hair and gently press her head to the desk. Draw my ruler arm back. Her eyes flick to the side and see what I have in my hand. She shivers, says, 'Oh, God.'

Thwatch! Thwack! Plack! Doctor Nichols writhes against the red wood. Stands on her tiptoes to ride out the heat from wood on silk-bound flesh. 'Still want me?' *Thwop! Thwap! Thwat!* Clenches her thighs together to feel the stickiness coating her thighs down to her stocking tops that will be stained. Groans, stretches her arms across the desk. Closes her eyes. Snakes one silky foot around my calf muscle to pull me closer. Shows me past transgressions.

She thinks of a secret place where certain women in this town are known to go. They wear masks in a place that is already dark. Teeter around on high heels and wear tight rubbery clothes. Allow blindfolded, groping men to service their needs in corners and in booths. Chaplain has been there too. It smells of sex. The cries of women and the grunts of men are partially concealed by loud, strange music that makes me think of machinery.

The thought of women not just going to this place but having such desires makes me shake. I hesitate no longer. Push the end of my cock against the little knot of pink muscle. 'Yesss,' she hisses and grips the far end of the desk top. The long body of this professional woman of science stretches over the very place where she makes decisions that decide the fate of many. She demands that I slip my erect self deep inside her. It makes me dizzy. She even let me spank her with personalised stationery. I clench the muscles at the base of my cock.

Standing between those long, parted legs, I slip inside. Slide deep. Hear her groan. Watch her face redden, mouth open, forehead crease, knuckles whiten to bone. And now the softness of her body is pressed into heavy wood, my thrusts send me further inside her and make her sensations blinding. I wonder about the travel of sound in this place with her making such noises – deep tummy growls and shrieks of 'Yess'. Her long legs lock; the fine coating of stockings on her legs shimmers in sunlight, toes lock, knees bend. Again and again, I slip and squelch in and out of her buttocks. She bites her fingers, makes a crying sound. I cannot hold back.

Two expulsions quake inside her. I pull out and palm the remainder of my thick chugging over her buttocks and stocking tops.

A few moments pass. She lies still through them. Then turns her head and smiles at me. 'You made a mess of me. I like that. Do it again. Soon as you're ready.'

Chapter Twenty

'Lawyer here to see you,' one of my carers shouts from outside. I hear the door unlock. Arnold, the bigger of the two who doesn't like looking me in the eye, pokes his head around the door. Scans the room. 'Let's move.'

I swallow a mouthful of the salad I chose for lunch. 'Lawyer?'

He shrugs; looks bored; is fed up with escorting me to and from therapy, following me around the grounds on my twice-daily exercise, delivering meals, watching me swim during the period when restricted-access inmates take turns to use the pool.

My stomach swarms with stinging, panicking insects. A lawyer means my parents are getting involved in my situation. Other than two uncomfortable conversations on the phone, I've had no contact with them. Which is fine by me; they are practically concussed with shock and disbelief that I have done anything to warrant being put in this place. Mercifully, all they know is general stuff that has come from the doctor. No names or details yet of the women I have been involved with. But with a lawyer involved they're sure to find out soon enough – the Chaplain, Melody Watson, Mrs Berry. I feel sick, light-headed, want to be anywhere but here. Stumble to my feet. Can you die from shame? I think so.

Arnold holds the door open for me. Leads me through long vanilla corridors towards the interview room on the ground floor. I take some deep breaths to clear my head, to still the raging of woe and fear in my head; it's like a plane with engines on fire in here.

Straight away, with a little composure – telling myself I'm not a kid any more, that everything has changed, that I'm going to get out of this place, be a musician – I begin to feel a little weird. Icy prickles that don't feel bad at all run over my skin. A familiar excitement kicks in – like opening a present, hearing a great guitar riff, getting a smile from a pretty girl, the chest tightness of having a crush. I'm short of breath. It can't be.

It can't be her.

Inside the interview room, I'm a little unsteady on my feet. Throat has dried up, heart rate budda-bings. This woman can even change the air – it goes cooler and zings with tension. Feels like the first time we met all over again. But who is that?

'That's your lawyer,' my carer says, and squints at the guest-book. 'Mrs D O Hancock.' He nods at the blonde woman behind the perspex screen of booth number six. Head down, she's peering through her glasses at a laptop computer open on the desk before her. Hancock? The name seems familiar. 'You just pick up the phone to talk. You got thirty minutes then I got to get your pervert ass up to therapy.'

'Fuck off,' I tell Arnold.

'No, fuck you. Who's wearing the nappy?' He sneers, then laughs.

'If you could do half the things I have, chump, you'd swap places in a heartbeat.'

'Better watch your mouth, Franky. We're getting real tired of you.'

I hold my middle finger up to his face, and then walk across to my lawyer. I take a seat. Mrs Berry looks up.

Even the colour of her eyes has changed to topaz. Make-up is different too and she has a tan. Still looks so good it hurts. I pick up the phone and want to tell her how good she looks, but I stop. A sense of danger that feels like a hot, red flood under my skull peppers my brow with sweat. Discreetly, she shakes her head. I receive another uncomfortable sensation of being watched and of someone listening to my conversation. Mrs Berry is sending these signals. 'Hello, Franklin, I'm Mrs Hancock. Your parents have asked me to be your legal representation.'

Hancock: now I remember the book of matches she was holding in my dream, in the booth of the bar with the red glass – DADDY O'HANCOCKS. I smile. 'Nice to meet you, ma'am. How are my folks?'

She returns my smile; relaxes now I'm clued up. 'Doing fine. Worried, naturally. You're facing some serious charges that have been made by some important people. So there will have to be a panel at some point in the future in which the best possible treatment for you will be decided. You will be asked to appear and will have to answer some questions. Difficult questions. Several witnesses and your doctor will give evidence. I'm here to help you with your defence.' *To get you out of this friggin' monkey house.*

I smile at hearing her sweet voice inside my head. 'OK.'

'Right, now let me find your file.' She looks at the computer screen as a diversion because I hear her voice again. *You have a lover in here. She's not to be trusted. She's halfway to bonding with you. Resist her.*

I nod. *I know*, I think back, staring at her beautiful head, feeling inspired by her.

If you bond with her, I'll kill her.

I swallow the cold lump that has suddenly formed in my throat. Mrs Berry looks up, smiling. *Maybe now you understand the precautions you must take. How your life must be. You are not ready to give to another.* 'Are they treating you well?'

'OK.' *Sorry. You mad with me? I screwed up.*

'Well, if there is anything you need, just put in a request with the administrator and it will be forwarded to me.' *You did better than you know. I'm actually quite pleased with you. But this place is too dangerous now. We have to get you out of town, out of state.*

'Sure, if I think of anything, I'll let you know.' *I'm ready.*

'Good. Well, I just wanted to introduce myself today. I'm taking care of the procedural end, but will have to come back soon to help you prepare.'

But how do I get out? The cameras? Carers? The leg tag? Fences?

Mrs Berry closes her laptop. *I'll come for you. Hold on. Do not go with the doctor again. For her sake.*

She's getting ready to leave. Seeing this makes my eyes swim with tears. Just as well I don't need my throat to speak with her now. *Why did you bond with me? Why me? I'm hopeless. I don't want the doctor, I want you. I love you but you can't love me back. My heart is broken.*

She looks at me. Her smile is so tender it makes me feel even worse. *We all suffer. Those who are chosen are also chosen by the broken-hearted. I chose you because you are special. I need you.* 'Well, until the next time, look after yourself.'

I nod, swallow. This is the time, in the movies about how bad things used to be before the Revolution, when people put their hands on the glass. I know why they did it.

Don't pout. I've told you before. She stands up and tidies the computer into her shoulder bag. Walks away to the door and depresses a button so the guard will let her out. Can't remember ever wanting her so much. I want to cry and I want to fuck her hard. My need is painful. I watch her bottom, tight in a pencil skirt. Her slender legs; flesh stockings shimmering under the strip lights, watch them streamline into the shiny spike heels.

I move about on the chair, uncomfortable with the pressure around my groin. Just for once, couldn't she have dressed down and given me a break?

The door-lock buzzes. Mrs Berry looks over her shoulder, smiles innocently. *Not my style, darling.* She disappears through the door.

Chapter Twenty-One

Lying on the leather couch, I stare at the ceiling, at anything but the doctor sitting opposite me. I hear her legs cross with a static rasp and feel arousal glow from my groin to my throat. Hard to take my mind off her, hard to concentrate on anything but her and the fact that she is mine for the taking. Only she is not; my Mentor has forbidden me to love her again. Any more of the desperate intimacy between us and we could bond. What I possess will pass to her; it cannot be given through duress. This I know instinctively; it will turn her into something terrible and Mrs Berry will kill her. But how do I say no? How do I control myself when she looks that good?

Never seen clothes like this before on a woman in Saviour Town. It's like she's brought her secret wardrobe to my therapy. Has dressed especially to tempt and please me; in here, she must have dressed before I arrived. Heels on her shiny knee boots are thin as pencils. Leather looks like a mirror as it clings to her long feet and calves. What I can see of her thighs are skinned in whispery black nylons with a seam up the back that I want to climb with my mouth open. Her tight-fitting skirt and jacket are made from a similar shiny material to her boots. Looks like fresh oil and must be as supple as thin rubber. Makes all the long lines and gentle curves of her body look like they have been cast in a mould. No blouse either; just a see-through bra under her jacket. And with lips so thick and wet-red, eyes dark as charcoal, cheeks blushed high and haughty, and her hair slicked back so tight, I want to crawl across the floor to lick her soles. Kiss my way up her boots. Slide along those nylon-slick thighs. Lap from her shaven lips. Press my face into her gauzy chest. Cover her painted face with lips and tongue. Slip inside that tiny pursed mouth between her white buttocks. I can almost taste the plastic of her wrapping, the perfume on her skin, the salt of her pussy.

My brace feels like a strong man's fist throttling the proud neck of a swan. Saliva bubbles around my gums. My teeth creak in anticipation of pure sustenance. I must not succumb to the unthinking, panting animal inside my restless skin. I feel dizzy from the thought of fast, hard, dirty, suffocating sex. It's like the moment of no return when your feet are slipping towards a terrible edge and you can suddenly feel the root of every individual hair swelling on your scalp; know you must fall and accept it with a terrible euphoria.

Am about to leap off the sofa when I think again of Mrs Berry and what she said: how I cannot endanger this woman's life. I settle back into the leather cushions. Yearn for my Mentor's self-control, her clear head, the clever tactics she uses to get what she wants without giving herself away.

'Franklin, I would like you to tell me about the visions. The images you see.'

'What do you want to know?' My voice is heavy with the sodden sulkies of one who cannot have what he wants.

'How do you receive them? Is it something you can create at will? Have you only to look at a person to know their secrets, their thoughts, their feelings?'

'Not that easy. Most of the time I don't know why it happens. I just start to see things, or feel things. But usually it's only with people who really interest me in some way. You know, I have to be inspired.'

Doctor Nichols scribbles with her fountain pen. Slim, white fingers, polished nails around bullet-shaped metal: the sight of it excites me. 'I see.' She puts the end of the pen against her shiny lips. 'So if you are aroused by me, for instance, then there's a good chance that you will know what I am thinking?'

'Maybe.'

'So do you like my outfit? You could say it is part of an experiment I am conducting.'

'You know what I am, ma'am. Didn't take you long to work it out either.'

She smiles. 'So what am I thinking now?'

'I'm not a magician. Don't do tricks.'

'I just want to understand your condition.'

'You might not like how I see you.'

'Try me. Speak freely. Say anything. It's confidential. Everything between us is confidential.'

I sit up, turn to face her, clench my fists between my knees. 'You are excited. That's the easy part. You enjoy having me here as your pet. You give your pet treats to get it to obey you. Because you want the same thing I have; the same abilities. You cannot stop wondering about how it will feel and what you will be able to see and do. As you believe you are smarter than everyone else, you're not afraid. This will give you an even bigger edge. It's going to let your secret darkness just pour out. You can hardly breathe when you think of the possibilities. You want to gorge yourself and get more control over other people too. You want to be a goddess. Beautiful, irresistible, all-knowing. You'll indulge your appetites, smash your enemies, be untouchable. There are some women in your life who you just can't wait to tear down. And you will, when you know everything about them.'

201

The doctor's face stiffens. 'You have a low opinion of me. We are all emotional creatures. We all have unacceptable thoughts, but we do not necessarily act on them. Well-adjusted people can rationalise these dangerous feelings. That is the difference between us – why I am a doctor and you are my patient.'

I shake my head. 'You're missing the point.' She frowns at me. 'It's not something you can control. You'll crash and burn straight away if you don't know what you're doing. Like I did. Just because you're older and better educated and a doctor and all, you think you will be able to control yourself. But you won't. You can't just catch this thing like a cold. You have to be in love to receive it. Otherwise it will mess you up.' This is further than I have gone with her before; but what I am saying sounds so crazy, no one would believe me to be anything but a nut if they read her notes. Maybe this warning will change her mind and she won't insist on seducing me.

She smiles, has a sexy look in her eyes. 'Why don't we find out? I'm ready for what you have to give, Franklin. Everything you care to put inside me.' She opens her legs and slides her hands up and down her thighs; shows me her naked sex. 'Come to me now, Franklin. Let me help you feel better, stronger. I know you do after we make love.'

'Not today. Don't feel like it.'

Doctor laughs. 'You're bursting out of your clothes, my dear. Haven't known where to look since you arrived. Now, come on. It'll be for the best. For both of us. We have a lot to offer each other.'

Shake my head. 'No. Can't.'

She cocks her head at an angle; her need is turning to frustration which will soon be anger. 'I must say, you strike me as a very ungrateful and confused young man. You could barely contain yourself before. What has changed?'

'It won't work.'

'All I'm asking you to do is fuck me, in that special place. And then to bite me like you did before. Quite simple really. We both enjoy ourselves. And this is important work I'm conducting here.'

First time I was with her I knew I'd taken too much. Already she has started to bond with me. But it's making her crazy. She's an educated, respected, decorated doctor of psychiatric medicine, but is now dressed like a forbidden sex image, trying to get a restricted-access inmate to fuck her in her study.

Kind of turns me on; just the thought of it. 'Unless you are in love, the bonding goes wrong. I just know it. It'll make you crazy, ma'am.'

'So you are in love with your Mentor? We're well aware it was her who engaged you in this biting ritual. You never stepped out of line before, but ever since you began seeing a Mentor, you've been sticking your cock in anything. Is that what you call love? I hardly expected you to be such a sentimentalist with all this talk of love.'

It's love, it's lust, it's obsession, you have to lose your mind. Because it opens the whole of you and lets the whole of something else slip inside. She is so used to having everything she wants, and being better than anyone else, she can't accept what I'm saying.

She sighs, disappointed. 'I can see that I shall have to work even harder. I thought my clothes would have been sufficient, but I know you are a young man with strange and very exacting tastes. I have something else that may tempt you.' She walks across to her desk and clacks the locks on the briefcase beside her antique table lamp. 'We have more in common than you think.' She turns to face me. 'You expect me to love you? Most of my patients do. A simple matter of transference that will pass. But without such a commitment, can we not still enjoy the fruits of both our natures in the right circumstances? What do you say? It could be an incredible journey. Unique between a doctor and her patient. I see this as an extraordinary opportunity that calls for a different ethical perspective.' She removes something rubbery from her case. Then something long and thin and black that reminds me of the Chaplain's secret cupboard. 'You like to assert your desires over well-heeled women. Am I right? And I occasionally enjoy the attentions of assertive young men. Neither of us wants to take such risks, but we are forced to. As you have seen while rifling through the journals of my mind. So we complement each other in this peculiar relationship. Made peculiar by your ability to read the mind of your analyst. The irony is not lost on me. Now, I shall need your help with this.' She holds up something the same size as a squash ball from which leathery straps trickle. A gag, like the one the Chaplain used on me to stifle my cries as she whipped me. 'So why don't we stop sparring and get down to what we both want? In some respects, I am your student, Franklin. And I believe in your power to instruct.' She holds up a rubber paddle with a handle like a ping-pong bat, but with a longer and thinner blade. 'This will serve both our interests better than a common desk ruler, I think. Though I applaud your ability to improvise.'

Like a moth about to charge its feathery fluttery energy straight into a fire, I rise to my feet and join her by the desk. 'Once you think I have had enough, I would like you to take me in the usual manner. As deep and as hard as you wish. And if you don't mind, I'm not averse to being called names. Bad names. So, if you wouldn't mind?' She holds out the gag to me on her outspread hands. I take the gag from her hands. Our eyes meet. She swallows. 'How do you want me?' she whispers.

'Over the desk. Legs apart.'

She smiles at me. Kisses my cheek and then turns around so I can buckle the gag behind her head. 'Open 'wide,' I say and thumb the ball between her perfect teeth.

'Mmm,' she murmurs, at the taste of rubber and the sensation of a man's hands taking control of her. Kneeling down behind her, I unzip her tight skirt. It feels sticky to the touch as I roll it down to the top of her stockings. I take a moment to inhale her fresh sex and to stroke her thighs. Lick her anus so her whole body quivers. When I reach over her back to retrieve the paddle, she rubs her naked buttocks against my stiff, insensitive groin brace. Immediately, I hear a familiar beep and feel it loosen inside my suit. After stripping myself naked, I take a moment to stare at the sheer deviant beauty of what is bent over before me, offering itself.

This successful doctor has dressed herself in tight rubber and seamed nylons and spike-heeled boots to tempt me – her prisoner. As if that is not enough to blow my mind, she wants me to commit verbal crimes against a woman. Crimes long outlawed in our state by threat of chemical castration and life imprisonment. Once I have fulfilled those requests I am to penetrate her in the ass and to bite her flesh. Again, two forbidden practices that guarantee a man the needle. The doctor wiggles her buttocks again. Lids her eyes at me. Peels her lips back to show me her teeth sunk into the hard rubber.

I have the hardness that makes me think my flesh has turned to wood. And I know that I will spend my whole life in pursuit of this buried treasure in a woman.

I bring the paddle down against her shuddering flesh. The sound of each blow changes each time. *Splack! Flack! Thuck!* My doctor claws at the desk; writhes her head about; stamps her feet; rubs her moist inner thighs together; turns and looks at me with soft eyes brimming with tears. *Plack! Plock! Thulack!* I paddle her white cheeks until they burn, until her eyes simmer with brine, until her head is scalded with shame. Flex my wrist. Strike her harder. Expel the frustration at being confounded and dumbfounded by women I crave and fear. She mumbles into the ball. Begins to moan in a rhythm, until I realise she's asking me, over and over again, to fuck her.

The muscles in my wood ache to be buried between her milky buttocks. I pause at my paddling, to show her the thick root that extends from my body. 'You want this now?' She nods enthusiastically. Her make-up runs in streams of tears. I nuzzle the head of my cock against her anus. Hold back from pushing inside. If I do, I will continue until completion. And then won't be able to prevent my mouth from finding a way into the goodness; will be unable to think of anything but satisfaction. She knows this. Has gone to extreme and extraordinary lengths to make sure I see this through. But if I do, the last thing in this world that the doctor will see is the thin, beautiful face of my Mentor. I know Mrs Berry would not joke about such a thing.

Doctor Nichols pushes her hips at me again while forcing a yearning, angry groan from her mouth: a demand for penetration. 'You dressed up to make me hard. Turned yourself into a slut to be paddled and then fucked.' Closing her eyes, she nods her head. 'You are a slut.' Begins to moan and rub her body against the desk top. I place my mouth close to her ear. 'After a hard day, you need a hard hand and a hard cock. Doctor to the world, but a slut under all the fine words and fine clothes.' Again she pushes her bottom at my cock. Makes the eager sounds of a woman aroused.

'Moo it. Moo it,' she cries out with a mouth packed with rubber.

Squeezing her buttocks around my cock, but not penetrating her, I rub myself to the point of climax. She raises her head, looks at me, frowns. I raise her from the desk. Place my hands on her shoulders and push her to

206

her knees. Cup the back of her head. 'My beautiful slut. This is all I have for you today.' She tries to pull away. I grip her hair. Hold her face at the right upward angle and then beat five long ropes of hot come on to her pretty face. Empty my pain and frustration and need all over the mouth and nose and cheeks and forehead of my oppressor, my master. Then step back.

Blinking and shaking her shiny, dripping face, she rakes at the slick with her long red nails. Mumbles curses and threats at me. I pick up my clothes. 'We can't always have what we want, ma'am. I'll be seeing you.'

Clawing at the buckles at the back of her head and screaming into the gag, she watches me step into my suit and then step out of her study.

Chapter Twenty-Two

I snap awake. Someone is in my room. From the outskirts of my dream I heard the door unlock – a beep, a whirr, the click as it opened, the clack as it shut.

Sitting up, I peer into the dark. Gradually the shapes of the furniture become visible in their places. Chair, desk, wardrobe, and a figure standing with its back to me, in front of the door. I squint. See the shape of a man in a white carer's uniform. Fear ices my spine. The figure turns about and looks at me. The blood slows in my veins. Pressing my back against the wall, I kick the bedclothes from my feet. 'Who?'

A torch clicks on and its light blinds me; bruises the back of my retina. 'Be quiet. Don't move,' he says, in a quiet but firm voice. Sounds familiar. A carer?

The light is removed and the man moves. I flinch. After I upset the doctor, perhaps the thick-armed bully has been sent to soften me up. He walks to the chair and takes it out from under the desk. He places it on the floor beside the door. Suddenly, I think of hanging in the old prisons before the Graceful Revolution. A carer has crept into my room to fake my suicide. I think of Isaac and look about my bed for a weapon. The bedside lamp?

The intruder stands on the chair, reaches for the camera and places something over the lens. He steps off the chair, turns to face me. I can see he has something around his face. A surgical mask. And a white peaked cap on his head. 'On your feet. Get dressed in these.' A canvas bag is thrown on to my bed.

My whole body and mind fill with the cooling water of relief; he's not here to hang me, but to break me out! But I'm still brittle with suspicion. I hesitate.

'Hurry!'

I snatch up the bag and unzip it. I wonder again about the voice. Suddenly realise where I've heard it before. 'You're . . .'

Man turns the torch back on and holds it under his chin. Raises the mask briefly, but holds a finger tight against his closed lips. But even with the mask still on, I would have recognised him by the cool, expressionless face and vaguely sad eyes: Mr Karl Berry.

Confused, I struggle into my favourite pair of jeans that were inside the bag, plus a smart new pair of cowboy boots and a black T-shirt.

'Put your uniform over the top,' Mr Berry says. He then opens the door with the ID card around his neck. 'Follow me. Don't speak.'

Blinking the last of sleep and panic from my eyes, I scuttle behind him. He moves quick, almost at a jog. I'm as scared as hell and real uncomfortable too; I've been playing around with this guy's wife and now he's busting me out of the joint. And he doesn't lead me down to the nearest fire escape or exit either, but up a staircase to lead me on the same route my carers take me for therapy at the doctor's office. I'm really confused now and doing my best to keep my mouth shut.

We stop outside the doctor's office. Karl Berry knocks four times, real slow. Then opens it. I follow him inside.

Dressed in a white uniform, hair tucked up inside her cap, is Mrs Berry. The doctor's files and papers are scattered all over the desk and room. She looks up at me and winks over her mask, before continuing to stuff some folders inside a canvas bag. 'Your doctor is over there,' she says, and nods towards the two sofas before the window overlooking the golf course. Immediately, I sense the presence of a troubled and angry presence on the couch in which I usually sit. I look over the back of the sofa. Feel my face freeze hard with shock.

Stripped down to her black underwear, Doctor Nichols lies on her side. Mouth filled with a gag of bundled pantyhose. Arms and legs tied close to her body by criss-crossing white rope. Loops around her ankles, thighs, tummy, chest and shoulders so she cannot do much beside rock from side to side. Sticking out from between her buttocks and protruding through the slit in her sheer panties is her favourite toy, that I have seen her use for pleasure in visions.

'Found all kinds of surprises in this big girl's bedroom. And then she was kind enough to invite us in here to show us more of her secrets. Give her a kiss goodbye, Franklin. You won't be seeing her again. Because if she's got any brains she won't come looking for you.'

But all I can do is stare at the doctor's frantic blue eyes. Though I feel my brace immediately tighten at the sight of that long body, all tied up in rope.

'Let's beat it,' Karl Berry says, from over by the door.

Mrs Berry nods, zips up her bag. Looks at me. 'Come on, lover boy. There are plenty more sharks in the sea.'

We walk real fast back the way we came, but detour to a service entrance soon as we hit the ground floor. Before Mrs Berry pushes it open, she grabs two automatic handguns out of her bag. Throws one to her husband. They tuck them inside the pockets of their trousers. I can hardly breathe. Am glad she never gave me one. Suddenly, I feel like a run – a real sprint – away from this place, this night, this world.

We make our way around the outside of the block and then walk up to the main gate. Karl Berry runs up the stairs and goes into the guard house, one hand behind his back on the pistol grip. There is an electric humming sound and the main chain-link gate starts to open. Mrs Berry and I walk through. Karl follows, walking backwards, watching the facility buildings.

After a quick jog down the main road, we stop beside a car I've never seen before. Mr Berry opens the back door. Takes a pet cage off the seat. I can see a dog inside. Melody Watson's pet! 'What?' Mr Berry motions for me to sit on the back seat. I climb inside. He pulls some steel shears from out of the bag.

'Give me your leg,' he says. 'One with the tag.' I offer my left leg and he cuts the electronic bracelet free. Opens the cage and pulls the squealing, frightened dog out. Ties the bracelet to the dog's collar and then says, 'Home. Go home.' The dog runs a few feet into the road and stops. Looks at us. Blinks. Ears down.

The Berrys slide into the front seats and put their guns on the dashboard. I look out the window. Melody's dog is taking a piss against a tree and sniffing around. Only once the doors are closed do they rip off their masks and hats. 'Thanks,' I say, finally recovering the ability to speak.

In the rear-view mirror, I see Mrs Berry smile. 'Don't mention it.' Mr Berry says nothing, but looks into the side mirrors.

'They won't follow tonight,' Mrs Berry says. 'No one ever escaped from there before. And this town isn't used to people breaking the big rules. But by morning the whole county will be after you. Couple of your old girlfriends leading the hunt like bloodhounds.' She laughs. A laugh that used to make me sulk. Now it's just about the best thing I can ever remember hearing.

As I fall in and out of sleep on the back seat of the car, I'm aware that we have been driving for a long time. Streetlights and headlights shine through my eyelids.

Sometimes I wake with a jolt and it takes a few seconds for me to realise where I am. Mr and Mrs Berry don't say a word to each other. I drift off again.

The slam of the car boot wakes me up. Frantic, I look about. Sit up. Greyish daylight fills the car. I cough. My mouth is dry. We are on the car lot of a highway motel. Parked in front of the door of a single-level bungalow. It looks old, run down, stuck in the last century. There are no other cars on the lot. In the office window, the sign reads CLOSED.

Mrs Berry is jangling keys by the door of a room. Karl is taking bags and cases out of the boot. Stretching my legs on the tarmac, I groan at all of the tight and painful parts of my spine from where I've been lying on the back seat. Mr Berry hands me a backpack. 'This is for you. Your dad packed it.'

'Dad? He knows?'

He nods. 'They know something. But not much. Better that way.'

I breathe out with relief. 'Thanks for, you know, everything you and your –' it's real hard to get the word into and then out of my mouth '– wife have done for me.'

Karl Berry stares at me, his face blank. 'She's not my wife.'

Mrs Berry turns around in the open door and throws another set of keys to Karl Berry. 'Franklin, you're in here with me.' She goes inside. I swallow. Nod to Karl. He shoulders his bag and walks to the next bungalow along.

I stand in the doorway to our room and look around the car lot and silent highway. Wonder where the hell I am. Feel too beat to think much more or to absorb many more shocks. I go into the dark room.

212

Chapter Twenty-Three

Mrs Berry comes out of the bathroom. Lights a cigarette by the little table holding the scotch bottle and two glasses. Curtains are closed, but by the light of the bedside lamp, I can see that the blonde hair and suntan have gone. The glasses she wore as my lawyer are nowhere to be seen either. She wears a long Japanese gown made from red silk, and scrubs at her wet hair with a towel. 'Sorry, have I shattered the illusion of glamour?'

'No way,' I say. 'I'd want you if you were wearing a paper bag.' I admire the fine bones of her face and shoulders. Can see half of a naked breast through the front of her gown. 'I missed you. You don't know how pleased I am to see you again.'

She smiles. 'I do. It's why you're always so easy to find. You think of me so much.'

I blush. 'Try not to. It hurts.'

She nods. 'I know, darling.' The smile comes back into her eyes that always used to make me feel good and warm inside when she came over to see my mom. 'But you kept yourself busy in my absence.'

I look down. 'You told me to.'

'You did it because you had to. But I might not always like your choice of girlfriend.'

'Sometimes there was no choice.'

She laughs. 'In time you'll be able to control your appetite. And you won't be anyone's bitch either.'

'Really?'

'Sure, you're still in your teens. That's why you want to fuck every six minutes.'

Thinking quickly back over all the trouble sex has brought me, I say, 'Never thought I'd be the one to say it, but a bit of self-discipline wouldn't do me any harm.'

'It will come. This is just a beginning.'

'Was it the same for you once?'

'Once. But I've grown into this life. Learned to deal with it in my own way. You will too.'

'What is it I've got? At the facility, they said it was an illness.'

'If you'd stayed there any longer, you would have started to believe that too. If you want to know what you are now, then listen to your instincts and pay attention to your dreams.'

'I know it's a bond between you and me. And all of the others that have gone before you.'

She smiles, pleased with me. 'But it's not all about fucking.'

'I kind of guessed there'd be a pay-off.'

'That comes next. This has been an initiation. To teach you how careful you must be. How clever. How stealthy.'

'Sink or swim. And I sink every time. Maybe I'm not cut out for this.'

'You do better than you know. In just a few weeks, you managed to seduce some of the most important and difficult women in Saviour Town. We can always use that kind of raw talent. You're a sweet little devil and the big girls can't keep their claws to themselves. Of course they'll want to own you; they know when they're on to a good thing. And in this place, they're used to getting everything they want. You're totally out of your league. But at least you showed potential. The rest you can learn. But there is no going back. I never gave you a choice. We can't. When we're sure we have found the right one to join us.'

'We? So who are you? And that guy I thought was your husband?'

'Members of a very exclusive club. Who fight a very dirty war.' She stubs her cigarette out. 'There are some people I'd like you to meet, very soon.'

'But what if I fuck up?'

'Then you fuck up.' She looks at me in a way that means she's not messing around and I just better accept it. 'I'll do my best for you when I can. But soon enough, you'll be on your own and will have to look after yourself. And from time to time, you will be asked to do things.'

My turn to not mess around. 'You and my buddy Isaac were lovers?'

Her face goes dark. She lights a cigarette. Nods. 'He was too wild. I was mistaken. Should never have bonded with him. And now I have to live with that. In the beginning, it's essential we all make mistakes. I knew I'd have to spring you out of some joint sooner or later. Better it was some candy-ass country club posing as a correction pen in Saviour Town than other places I know of, out of state. But Isaac ran before he could walk. And I didn't get there in time. Your doctor girlfriends killed him. They're all lucky to be alive.'

I have a feeling Doctor Nichols is only alive because Mrs Berry didn't want to scare me. 'We will do anything to survive. And so will you, darling. In time.'

I sit there like a dummy, trying to take it all in. Already worrying about the things I will be asked to do by her and her friends.

'You're free. Enjoy the moment. Enjoy all the moments. They count the most.'

'I guess.'

She leans on the table. 'You stink of that bitch who calls herself a doctor. Go take a shower. Then we'll get reaquainted.'

Chapter Twenty-Four

I can hardly believe it's true; lying on a bed in a motel with Mrs Berry beside me. Those long white limbs slipping out of the silk gown; one breast, half revealed; a pink nipple drawing my lips towards it; perfect feet, nails red as blood, mounted on high heels; sly smile on her handsome face; pretty eyes seeing inside me, knowing. Prepared; waiting for me. She touches my face with gentle fingers. Polished nails tickle my cheek.

'So everything is a cover? Karl isn't your husband?'

She just smiles.

'Do I even know you?'

'Intimately, in some ways, darling. But there is a need for secrecy, as you will see, in time.'

I lie on my back and sigh. Close my eyes.

'You worry about your parents?'

I nod. 'What the hell do I do now? Will I see them again?'

She strokes my chest and puts her lips on my cheek. 'I never expected you would have to leave your home so soon. I thought there would have been more time for you to adjust to this life. But events take over. You made certain selections.'

'Don't keep reminding me.'

She laughs. 'It's hard for a man to keep secrets in this town. You did your best. But you have to leave now. It would be dangerous to go back, foolish. But you will see them again, sometime, I promise.' She kisses me. 'I'm still surprised at your taste in lovers.'

'Give any guy the ability to seduce women and what do you expect?'

'Trouble.'

'There you have it.'

'You're far more cautious than many. More intuitive than most. You are right for this life. These are some of the reasons why I chose you. And this is another.' Her cools fingers close around my sleepy cock. Immediately, it thickens to life and rises.

I think of the life, of the pleasure it brings me: intoxicating, addictive, maddening. 'Will I always have these abilities?'

'Always. They can only get stronger.'

'The sex. Will I always need so much?'

Her hand strokes my wood. Fingertips trace the contours, then tickle my balls. 'The appetite never weakens. But your ability to go without will increase, in time. Eventually, it can be months before you need love.'

'Do you go without for that long?' I ask, wanting to be hurt.

I sense her smile. If I looked at her, the wickedness in her eyes would be too much to bear. 'I choose not to. You can call me a slut if you like.'

I turn my head and look at the lips that have been so much a part of my damnation. 'You are. Yes, you are.' Up and down, her hand works my erection. Shivering, I arch my back. There is magic in her hands.

'It hurts you to think of me with others. But sometimes it is a sweet pain. Excites you to think of my hunger. Makes you want me even more. That is how it should be. There is always madness in love. But those of us who have the bond cannot afford to be so jealous. For some, the idea of sharing has been too much. It has

217

destroyed them.' Her mouth covers my cock. Gentle, wet, warm pressure makes me writhe on the sheets and already think of release. It is uncomfortable to feel so much pleasure. And then to see her face in profile – eyes closed, nose thin, lips stretched and painting my skin pink – I struggle to hold back. I suddenly want to hold her head and pump every drop of myself deep inside her throat while shouting, 'Go on, take every bit of me.' But I don't; I have learned to lengthen the exquisite moment when life is at its most intense. 'Steady. It's been a while. I was on a promise with the doctor, but I had to turn her down.' I mention the doctor like a sulky child, intending to strike back at someone who has just put me in my place.

Mrs Berry releases my cock with a pout. Narrows her pretty eyes. 'And now the bitch is tied up with other things. And she's still there, riding that false cock because everyone is too scared to enter her room. While I have what she desires most.'

Her head falls to my meat again. I roll on to my side and she clings to my buttocks and I push, slowly, in and out of her mouth. She breaks away to breathe, but moves her soft hand up, over and then down my erection. Repeats the action. Looks me in the eye. 'Did you miss me?'

'You don't know how much.' She knows I've missed her. Regardless of the others I took, having her on my mind so often is how she managed to track me. 'But it's weird. Something about the others reminded me of you.'

'It was me you looked for in others.'

'Yes.'

'That is the way of the bond.'

'Who passed the gift to you?'

For a moment, her face stiffens as if from the sudden recall of an old heartache. Her hand continues to stroke me, its touch much fainter. She looks past me. 'Someone I loved. And will always love.'

218

'We're both trapped by this, aren't we?'

'By heartache and longing, for ever.' She looks up at me, smiles. 'I've tried hard to make it easier for you, my sweet boy. I never tore anything from here –' she touches the skin of my chest, above my heart '– as others have done.'

I feel sorry for her; it's the first time anything resembling age has crept into her face, her eyes. Never met a person as strong or clever as Mrs Berry, but now she looks frail as an older lady and as vulnerable as a young girl. I hold her. Kiss her mouth. Press my nose into my hair. 'We love to ease the pain of a separation that has to be. And we love to remember. Love to relive the beginning of the love that lasts always.'

'Always,' she says, and closes her eyes on a tear. Part of it runs down her cheek. I squeeze her slender body more tightly.

'I love you, ma'am. Always will.'

She sniffs, smiles. 'About time you called me Val.'

I shake my head. 'No. You are my Mentor. Mrs Berry. That's how it was at the start, in Saviour Town. That's how it will always be. You are my Mentor. And I won't let myself go crazy without you. Because you're always here –' I place her hand back on my chest. 'My time with you has given me so much. It's up to me now, I know it. I won't make a mess of it. Everything I do will be for you. And I want to make music about this life.'

'You will,' she says, a smile appearing in her eyes, the tear blinked away. 'About the love and the pain. Pleasure or death. And through music you will be able to live this life.'

'Yes.' My imagination suddenly bustles with images and fragments of dreams; of how it will be. Stages and clubs and after-show parties; records and tours and a thousand pretty faces staring at me with longing, their eyes painted and framed by long silky hair; their legs long and tapering into shiny heels. And through them, and up through my whole body, the songs will quiver and rush and finally break out. 'Oh, yes,' I say, as Mrs Berry begins to suck me with great enthusiasm. Moving her whole head and shoulders. Adoring this part of me. Moaning through her nose and sending little vibrations along my cock and into my tummy.

'I want you now. Need you. Been too long.' Pleasure or death; love to take away the pain.

I roll Mrs Berry on to her back. She giggles with surprise but immediately places her ankles on my shoulders. Claws the bedclothes. Half lids her eyes. Moistens her lips. And through her I sink. Every muscle and sinew in my body taut to control the excitement, to make it last. No woman feels this good around me. Her nails cling to my forearms and she shuffles down the bed to meet my thrusts. Begins to move with the rhythm of my lunges between her thighs. 'I liked you blonde, as the lawyer. Will you dress up for me again?'

She laughs. 'Of course, darling. I'm going to be around for a while. To launch you. Out there.'

'You better aim to show me a few useful things.'

'You can be sure of that.'

'Because you're still my Mentor. Still responsible for my development into a responsible young man.'

'Just don't expect me to teach you how to bake. Now fuck me. Really hard. You know how I like it.'

'How you get it.'

'All the time.'

And against the wall the motel bed thumps. Up and down the mattress I move her body by the sheer force of my thrusts. She lets go of formality, decency, eloquence. 'And harder. Harder. In me. Fuck your big cock into me. Right down. Deep.'

And I obey her. Hold her legs behind the knees and thrust and thrust so we make a slappy meaty sound until she becomes wordless with an open mouth. Her body locks. Her hands fist the sheets; a lithe, feline creature clinging to a tree in a storm. Bucks, groans, tilts her head right back. Feels me pulse and clench deep. Knows the white surge of all my energy, vitality and strength is inside her. Where it belongs. Where she craves it. Deep.

Chapter Twenty-Five

In the afternoon, pizza was delivered to our room. When I asked Mrs Berry if Karl wanted to eat with us, she said, 'He's gone.' After we ate, we took another long drive and I crossed the state line for the first time in my life. There was a checkpoint. From where I hid inside the trunk, curled around the spare tyre, I heard cars being searched and papers being rustled. Mrs Berry played it real cool. We were just waved through after her papers were looked over. She used a fake ID for one of her aliases, and even if the border police had a photo of her, they wouldn't have recognised her in the red wig and the prosthetic nose. She told me later that this alias was real important in some Saviour Town bank, so she never gets any hassle.

She let me out of the trunk a few miles down the highway, but the country didn't look too different from home. I wanted to take her on the back seat right away because she looked so hot in the black suit and red hair. First time she ever rejected me, but she did let me stroke her legs in the shiny black stockings while she drove. I eventually gave up on trying to seduce her and climbed into the back to sleep for a few hours.

And the strange journey continued for a week. But sometimes she let me drive on the long straight roads when I was getting restless. Can't even say I saw much of my new world. Desert highways, empty motels, back roads, avoiding the cities and big towns. Sometimes we drove all night to reach the next safe place. Besides the trucks and military convoys, there was never much traffic; hardly any private cars. And because of the great drought and all the weird storms, not many people lived in this part of the country. Nothing grew in the fields; everything was flat and brown and dusty; it was becoming a desert aiming to join up with all the other deserts. But Mrs Berry still preferred it to the Saviour State, and out here there are the biggest skies that turn all kinds of colours throughout the day. She has a place in this country.

Six days after she broke me out of the Reformatory, we turned off a main road and drove up a dirt track to a farmhouse. Old wood and shingle affair with a porch and two levels. Some kind of safe house she and her 'people' use from time to time. I get the impression they don't belong anywhere and are soon fugitives from any place else they go. Thought of it kind of makes me sick with nerves.

'This is your new pad,' she said with a smile, when we were standing outside the car. 'And a place to get to when you're in trouble deep.' She put a key on a silver chain around my neck. But looking at this lonely house from the outside, while the sun sank blood red into the distant fields, made me feel real low. Big fist of grief just pushed out of my guts and into my throat. I started to miss my folks. Tried real hard to suppress it, so Mrs Berry wouldn't think I was a pussy, or ungrateful, or something.

But soon as we went inside, I started to feel better. It looked real nice; has a good stereo and a games room with a pool table and little cinema and cool leather sofas. There was a generator in the barn and a big storm cellar outside, full of supplies. No clutter at all in the rooms of the farmhouse, just wide spaces and wood

223

floors, simple furniture. Had a sense of people coming and going here all the time; leaving nothing but a sense of relief. I felt the excitement build: my own pad! My first pad and all this space.

Two days after we arrived, it just got better and I had the biggest surprise. Mrs Berry never mentioned anything about it before. She was real relaxed here. Talked a lot more and made some great chillies, but only smiled when the big delivery truck pulled up in the yard. Back of it was full of amps and recording equipment, some effects boards and some new guitars. 'Just to get you started,' she said, sitting on the porch and smoking a Winston Red. A complete mobile studio that had come all the way from Memphis. 'Thought it was time I spoiled you,' she said, and I know she was feeling guilty about taking me from my parents and home. But she always took my music seriously. Never laughed at me or thought it was something childish I had to grow out of. 'But you got some work to do,' she said, while the guy was setting it all up in the barn. 'You need an album by the fall.'

I couldn't even answer that, or even think of a question. My face just said, who, what, where, why.

'What you always wanted, wasn't it? To be a rock star. This is your chance. Suggest you take it.'

'Sure. But . . . On my own?' I could play all the guitar and bass parts to our songs, but I was pretty clueless about drum tracks, recording and mixing. That was always Gretchen's job.

'Leave the rest to us.' She smiled, and once the truck was gone, she went out back and got into her target practice. Never known a woman love guns so much. Few too many of them at the farm for my liking too. I prefer guitars. So does Gretchen. So when Karl Berry showed up two weeks after I started fiddling with the equipment, he'd brought his own strange load along, in the back of a station wagon. When I heard him park in the yard, I came out of the barn and heard two doors slam.

'No way,' I said to myself. 'No way,' I said out loud. And I just stood in the dust blinking my eyes to make sure this wasn't some vision or mirage.

'Uh-huh,' Gretchen said, standing near the porch, holding a rucksack in one hand and his guitar case in the other. 'No way you're gonna be making records without me, buddy.'

Chapter Twenty-Six

And as we play our guitars together – something rocking with a shimmy of country running through it – the pretty ladies dance. Sweeping around the floor, but making no sound, Mrs Berry's black dress shows off her pale shoulders and one of her dark legs that occasionally glimmers through a slit at the back. Holding her tight around the waist is a girl called Missy.

Guy called Hank turned up yesterday in an old Pontiac rag-top and dropped her off. He never said a word or even got out the driver's seat, but Missy kissed him real hard with tongues before he drove off. As she leaned over the side of the open top, her gingham dress rode right up the back of her pretty legs; wearing those old-style nylons that Mrs Berry likes. Me and Gretchen followed those seams with our eyes, right up to the top of her thighs until our mouths were dry as the land out here. She raised one foot in a red high-heeled shoe that caught the sunshine and I think Gretchen went cross-eyed watching that patent leather spike.

When Missy came up to the porch, we thought it was Marylin Monroe, but she couldn't have been a day older than seventeen. She was so pretty, all the words just evaporated off my tongue and left only a stutter behind. 'How y'all doin'? she said with a curtsy.

Gretchen and I banged heads trying to get that little red suitcase out of her hand. We're Saviour City boys,

presentation of tight corset, nylons and high, high heels; a movie star, a vision from the past, right before our eyes. What have two boys from the Saviour suburbs done to deserve such a floor show? Whatever is it, we both intend to keep on doing it.

'Dude, this ain't happening,' Gretchen says, when Missy kneels down and puts her blood-red lips on to Mrs Berry's shaven sex. Stroking the back of her seamed stockings and just eating my Mentor like a hungry kitten. And if that surprised him, when Mrs Berry lies on the rug and puts her legs over Missy's shoulders it must look like a miracle to him. Never seen my Mentor get so aroused so quickly; Missy knows right where to go with her mouth and what to do with it when she gets there. Moving her pretty blonde head around between Mrs Berry's shiny thighs does something to me. If Gretchen was still back in Saviour Town, I may have strutted right on over there and just joined in.

Missy just licks and laps and purrs through her snubby nose while stroking Mrs Berry's kicking legs with her hands, until, with a whimper and a jolt, Mrs Berry bites her fingers and comes on that beautiful smudged girl mouth. Missy slides her open hands up Mrs Berry's body until they reach her breasts and keeps on kissing that sweet place until Mrs Berry looks like she's in pain. When Mrs Berry tries to roll away, this bad kitten in the corset climbs on top of her and they kiss so hard I can imagine the taste of pussy and lipstick in their mouths. My balls start to feel so heavy with sap and my cock is hurting to be free.

When Missy turns to face us, her blue eyes are so full of lust and need it's a shock to look into them. Strokes one hand down Mrs Berry's thigh and says, over her shoulder, 'Don't know about you, girl. But I could sure use something young, hard and man-size right about now.' She rises from my Mentor and teeters across the floor towards us. Extends a pale, slender hand to Gretchen and says, 'Dance with me, baby. See if you can play me well as you play that ole guitar.'

Gretchen looks at me, looks at the floor, looks at Missy. 'Sure,' he says, like a choirboy. I give him some elbow and he gets to his feet, shaking like something that's just come out of a jelly mould. Missy seems to just weave around him and dance him away towards the stairs. Until they vanish up to his room, he never breaks his stare once from her big eyes; I know how that goes.

I walk over to the mess she's made of Mrs Berry; lying still, one leg drawn up, eyes closed. Looking down at her, I slip out of my clothes. Kneel down. Slip each pretty foot into the air and then slide my cock deep into a place made so recently wet by another woman's mouth. 'Ought to spank you like a schoolboy for being such a slut when we got company.'

Mrs Berry just smiles and then writhes around as if my cock is filling her whole body. 'So what's stopping you?'

'A need to get real deep and to go real hard inside you. Then I'm going to bite someplace soft and white. Just eat you alive, ma'am.'

'Leave something for Missy. Been a while since she's danced with me. And she likes the way I taste.' Holding her legs straight so I can watch the dark seams over her white skin, I just go at her; thrusting so the whole house seems to shake around us. 'Gonna keep you up all night, ma'am. Teach you a lesson for giving me a taste for all the bad things in this world.' Little while ago, I still had posters on my walls and kid's stuff in my room, ran track and field and lowered my eyes every time a woman so much as looked my way. Now, with the taste of wine in my mouth, the feel of six silver strings under my fingertips and the sight of a beautiful woman beneath my body, I can feel all the fears and doubts just dropping away. No limits, no barriers, nothing holding me back while I shoot like a comet across the sky. Never going back. I'm just gonna burn up when my star hits the atmosphere.

To be continued.

NEXUS NEW BOOKS

To be published in June 2005

STRIPPED BARE
Angel Blake

A policewoman who will do anything to keep her job; a nurse who loves to show it all off; a stewardess who takes revenge on a passenger with no self-control. These are just three of the ten stories that show what happens when the uniforms are stripped away and women's darkest desires exposed. Ten stories that show the perverse pleasures that lie under the surface, from the prim smugness of the cosmetics stand to the adult sleaze of a school-themed disco.

£6.99   ISBN 0 352 33971 3

TEMPTING THE GODDESS
Aishling Morgan

Tempting the Goddess follows Nich Mordaunt's elaborate schemes to replace the Pagan leader Ariesian's bland and commercial festivals with ones of his own invention, featuring the deflowering of virgins, together with lurid orgies and sacrifices. However, Nich must negotiate the bitter sexual rivalries among antagonistic priests and priestesses, and all the while the lewd and unctuous Mr Pedlow is watching.

£6.99   ISBN 0 352 33972 1

THE BLACK WIDOW
Lisette Ashton

Spurned by her husband, and cheated of her inheritance, the Black Widow feels justified in seeking revenge. Determined to lay claim to the Elysian Fields, a health farm with a unique doctrine of sensual pleasure and erotic stimulation, the Black Widow wants what's rightfully hers.

Indulging a new-found passion for sexual domination, she is only too pleased to deal with those that get in her way. Punishments are cruel and explicit as she forces subordinates to do her bidding. Only the brave dare beg for mercy and their cries invariably go unheeded. Caught in the middle of this hostile takeover, private investigator Jo Valentine find herself entangled in the Black Widow's web.

£6.99   ISBN 0 352 33973 X

If you would like more information about Nexus titles, please visit our website at www.nexus-books.co.uk, or send a stamped addressed envelope to:

Nexus, Thames Wharf Studios,
Rainville Road, London W6 9HA